Praise for Jessica Clare

"The residents of Painted Barrel are just as lovely as ever."
—*Publishers Weekly* (starred review)

"[A] steamy holiday confection that equally delivers heart-warming laughs and heart-melting sighs." —*Booklist*

"Great storytelling. . . . Delightful reading. . . . It's fun and oh-so-hot!" —*Kirkus Reviews*

"Jessica Clare found a balance in developing the characters and romance with banter, heart, and tension. [She] introduced colorful new characters along with Eli, Cass, Clyde, and the dogs from *All I Want for Christmas Is a Cowboy*."
—Harlequin Junkie

"[Clare is] a romance writing prodigy."
—Heroes and Heartbreakers

"Blazing hot." —*USA Today*

Titles by Jessica Clare

Wyoming Cowboys

ALL I WANT FOR CHRISTMAS IS A COWBOY
THE COWBOY AND HIS BABY
A COWBOY UNDER THE MISTLETOE
THE COWBOY MEETS HIS MATCH

Roughneck Billionaires

DIRTY MONEY
DIRTY SCOUNDREL
DIRTY BASTARD

The Billionaire Boys Club

STRANDED WITH A BILLIONAIRE
BEAUTY AND THE BILLIONAIRE
THE WRONG BILLIONAIRE'S BED
ONCE UPON A BILLIONAIRE
ROMANCING THE BILLIONAIRE
ONE NIGHT WITH A BILLIONAIRE
HIS ROYAL PRINCESS
BEAUTY AND THE BILLIONAIRE: THE WEDDING

Billionaires and Bridesmaids

THE BILLIONAIRE AND THE VIRGIN
THE TAMING OF THE BILLIONAIRE
THE BILLIONAIRE TAKES A BRIDE
THE BILLIONAIRE'S FAVORITE MISTAKE
BILLIONAIRE ON THE LOOSE

The Bluebonnet Novels

THE GIRL'S GUIDE TO (MAN)HUNTING
THE CARE AND FEEDING OF AN ALPHA MALE
THE EXPERT'S GUIDE TO DRIVING A MAN WILD
THE VIRGIN'S GUIDE TO MISBEHAVING
THE BILLIONAIRE OF BLUEBONNET

The Cowboy *Meets His* Match

JESSICA CLARE

JOVE
New York

A JOVE BOOK
Published by Berkley
An imprint of Penguin Random House LLC
penguinrandomhouse.com

Copyright © 2020 by Jessica Clare
Excerpt from *Her Christmas Cowboy* copyright © 2020 by Jessica Clare
Penguin Random House supports copyright. Copyright fuels creativity, encourages diverse voices, promotes free speech, and creates a vibrant culture. Thank you for buying an authorized edition of this book and for complying with copyright laws by not reproducing, scanning, or distributing any part of it in any form without permission. You are supporting writers and allowing Penguin Random House to continue to publish books for every reader.

A JOVE BOOK, BERKLEY, and the BERKLEY & B colophon are registered trademarks of Penguin Random House LLC.

ISBN: 9780593101988

First Edition: June 2020

Printed in the United States of America
1 3 5 7 9 10 8 6 4 2

Cover photo © Brandy Taylor/iStock
Cover design by Sarah Oberrender
Book design by George Towne

This is a work of fiction. Names, characters, places, and incidents either are the product of the author's imagination or are used fictitiously, and any resemblance to actual persons, living or dead, business establishments, events, or locales is entirely coincidental.

If you purchased this book without a cover, you should be aware that this book is stolen property. It was reported as "unsold and destroyed" to the publisher, and neither the author nor the publisher has received any payment for this "stripped book."

For Mick and Jen—
we've emailed one another a million times, and
may we email one another a million times more.
Please know I'm singing the Golden Girls *theme*
in my head at this moment.

CHAPTER ONE

February

Sometimes it was hard to live in a town like Painted Barrel. The community was small and intimate and supportive, but it was impossible to have secrets. Worse than that, everyone seemed to think they knew what was best for you, even if you didn't agree.

Which meant Becca heard a lot of well-meaning advice daily, no matter how many times she tried to escape it.

"You really should get out there and start dating again," Mrs. Williams told her for the seventh time in the last hour. "A pretty thing like you? You don't want all your good years going to waste. If you want to start a family, you need to move fast."

And wasn't that just depressing? Becca did her best to smile as she plucked foils off Mrs. Williams's head, as if the woman's kind words weren't stabbing her in the heart. "I'm not sure I'm ready to date. I'll know when I meet the right person."

Her customer tsked. "Like I said, don't wait too long.

You don't want to be the oldest mother at the PTA meetings." She nodded into the mirror at her reflection as if this was the worst thing in the world to happen. "It's very difficult for the children."

"I'll keep that in mind," Becca murmured as she pulled the last of the foils off Mrs. Williams's head. "Let's wash now, shall we?"

The good thing about washing was that because the water was going, it meant Becca didn't have to talk—or listen to Mrs. Williams talk. Thank goodness for that, because she needed a few minutes to compose herself. Becca had always thought that two years would be enough time to mend her broken heart. Two years surely should have been enough time to get over the man that left her on the eve of their wedding. It should have been enough time to get over the bitterness that swallowed her up every time she paid the credit card bills that she still had from the wedding that had never happened.

Instead, it all seemed to just irritate her more and more.

It didn't help that everyone in Painted Barrel still asked about the Wedding That Wasn't. Of course they did. Becca being left at the altar (well, practically) was the biggest scandal that Painted Barrel had had in all of the town's uninspiring history. She'd always been popular around town. She was moderately cute, tried her best to be friendly to everyone, ran her own local business, and, for ten years, she'd dated the ex-captain of the local football team, handsome, blond Greg Wallace.

Oh, Greg.

Greg was not good at making decisions about what he wanted in life. It had taken her ten years to figure out that particular tidbit of information, but once she had, it had explained so much. It explained why Greg never finished college, and why he'd never held down a job for longer than a year or two. It explained why he'd gone back and forth on their relationship, first wanting to see other people, then wanting Becca back, then getting engaged, calling it off, getting engaged again, and then deciding a few days before the wedding that he'd changed his mind and he was in love with another woman.

She'd been a damned idiot for far too long.

Becca scrubbed at Mrs. Williams's hair, asking about the woman's grandchildren without listening to the answer. Her thoughts were still on Greg. Why had she wasted so much time with him? Was she truly that stupid?

But, no, she supposed it wasn't stupidity as much as it was a soft heart, a fear of being alone, and the fact that Greg was a terrible decision maker but a great apologizer. He'd been so sweet every time he'd come crawling back that she'd felt like the world's worst person if she said no. So she said yes . . . and yes, and yes . . .

And now look where she was. Becca Loftis still had her salon in Painted Barrel, but she was turning thirty, she was utterly single, and now she was being warned that her womb was aging with every day that passed.

For someone that had always said she didn't want to turn into her mother, she sure was doing a terrible job of breaking that pattern. Heck, according to Mrs. Williams, she was failing children she hadn't even had yet and—

"Too hot," the woman under the water cried out. "Too hot, Becca!"

"Sorry," Becca said quickly, turning the water cooler and trying not to feel too ashamed. Even now, Greg was ruining her life, wasn't he? "You were saying it was Jimmy's sixth birthday last week?" She was relieved when Mrs. Williams settled back down in the salon chair and began to talk once more.

Enough Greg. She had customers to take care of.

* * *

Becca was sweeping up underneath the chair after her last appointment of the day when the door to the salon chimed. She looked up and inwardly felt a little stab of emotion when Sage Cooper-Clements waddled in, looking like a plump penguin with her puffy jacket and pregnant belly. The new mayor was the nicest woman, and once upon a time, Becca had thought she was the loveliest, most giving person, sweet and shy and eternally single.

Then Greg had decided he wanted Sage instead of Becca.

Then Sage had turned around and married some tall cowboy and immediately gotten pregnant.

Now Sage was the mayor of Painted Barrel and the new darling of the small town. Everyone loved her. Everyone touched her belly when she walked in and asked about her new husband. They asked about her family's ranch. They gave her advice and doted on her.

And Becca didn't hate her. Not really. It wasn't Sage's fault that Greg had bailed on Becca because he'd thought he was in love with Sage.

It was just that . . . it was hard not to be envious of someone who suddenly had everything you'd always wanted. Not the mayor thing, of course, but a loving husband and a baby? God, Becca had wanted so badly to be in her shoes.

She gave Sage a wistful smile. "Hey, Sage. How can I help you?"

Sage beamed at her and lumbered forward, all pregnancy belly and layers of warm clothing. She thrust a flyer toward Becca. "I just wanted to let you know that we're having a Small Business Summit next year to promote local tradesmen. All of the shops in Painted Barrel and the neighboring towns can rent booths in the gym and we're going to make a big festival of it. There'll be food and drinks, and everyone can sell goods from their booths. I wanted to invite you personally since you're on Main Street and one of this town's mainstays. I know it's not for a while, but I want to drum up enthusiasm ahead of time."

The pregnant mayor beamed at her, and Becca did her best to take the flyer with a modicum of excitement. It was just as Sage said, a festival featuring small businesses. "I'm not sure if I can do a haircutting booth," she admitted. At Sage's crestfallen look, she hastily amended, "But I'm sure I'll think of something! Maybe quickie manicures?"

"Wonderful! Just fill out the form on the back and turn it in at city hall and I'll make sure we save you a booth, okay?" Sage glanced around the hair salon awkwardly, her hand on her belly. She looked uncomfortable, but Becca kept smiling, even though it felt frozen on her face. They'd been friends before the Wedding That Wasn't, and now it was a little tricky finding the right footing once more.

They smiled at each other for a moment longer, and silence fell.

Please don't say anything about Greg, Becca thought. *Please don't—*

"I'm really sorry about how things turned out, Becca," Sage said softly. She bit her lip, her hand running up and down the large bulge of baby belly under her sweater. "You know I had no idea that he was going to do that."

Becca somehow found it in her to keep smiling. "Don't apologize, Sage. It was all him, okay? No one should have to make excuses for Greg." That big walking human turd Greg. "He's a grown man."

"Yeah, but I feel responsible—"

"You're not." She cut the other woman off, just wanting the conversation to end. Couldn't Sage see that this was the last thing that Becca wanted to talk about? With anyone? Certainly not with the happy, glowing pregnant woman Greg thought he was in love with? "Please. Let's just not bring it up ever again, okay?"

"Okay, so, uh, I'm going to go," Sage said, thumbing a gesture at the door.

Becca held up the flyer. "I'll make sure and get this filled out, I promise."

"Great. Awesome." Sage turned toward the door, waving. "I'll talk to you later!"

"Bye." She stayed in place, clutching the broom handle in one hand, the flyer in the other, until Sage headed out of the salon and down the cold, snowy sidewalk of quaint Main Street. Once the other woman disappeared, Becca returned to calmly sweeping . . .

For all of a minute. Her hands were shaking and she gave up, setting the broom down and then walking to her small office at the back of the salon, where she kept her bookkeeping items and the tiny refrigerator with her lunch. She shut the door behind her, thumped down on a stool, and took a long, steeling breath.

She would not cry.

She would *not* cry.

Greg didn't deserve her tears. He'd had ten years of her life, keeping her on hold and promising her that they'd get married soon, soon, soon, and then soon finally had a date . . . a date he'd never gone along with. She'd given him enough of her time and energy. She wanted to move on.

Why wouldn't anyone let her freaking move *on*?

She swiped at the corners of her eyes carefully, proud that there were only a few stray tears instead of the normal deluge. Good. That meant she wouldn't have to go to extremes to fix her makeup, just a little touch-up here and there. She could end the day on a high note, in case she had any walk-ins. Of course, if she did have one, they'd probably just ask her about Greg again . . .

Her lip wobbled. Damn it.

As Becca sniffed and dabbed her face dry, the door opened in the main area of the salon, the bell chiming.

Crap. Sage had probably come back to apologize again, and that would make Becca cry even harder and ruin her evening. She'd just have to somehow tell the well-meaning pregnant woman that really, truly, she was fine and really, *honestly*, she did not want to talk about it. Gritting her teeth, she forced a bright smile to her face, pinched her cheeks so the rosiness there would hopefully distract from her red eyes, and opened the door to face Sage.

Except . . . it wasn't Sage.

The hulking man that stood in the doorway wasn't anything like the mayor. In fact, Becca had never seen this man in her life. That was something interesting in itself, considering that Painted Barrel was a small town nestled in the less populated north of Wyoming, and most of the people that lived here tended to be lifers. Becca had grown up here, and she knew everyone in the small town. It was both comfort and annoyance—and lately it had been far more of the latter.

This man was a stranger, though. She stared at him, doing her best not to gape. He wore a light jacket, and under it a faded black-and-red-checked shirt. The jacket seemed almost too tight for the massive breadth of his shoulders. He was tall, maybe six and a half feet, but more intimidating than that were his arms, which seemed like tree trunks, and his black beard, which seemed like something out of a Paul Bunyan storybook. He wore jeans and big, muddy work boots, and a dark cowboy hat covered longish, unkempt hair. It was light wear for the snowy weather they were having, really.

He really did seem like Paul Bunyan come to life if Paul Bunyan was a cowboy, but wasn't Paul Bunyan friendly? This man had a massive scowl on his face, as if he hated the world around him.

Becca blinked and tried to size the man up, thinking fast. There weren't many outsiders in this part of town right now. Either he'd gotten lost and needed directions or he was one of the new ranch hands. Not at Sage's ranch, because Becca had met those nice gentlemen—former soldiers looking to start a new life. The only other "outsiders" in the area were the three new ranch hands at the Swinging C up in the mountains, and those were Dr. Ennis Parson's nephews. She hadn't met any of them, but rumor had it that they were from the wilds of Alaska, here to help out for a year.

This man definitely fit the Alaska stereotype. He didn't look like a typical customer. Heck, he didn't even look like he'd ever been to a salon. That beard was untamed and so was the hair under the hat. She'd bet his nail beds were rough and his hands were covered in calluses.

It was a mystery why he'd shown up in her salon. Becca was just about to open her mouth and ask if he was lost when something pink behind his massive jeans-clad thigh moved.

Then she saw the little girl.

The big cowboy was holding the hand of the tiniest, daintiest little creature. Becca's heart melted as the small face peeped around his leg and her thumb went into her mouth. The girl in the little pink parka watched Becca with big eyes, not moving out from behind her protector's leg.

Well. This must be the daddy. It was clear he was here not for himself but for his little girl. That did something to her heart. For all that he was slightly terrifying, Paul Bunyan was a dad and this little one wasn't scared of him.

"Hi there," Becca said brightly to the two of them.

The man just gazed at her with dark eyes. He said nothing, and after a long moment, he gently tugged on the hand of the little girl, leading her forward a step.

All right, he wasn't much of a talker. Ranching took all kinds, and she wasn't surprised that this one was a silent type. It was kind of ironic if he was related to Doc Parson, though, because that veterinarian was the nicest man but definitely a talker. She studied the little girl, who stood in front of her enormous father, sucking her thumb. Her cheeks were fat and rosy, and she wore the most adorable little pink coat. Underneath it, Becca could see striped pink-and-white leggings. Her hood was down and the soft golden curls atop her head looked haphazard, pulled into a high, tight knot.

"What can I help you with?" Becca asked, crouching to get to eye level with the little one.

The girl just stared at Becca, intimidated.

"Gum."

Becca looked up in surprise. The big, silent behemoth had spoken. "Gum?" she echoed.

He nodded and nudged the little girl forward again.

The thumb popped out of her mouth and the girl spoke. "I ate all of Grampa's gum and went to sleep and when I woke up my gum was all gone."

Oh. And she was here at a hairdresser. That wasn't a good sign. But Becca kept the smile on her face and put her hand out. "I bet I know where it is. Shall we take a look?"

The small, adorable creature put her hand in Becca's and gave her a triumphant look. "It's in my *hair*! And Daddy said you'd be able to get it out."

Eek, had he said that? Becca cast the man an awkward look. "Well, let's see what we can do, shall we?" She led the little girl over to the salon chair and helped her out of her jacket, then lifted her into the seat. "What's your name, sweetheart?"

"Libby." She looked on eagerly as Becca pulled out a bright pink cape and tied it under her chin.

"How old are you, Libby?"

"Three."

"Four," corrected the man gruffly.

"Four," agreed Libby, kicking her feet under the cape.

"I see," Becca said as the man sat down in the other

salon chair next to Libby's, his big legs sprawling out in front of him. "Four is a great age. That means you're a big girl." She reached for the ponytail holder to pull it out of the girl's topknot, only to realize the gum was twisted into it as well. Oh dear. Normally, she'd pick through the loose hair to check for lice—because you never knew with kids—but this was going to be . . . interesting. She touched a few strands, trying to determine how it had happened. Gum really was everywhere. Long strings of it seemed to be melted into the delicate curls, and all of it was mixed in with the hair tie. The entire thing seemed to be glued together with a light brown substance she couldn't figure out. After a moment, she sniffed. "Is this . . . peanut butter?"

She looked over at the big man, but his jaw clenched and he remained silent. After a long moment, he shrugged.

"Daddy tried to help," Libby said brightly. "But I didn't tell him about the gum for two days and he said that was bad."

Two days? Well, that explained the rancid knot atop Libby's little head. "I see."

"Late night," the man said in a gruff voice. "Sick cattle."

"I wasn't judging," Becca replied gently. She moved to the counter and grabbed a large bottle of hair oil. "Sometimes it's hard to get away from work. Trust me, I know." She crooked a smile at him, trying to put him at ease. "Emergencies come up, even at a hair salon." And she gestured at his little daughter.

He just stared at her.

Right. Okay, so that was awkward. She turned back to Libby. "Daddy was off to a good start with the peanut butter," she told the little girl. "We're going to put more oil in your hair and see if we can't work some more of this gum out, all right?"

"Okay," Libby said brightly.

"Why don't you tell me about yourself," Becca continued, dousing the girl's head with oil and trying not to worry about how the heck she was going to salvage this little one's hair without shaving it down to the scalp. "You're a big girl of four. Do you have any brothers or sisters?"

"I have two uncles! They're big and hairy like Daddy."

"Two uncles," Becca repeated, grinning. This was definitely one of Doc Parson's nephews. From the rumors around town, all three had come down from Alaska. "What about your mommy?"

"I don't have a mommy," Libby said, kicking her legs some more. "It's just Daddy and Uncle Caleb and Uncle Jack and Grampa Ennis."

"I see." She discreetly glanced over at the girl's father, but the man didn't make eye contact with her. Kept his gaze on his daughter as Becca tried to work the hair tie free. Her heart squeezed with sympathy, just a little. A single dad with a young daughter? No wonder he hadn't noticed the gum in her hair until it was a disaster. She imagined that raising a child alone was hard, and with no women to lean on? He was doing a great job.

Libby rattled on and on as Becca picked and fussed at the knot on her head. Long minutes passed, but Libby wasn't much of a squirmer compared to some of the other kids Becca got in her chair, which was a good thing. She was content to talk and talk, asking about all the hair products on Becca's counter and if she liked cartoons and flowers and everything else under the sun.

"Is this your daddy's shop?" Libby asked as Becca's oily fingers worked out another strand of hair.

"No, it's my shop. I started it myself."

"So you can play with pcoplc's hair all day?"

She chuckled. "Yes, that's right. I like playing with hair. Especially little girls' hair."

"Do you have a little girl?"

Her heart squeezed. "No."

"A little boy?"

"I don't have any family," she said brightly. "No kids, no husband."

"Daddy doesn't have a wife, either."

"Libby," the man growled.

Becca chuckled. "It's fine." Her cheeks were heating, though. She peeked at the man again. He was big and brawny, and under that crazy beard, he just might be handsome. Not that it really mattered all that much—she hadn't paid attention to any man but Greg for the last while, so her radar was off. This particular guy wasn't much of a talker, but maybe he was just shy. He did have a cute daughter, though.

Maybe . . . maybe this was a step in the right direction. Maybe she should take the bull by the horns and rustle herself up a date. Then everyone would realize she was over Greg and they weren't getting back together, and they'd stop treating her like the bastion of lonely spinsterhood. She could show everyone she'd moved on.

All it would take was one date. They wouldn't even have to have chemistry. It just had to be dinner, enough to show that she'd continued on with her life and everyone should forget about the Wedding That Wasn't.

She didn't jump on the idea right away, though. She needed time to mull over it, and working on Libby's hair was the perfect distraction. The gum was so entangled that she'd spent a good half hour on the child's hair and was just now starting to work the hair tie out of the knot. She was pretty confident she could get this done, but it would take a while.

Unless he'd rather shave her head and be done with the mess.

Pursing her lips, Becca wiped her hands on a towel. "Can I talk to you for a minute, Mr. . . ."

He didn't offer his name, just got to his feet and followed

her as she headed to the far end of the salon, by the front door. It was getting dark outside, the chill seeping in through the windows, and it was long past time for her to close up shop. She kept wiping her hands on the towel, her thoughts all over the place.

The man just kept watching her, waiting.

Okay, she was clearly going to have to carry the conversation. "I think I can get most of the gum out of Libby's hair, but it's going to take a while."

He grunted.

"Like, hours. I have to go slow because her hair's very fine and I don't want to pull on it. The other option is to shave her head, but I'm not sure how you feel about that."

The big cowboy looked over at his daughter, then back at Becca. He rubbed his bearded jaw. "She won't like it shaved."

"Well . . . I have time if you have time." She gave him a bright smile.

He paused. "Is . . . this an inconvenience?" The words seemed as if they were being dragged out of him.

"No, like I told Libby, I don't have anyone waiting at home for me. It wasn't how I planned on spending my evening, but that's all right."

The big man grunted again. "Appreciated."

They both paused, and Becca took in a steeling breath. This was her moment. This was the chance she should take. She could ask him out on a date and shake off the specter of Greg and the Wedding That Wasn't once and for all. So she toyed with a lock of her hair and hoped he found her reasonably attractive. "Is it true what Libby said? That you're not married?"

The dark eyes narrowed on her. Intense. Scrutinizing. He glanced at her, up and down, as if sizing her up.

Becca flushed. She charged ahead. It wasn't about this guy in particular. It was any guy, just to change how the town viewed her. She needed to change the conversation, period. "I know I'm being forward. I hope you don't mind. But . . . I figure now's as good a time as any to ask. Want to go on a date?"

He stared at her, up and down again. There was a long, awkward pause. Then he spoke a single word.

"No."

CHAPTER TWO

Hank said nothing as the pretty woman worked on Libby's hair. He knew it was a mess. Knew he'd somehow failed his little daughter in a way he'd never even considered. When he was a boy, if he got gum in his hair, he'd had the entire chunk hacked out, and then his head was shaved. But one look at Libby's tearful little face and he didn't have the heart to do that to his daughter. It was his job to keep her safe and take care of her, and if that meant he was going to sit in a girly salon all night, then he would.

He hadn't counted on the salon lady asking him out on a date, though.

He didn't trust it. Women didn't ask him out. Not that he knew a lot of women. Up in the remote wilds of Alaska, there weren't a lot of women, and the ones that were there tended to be as rough as the men. Ever since he and his brothers had come down to Wyoming, he'd seen the looks people gave him. He knew he didn't fit in. He scared people. His silence just made things worse.

So a pretty little thing like the salon lady asking him out? Had to be a trick.

She was nice, though. He watched her out of the corner of his eye as she patiently worked through strand after strand of Libby's hair, her oil-slicked fingers moving deftly and separating bits of gum and peanut butter and lint. She chattered in a bright voice, talking about dolls and horses and keeping Libby laughing and smiling.

His little bit was normally a happy child, but he'd never seen her light up so much around another person. Made him a bit jealous, really.

But she was working out a large section of Libby's hair from the gum, so he'd shut his trap and endure for his baby girl.

Hank peered over at the woman from under his lashes. Short little thing, maybe five feet in height. Long, pretty brown hair in big curls that fell down her back. Big eyes. Nice figure, too. Kinda rounded but with good hips and tits.

Not that he should be looking, but she had asked him out on a date. He was only human. No ring on her finger. She liked to talk, and she was pretty. Why wasn't she married?

Better yet, why was she asking *him* out? He was big and ugly and shit at conversation. He wasn't rich and he had a young daughter and no wife. He wasn't a prize by anyone's standards.

Had to be a trick.

Hank glanced at the clock as the minutes ticked past. His phone had buzzed with a few texts, but he ignored it. Seemed rude to act all distracted when this stranger was entertaining his child as she worked. His gaze fell on a neat stack of business cards on the counter, tucked between combs and bottles. *Becca Loftis, Beautician.*

She looked like a Becca. Not that he'd met a lot of Beccas.

Not that he cared. But he reached over and took one of

the business cards anyhow, just in case Libby had another gum incident.

The woman—Becca—didn't notice his movements. She was too busy concentrating on Libby's hair as his daughter yammered on and on about some sort of baby shark, her comb gently moving through the mess on Libby's head. He kicked back, their jackets in his lap, and watched Becca work, since this beat mucking stalls or listening to Uncle Ennis tell another one of his stories. It was kinda nice to sit down for a while and listen to Libby's laughter as she talked.

And then he nodded off.

He jerked awake a short time later, when a hair dryer turned on. Running a hand over his face, Hank sat up and glanced at the clock. Damn. It was nearly ten at night. Had he fallen asleep that long? Had this woman—Becca—been working on Libby's hair the entire time? He looked over at his daughter, and her little face was beaming into the mirror as Becca worked the child's pale curls into big sausage-like rolls and then carefully pinned them atop her head until they looked like puffs. Then she got out a pink canister and sprayed some pink glittery shit all over the kid's head. He wanted to tell her to stop, that he wasn't gonna pay for that, but the look on Libby's face kept his mouth shut.

His little tomboy daughter, who knew how to bait a hook and scale a fish, who played in mud and laughed hysterically when his horse pooped, who had always said she wanted to grow up and be a cowboy like her daddy, looked utterly entranced at her ridiculous pink hair. Her mouth gaped and then she looked over at him, full of joy. "Daddy, I'm a princess!"

And his chest gave this funny little squeeze, because in that moment, Hank knew he was completely and utterly out of his depth. He knew fishing, and he knew ranching. He knew trapping and how to survive in the wild on limited supplies for months on end.

He knew absolutely nothing about princesses. Or pink hair. And clearly these were important things to Libby, and he had no idea what to do. Uncle Ennis always laughed and said that a girl would be the death of him, but he'd just brushed it off. Now he suspected the old man was right.

"You're a very beautiful princess," he said gruffly, and put his hand out. "But it's past your bedtime."

Libby hopped out of the chair the moment the bright pink cape left her shoulders, and she bounded over to him. "Daddy, can I come back and play princess with Miss Becca again tomorrow?"

His throat locked up. Play princess? "Little bit, I don't think—"

"It might not be tomorrow, but the next time you're in town, I'll be happy to do your hair, Miss Libby," the beautician said, smiling. "As long as you promise to stay away from the gum!"

Hank clenched his jaw. He couldn't shell out hundreds of bucks to fix a kid's hair, no matter how cute his kid was. How much did a hairdo cost, anyhow? He always shaved his own head when it got too annoying in the summer. He didn't know anything about girl hair. Even so, he had to say no. He held Libby's coat out to her. "Libby, she's busy."

"It's all right," Becca said. Her smile was tired but pleased. "It doesn't take long and she's so cute I don't mind. As long as you don't tell my other customers, it's on the house." And she winked at his daughter as if they shared a secret.

Libby just giggled wildly as she shoved her arms through her coat.

Right. Well, that answered that. He pulled out his credit card and held it out to the woman.

Becca held a hand up. "No charge."

Did she think he was poor? Gritting his teeth, he held the card out again. "We took up hours. I can pay."

She shook her head, ignoring his surly mood, and went around him to get the door of the salon. "I didn't have plans this evening anyhow, and I got to make a new friend. I'd say we're even."

A friend? Him? That was an odd thing to say to a fella you just asked out. But then Libby giggled and Becca looked down at his daughter, and he felt like an idiot.

Not him. His kid. Right.

His face burned. "Sure I can't pay?"

"I'm sure." She beamed at him. "Have a good evening."

And that was that. He took Libby's hand and led her out to the truck, and his daughter was practically asleep before he even put the seat belt on her. She sucked her thumb as she slept, a habit he knew she needed to break but couldn't seem to get her to stop. And she was so damn sweet that his heart ached.

Best thing in his life, this little bit. He hoped he wasn't messing things up. He thought about how she'd lit up when talking to the woman at the salon. How she'd been so delighted to have her hair made all pink and cute. He'd always told himself he'd be a good-enough dad so that it wouldn't matter that she didn't have a mom.

Now he was worried that it did.

Hank drove back up the snowy pass and down the narrow, dark road that led up to the Swinging C Ranch. It was scenic here, but not much like home. Back home, he'd lived near a creek that ran down from the mountains. In the summer the meadows were filled with flowers and wandering elk, and in the winter it was nothing but snow. Here . . . well, okay, it was similar with all the snow, but there was a lake instead of a stream, and the only things wandering the valley here were cattle. Lots of 'em. He missed Alaska. Missed it a lot, really. He'd only come down because Uncle Ennis needed help with the ranch, and he'd offered Hank and his brothers a dollar amount that would buy supplies for years and new snowmobiles for each of them. Maybe even a plane, if they could figure out how to fly it. That'd be handy to have, a little two-prop to fly in and out of Anchorage when he needed something.

The longer he was in Wyoming, though, the more he felt . . . well, he felt like a failure.

He'd always thought of himself as a good dad. He made sure Libby ate three square meals a day and she knew how to take care of herself. She brushed her teeth and could dress herself, and he'd even taught her the alphabet song. But meeting the lady at the salon had rattled him. How was he supposed to give his daughter everything she wanted when he didn't even know some of this shit existed? Princess hair? It apparently wasn't enough to comb her hair. It had to be princess hair.

Maybe he should have taken that lady up on her date—trick or not—and picked her brain about kids. She seemed to be good with Libby.

He was still thinking about the woman—Becca—when he carried his daughter inside and up to her room. Hank tucked her into the bed, brushed the curls off her brow, and kissed her forehead. When he held her favorite teddy bear up, she reached for it without opening her eyes and rolled over, going to sleep. That was his kid, all right. She slept heavy. He watched her for a little longer, reluctant to leave her side, because it felt like if he turned around and walked away, she'd be eighteen in the next moment and leaving him. He wasn't ready for that.

Not at all.

Hank eventually left the room and headed downstairs. The Swinging C Ranch boasted a large house with additional cabins out along the path for the ranch hands. His brothers were staying in two of the cabins, but Hank was staying in the house because it had a tub instead of just a shower, and Libby needed baths. He headed into the kitchen for something to eat, and it wasn't empty. Uncle Ennis was seated at the table, doing a crossword, a cup of coffee at hand despite the late hour.

Well, hell. Uncle Ennis was a chatty sort, and that meant Hank was going to get trapped into a conversation.

Just what he needed.

"Late night," was all his uncle said as Hank moved into the kitchen and opened the freezer, looking for something to eat.

If he was in his cabin in Foxtail, he'd fire up the griddle and make himself a stack of pancakes because pancakes were easy on the supplies and he had to make them last. But he was tired and preoccupied, and the last thing he wanted to do was spend more time in the kitchen. So he grabbed a frozen dinner, shoved it in the microwave, and crossed his arms, glaring at the thing as it spun around, cooking his food far too slowly.

"Everything okay?" Ennis asked.

Hank grunted a response.

"Libby okay, too? I noticed she was out with you."

He clenched his jaw. "She's fine. Had gum in her hair."

"You try peanut butter?"

Hank reached over and pulled out the empty peanut butter jar that was still sitting on the counter from where he'd left it earlier and showed his nosy uncle. He knew the man meant well, but, damn, he was acting like Hank didn't know how to be a dad or something. "Took her to the hair lady."

It was the wrong thing to say. Uncle Ennis lit up. "You saw Becca? She's the nicest young lady, isn't she?" He shook his head, leaning over his crossword. "Pretty little thing, too. Shame about the fiancé."

He thought about the short, curvy woman at the salon. How she'd asked him on a date. Now he had to know more . . . which meant talking to Uncle Ennis for longer. Damn it. It wasn't that he disliked Ennis . . . but the man was a busybody and it crawled under Hank's skin sometimes because he wanted to be involved in everything.

His dinner beeped.

Hank took it out of the microwave and slapped it down on the table. He grabbed a fork in silence and began to eat. He wasn't going to ask. He wasn't. He knew it was a trap, Ennis's way of getting him to converse when he didn't want to converse.

He took a bite.

Waited.

Took another bite.

Damn it. "Fiancé?" he asked as Ennis wrote something down on his crossword.

"Mmmhmm." He didn't look up. "She got left at the altar, you know. Man broke up with her for the mayor. Well, she wasn't the mayor at the time. She's the mayor now. Anyhow, poor Becca was so humiliated. Everyone felt just awful for her." He shook his head. "Nicest girl. She deserved better."

Hank grunted again. Took another bite. The food was awful. He took another forkful and then pushed it aside. "She asked me on a date."

Ennis sat back in his chair, his expression one of utter surprise. "She did?"

Hell. He knew he shouldn't have said anything. Hank shrugged.

Ennis smiled. It wasn't a normal smile. It was slow and sure, and far too pleased. "Well now. When are you two going out?"

"Ain't. I said no."

Uncle Ennis opened his mouth to protest, a look of confusion on his face. He must not have noticed the warning glare on Hank's face that told him he needed to let it go. Instead, his eyes focused on the door behind Hank. Two seconds later, the screen slammed and Hank's younger brother Jack sauntered in. He headed for the fridge and stared inside it, not greeting either one of them.

"Hank was asked on a date by a pretty young woman in town," Uncle Ennis announced.

Hank gritted his teeth. He shoulda kept his mouth shut, damn it. Now Uncle Ennis was going to tell everyone he ran into all about Hank's business.

Sure enough, Jack jerked around, his eyes going wide. He stared at Hank, then at Uncle Ennis. "A date?"

"Sounds like."

"Was she blind?" Jack asked.

Hank scowled. He wasn't that ugly. "Go away, Jack."

"Even more than that," Uncle Ennis said, tapping his pencil on the crossword. "He turned her down. She's real pretty, too. I've known her since she was a baby."

Jack moved over and put his hand on Hank's forehead, pretending to feel for a fever.

Hank swatted his hand away. "Cut it out."

"Just wondering why you turned her down if she's attractive." His eyes widened. "She was ugly, wasn't she? That's why she wanted you."

"She wasn't ugly," he gritted out. "She was real pretty. She was . . . short. Nice." He tried to remember the woman's features. He remembered her hair, her smile . . . and the way her tits moved when she shifted. Not that he was supposed to be thinking about that sort of thing. Didn't seem right.

"But you didn't wanna go out with her," Jack restated, grabbing a chair and flipping it around, then straddling it. He sat at the table and gave his older brother a hard stare. "Did you pull a Caleb?"

Caleb was their other brother, and he was quiet and polite . . . most times. Around women, he got all red-faced and said nothing at all—and when he did say something, it usually came out wrong. Jack still liked to tease poor Caleb about the last time he liked a woman—Tina Tattersall was wearing a pretty, low-cut blouse and tending bar back in Anchorage when they'd stopped in for supplies one time. After dreaming about her for six months, Caleb had walked up to her and instead of saying, "Hi, Tina," he'd said, "Hi, Tits," and then turned around and walked out of the bar.

He'd never gone back.

"Becca isn't ugly," Uncle Ennis declared. "She's a very sweet girl. Very lovely. And she hasn't dated anyone since Greg left her at the altar." Ennis patted the table. "I think you should go out with her."

"No," Hank said quietly again. "Not interested."

"If she's so pretty, maybe I'll go say hello to her," Jack said, scratching at his unkempt beard. "She can't be all that picky if she asked you out, and I'm of a mind to start datin' since I'm here."

That was enough conversation for him tonight. Hank got to his feet, glared at Jack, glared at Uncle Ennis—who was grinning like a fool—and headed up to his room. At the top of the stairs, he pushed Libby's door open wider and checked on her. His little girl was asleep, thumb shoved in her mouth, clutching a teddy bear, the blankets kicked off. He tiptoed in, replaced the blankets, smoothed her hair . . . and realized too late that he'd just gotten glitter on his hand.

Pink glitter.

Damn it.

Hank quietly left the room and went to the bathroom to wash off the glitter. Shit was everywhere, and somehow it had gotten into his beard in the last thirty seconds. How the heck did that happen? Frowning at his reflection, he scrubbed at his beard and then stared at himself. He saw a deep scowl, heavy, dark brows, and a long beard. Nothing that would entice a pretty, sweet woman like Becca to instantly ask him out on a date.

Had to be a trick. Had to.

He thought of the first and last woman he'd fallen for. Well, "fallen for" was the wrong phrase. But he'd been mighty sweet on Adria Young every time he went into town. Tried to go out of his way to say hi to her. She always gave him welcoming smiles and flirted with him when he went to the bar. One night, he'd had a few too many to drink, Adria had been real friendly, and the next thing he knew, they were in bed together. It had been his first time with a woman—twenty-six was old for that sort of thing, and it was bothering him, but remote Alaska wasn't crawling with eligible ladies. He'd thought Adria was amazing. Stunning. Maybe a little too sly for his taste, but that didn't matter after a few beers. She'd curled up in bed with him, and in the morning she'd asked for money for a pack of smokes. He'd offered her his wallet and she'd smiled cutely and took a couple hundred.

And because he was an idiot that had gotten laid, he let her.

That went on for about a week before he realized she was always taking money out of his wallet the moment he had his back turned. One of the drunks at the bar had commented on how she'd done that to him last season—how she picked a mark and cleaned him out when he came into town with his savings—and Hank realized he'd been made a fool. She'd cleaned out his savings, sure enough, a few bills at a time out of his wallet.

He'd packed up his supplies and left town that same day, spent all winter at his remote cabin, throwing himself into daily chores and wishing he'd never met Adria. He'd piled up more pelts than ever before, worked harder, and repaired the log cabin so many times that Caleb and Jack got irritated every time he picked up a hammer. Eventually it was time to go back into town, and he had . . . and had woke up one morning to Adria on the doorstep of his motel room with a fat baby in her arms.

"This is yours. I don't want it. She's cramping my lifestyle." She'd dumped the baby in his arms and left.

Hank hadn't known what to do. Adria wasn't at her apartment and he didn't know where else to find her. He'd gone down to the police station with the infant in his arms and they'd chuckled at him because they all knew Adria. They'd politely suggested a DNA test.

He'd taken it and left with the baby girl to wait for the results. Before it had even come back, he'd fallen in love with the poopy little angel. She'd vomited all over his shirt and made disastrous diapers and cried so much he hadn't known what to do. But when she settled down and held his finger? And smiled up at him with those toothless gums? He'd felt . . . something special.

The DNA test had said she was his, but it didn't matter. Liberty Marie Watson had been his the moment she'd grabbed a fistful of his beard and giggled in delight.

She was the only female he liked and trusted. The only one whose smile was completely innocent.

He'd never seen Adria again. He'd kept going into town for a while, wondering if she missed Libby or wanted to see her. She never showed up, never responded to texts or emails, and last he heard, she'd moved to Dutch Harbor, because crab fishermen normally had loaded pockets.

So, yeah, Libby was his and that was all there was to it. Libby was the only reason he was here now. If it was just Hank, he'd have stayed high in the mountains in Alaska and never come out. But he had a tiny daughter to think about. Towns had books and dentists, and he figured Libby might need those things. When Uncle Ennis said he needed help at the ranch, he'd thought long and hard and eventually decided to go. It wasn't just the money or that Ennis was family. It was that he needed to know if Libby needed a community. He'd give Painted Barrel some time, determine how Libby handled being around so many townsfolk and adjusted to life on the farm, and then see how things shook out after calving season.

If she wanted to go back to Alaska, he'd take her.

If she wanted to stay in town, well . . . he'd endure it. He'd do anything for his baby girl.

Maybe not date the local hairdresser, but . . . most anything.

CHAPTER THREE

Four Months Later

All was quiet in the salon, even on what was normally a busy weekend. Becca flipped through a magazine, eyeing the hairstyles. She wasn't worried. As the only hairdresser in Painted Barrel, she had a captive audience. Unless they wanted to drive a half hour up the road just for a trim, everyone would come in sooner or later. Right now, it was "later" because it was right in the middle of calving season, which meant that every rancher with two hands had them full right about now. Happened every spring. The cattle all seemed to want to give birth at the same time, which meant the ranchers didn't have time to breathe, much less head into town for some grooming.

She didn't mind. It was a regular occurrence, and work would pick up when calving slowed down. Until then, she just had to entertain herself.

The door opened, and one of her weeklies stepped inside with a gusty sigh. "This place is like a ghost town!" Hannah said dramatically. She set her purse on the floor and then hopped into the chair next to Becca's. "Calving season always makes this place feel deserted."

Becca's lips twitched with amusement. As the local hotel owner, Hannah wasn't affected by calving season that much, but she loved to be dramatic. She also loved gossip, so Becca did her best to be careful about what she said to her. Hannah didn't have a mean bone in her body, but she also didn't have a private one, either.

Becca got out of her seat and put a cape on Hannah's shoulders. "Is your husband helping up at Price Ranch?"

"He is. That old fart." She shook her head, smiling. "Still thinks he's not a day over eighty."

Becca giggled. Hannah and her Clyde might have found each other late in life, but they were determined to make every day count. She'd never seen a pair so very happy with each other. It was nice, though. It reminded her that love was a real thing that existed. Sometimes she needed that. She let Hannah complain for a bit before taking her over to the sink to wash her hair. She then started to blow-dry the short white hair into the puffy curls Hannah preferred. As she worked, Hannah rambled on about the town's gossip, whether Sage's baby would be a boy or a girl, or who was driving into town extra late on a weeknight.

"I saw Jimmy Irons bought some fresh paint at the hardware store, you know." Hannah met her gaze in the mirror. "Everyone's keeping busy with spring projects during calving season except you."

Becca smiled as if the comment didn't bother her. She'd been expecting it, really. "It has been a little quiet around here."

"You need something to do or you're going to go stir-crazy."

"Oh, I still have some clients coming in. It's just quieter." She shrugged, teasing a white curl with the iron. "Until then, I'll catch up on my reading."

"Reading? You should be chasing after children or looking after a husband." She shook her head, messing up Becca's careful work. "I told my Clyde that it isn't normal for a young thing like you to be all alone. Surely there's got to be someone you can date."

Jeez, Hannah made it sound like she was a leper. "I'm not sure I'm ready for that."

"It's been two years, Becca. You need to get back on the wagon." Hannah gave her a knowing look in the mirror. "I heard Greg's chasing down that new teacher. Miss Amy."

She'd met Amy a few times when the woman came in for a trim. She seemed very soft and sweet, with gorgeous thick mahogany hair and naturally long lashes that framed bright blue eyes. That seemed unfair, but Amy was kind. Besides, it didn't matter to Becca who that loser Greg dated. She was done with him. "Good for them. I hope he makes her very happy."

Hannah just watched her in the mirror. "Mmmhmm," she said knowingly. "Just seems wrong to me that he kept you on hold all your best years and now he's going to hitch up with someone new lickety-split."

Gosh, she hated these conversations. She said nothing, spritzing a layer of hairspray on the perfect puff of curls adorning Hannah's head. "You want to get your nails done this week or next week?"

Hannah threw her hands up, her expression that of a martyr. "Oh my goodness, it has to be next week. I'm so very busy today."

"Oh? New guests at the hotel?" Was she pouncing on the conversation change? Probably. Did it matter? Nope. If there was an opportunity for diversion, she'd take it.

"Mercy, yes." Hannah rolled her eyes. "The repairman is coming for the washer, and I have a ridiculous amount of dirty linens waiting to be cleaned. I have new guests coming tonight and Chelsea's on vacation this week and Clyde's helping out over at Price Ranch, and I promised Doc Parson that I'd drive groceries up to him. I'm just . . . swamped!"

Becca's lips twitched. Hannah was swamped because she loved being in everyone's business. If she spent more time working and less time gossiping . . . well, Becca wouldn't even have a client today. So she couldn't complain. She adjusted one last curl, absently noting, "You're driving groceries up to Doc? Are they too slammed to get to the store?"

Hannah's eyes went wide. "You know he broke his foot, right? Poor man can't drive until he gets the cast off!"

"He broke his foot?" Becca thought of the elderly vet up at the Swinging C, who everyone called Doc. He was a staple of this town as much as she was, friendly and outgoing, and always had a helping hand. Heck, he'd changed a tire for her when she'd gotten a flat and ended up stranded on the side of the road outside of town. Greg had been "too busy," but Doc had driven past, seen her, turned around, and changed it without letting her raise a finger. He was like everyone's favorite uncle.

Come to think of it, he hadn't come in for a haircut recently, either, but she'd thought it was just due to calving.

"Oh yes, slipped on a step a few weeks ago. Right foot, too, so it's twice as bad." Hannah shook her head, tsking. "Those big nephews of his took him to the hospital in Casper and got him fixed up, and he's stranded up there for now. Normally one of them goes and gets groceries, but he called me earlier today and asked me to do him a favor, what with them being so busy and all. I just didn't have the heart to tell him I was busy, too." She waved a hand in the air. "I'll make it work, though. Somehow."

Becca glanced at the clock. She didn't have another appointment this afternoon and walk-ins were few and far between at the moment. "I'm not all that busy. You want me to get the groceries and take them up there?"

"Would you? That would help me so much!" Hannah beamed at her as Becca pulled the cape off her shoulders. "He gave me a list. It's nothing too big, just coffee and sugar and a few other staples."

Becca smiled as Hannah pulled a paper out of her pocket. "I'd be glad to."

"You are such a sweetheart, Becca," Hannah gushed, handing over the envelope with the grocery list written on the back. "That Greg was a fool to let you go."

Becca kept smiling through that, somehow. Someday, she hoped Greg's name would never be brought up again. Today, it seemed, wasn't that day.

A few hours later, Becca parked in front of the Swinging C Ranch behind a few trucks on the long gravel driveway. She'd been up to the ranch a couple of times in the distant past as a young girl, but not recently. It looked the same as it ever did, right down to the milling herd of cattle munching on hay in a nearby pasture. There wasn't a lot of snow on the ground, being that it was spring, but it was slushy and muddy, and she tiptoed her way toward the porch while carrying two big paper bags, along with her purse. She'd brought the groceries requested, plus a few treats from the local bakery since it was near the end of the day. Doc had a sweet tooth, and what better to go with some coffee than fresh doughnuts? His mood had to be down considering he had a broken foot during the busiest time of the year. She'd also brought a hair-trimming kit so she could fix him up while she was here.

After all, she had nothing else to do with her evening other than watch *Real Housewives*, and being a good neighbor seemed like the right thing to do.

It had nothing to do with the big, burly cowboy she'd asked out four months ago. Or his cute daughter. Nope.

Okay, so it did. She couldn't even lie to herself. Truth was, she was mighty curious about him. Not in a creepy way; she just wanted to see how things were going. See if he was still around. If he was as intimidatingly large as she remembered.

She also remembered him having really nice eyes and a firm mouth, but that might have been her hormones playing him up. Then again, everyone probably looked amazing after Greg, and wasn't that catty of her?

She hoped Greg was very, very happy with the new teacher, she thought bitterly as she rang the doorbell, and then realized Doc probably would have a heck of a time getting up to answer the door. So she knocked and then opened the front door, sticking her head in. "Doc? It's me, Becca Loftis. I brought your groceries. Hannah was busy."

There was no answer.

"Are you . . . here? Hello?" The lights were on in the front parlor area, and the kitchen looked messy enough that someone was in the house. But no one came out to greet her.

Well, perhaps he was taking a nap. Becca set the groceries down in the kitchen and then began to put them away in the fridge. She straightened up the counters, filled the dishwasher, and plated the doughnuts. A quick touch told her that the coffee was lukewarm, so she made a fresh pot, humming to herself as she scooped grounds into the basket. Even if Doc was asleep, he'd appreciate a fresh cup of coffee—

"What are you doing here?"

The deep, growled words startled her. She yelped, whirling around and sending coffee grounds flying everywhere. Behind her, in the doorway, was her cowboy.

Well, not *her* cowboy. Someone's cowboy.

But it was the same man that had brought the little girl to the salon. And her memory had not done him justice. He loomed over her, all black brows and thick beard, and she noticed absently that she didn't even come up to his shoulder. He'd have to stoop over to kiss her—not that they were going to be kissing, of course.

Great. Now she was thinking about kissing this mountain man instead of fearing for her life.

He stared down at the coffee grounds she'd rained all over the clean tile floor.

"You startled me." Becca clutched at her chest. "My goodness. Warn a girl if you're going to sneak up on her."

He scowled in her direction. "Why are you here?"

"Doc asked Hannah to bring groceries up. Except Hannah was busy. Her dryer—no, wait, her washer. Yes, it was her washer. The repairman was coming by later today and she had a bunch of sheets to wash and new customers tonight and since the salon wasn't busy, I figured I'd help her out. I bought the groceries and didn't see anyone inside and figured that—" Oh mercy, but she was babbling like an insane woman, wasn't she? But she couldn't seem to stop. "I figured that coffee would go great with the doughnuts and since Doc can't get around, it would be the neighborly thing to do to clean up the kitchen and . . . yeah." She exhaled slowly. "Yeah, that's about all of it."

The big guy glanced down at his boots.

She did, too. The leather was wet, she noticed, and where it was wet, grounds were sticking to them.

She giggled.

He made a sound in his throat that was like a *hmph*.

But that was it. And she decided he wasn't all that scary. Not really. Large, sure. Bearded, sure. But she'd dealt with her fair share of taciturn men and she could always charm them. She'd look at him as just another snarly customer she needed to win over. "Well, if you wanted a cup of coffee, there are easier ways to get one," she told him breezily. "If you'll wait a few minutes, I can clean up the floor and get the coffee started."

He stared at her.

"To go with the doughnuts."

He blinked.

She winked at him. "Trust me, you'll like them. Then I can do a little cleaning up while we wait for Doc to wake."

He blinked again. Looked over at the table and the pretty plate of doughnuts she'd set out. Looked over at her. Then he moved over to the table and picked up a doughnut with pink icing and sprinkles and set it carefully on a napkin. "Save that one for Libby," he said gruffly. "And follow me."

Mystified, she set down the coffee filter basket and followed him as he turned and left the kitchen.

CHAPTER FOUR

Hank was starting to wonder if fate was working against him.

That had to be the reason that the pretty hairdresser he'd turned down months ago was in the ranch's kitchen, humming and making coffee. He'd done a good job of avoiding town up until this point specifically because she was there. He'd done his best to forget about her and the soft fall of her long hair, the bright smile, the curvy figure.

He wasn't the type to dwell on what could have been. He'd thought the date request was a joke, he'd turned her down, and that was that.

Didn't matter that maybe he thought about her when he was in the shower. Or when Libby was talking a mile a minute in his ear. Or when he brushed his too-long, overgrown hair and wondered what she'd think of it. She was not his type. She wouldn't last a day in the wilds of Alaska, and he was going to head back there soon enough.

Theoretically. He still hadn't figured that part out yet.

And now Becca Loftis was here. Her name was just about imprinted in his mind, because he thought about it often, just like he thought about the pink curve of her lips and the soft eyes that even now smiled up at him.

She'd looked just as surprised to see Hank as he was to see her, and her gaze had gone to his mouth, hovering there so long that he couldn't help but notice.

And that made him feel . . . things. Things he'd sworn off for good. It was bad that he was noticing the way she looked or how she smiled. He couldn't get involved with a woman, especially one as soft and probably helpless as her.

So he scowled in her direction and gestured that she should follow him.

"I promise I'm not trying to be intrusive," she chattered as he led her down the hall and toward the far end of the house, where Uncle Ennis's vet clinic was set up. "I just knew Hannah was busy and I wasn't, so I thought I'd help out. I'm sorry if it felt unwelcome. I really did mean no harm. I just figured while I was bringing groceries, maybe Doc would want a haircut, or some company. He's a good man, you know."

The woman wasn't wrong. Doc probably would love the company. It was just . . . did it have to be her? But he supposed it wasn't his call to make.

"I feel like you're uncomfortable around me and that wasn't my intention," Becca said as he opened a door and led her through. She paused in the doorway and looked up at him. "Can we just forget that I asked you out? I'd rather that we were friends."

Hank stared at her. Friends? With a woman? He wasn't sure he knew how to be friends with someone like her. Her hair smelled like fruit, and her lightweight jacket had a ruff of white fur on the collar. She was wearing boots with tiny little heels, for fuck's sake, boots that would sink into the mud immediately and did nothing for her height. If she was wearing plaid and had a skinning knife at her belt, sure, maybe they could be friends. As it was, he wouldn't know the first thing to say to her. And friendship meant . . . expectations.

"I don't think so," he said.

Becca stared up at him, clearly shocked at his refusal. "Have I offended you in some way?"

Couldn't she just take no for an answer? He sighed and stared down at her, trying to figure out what to say. She looked up at him with the prettiest blue eyes, her arms crossed under her breasts, and for a moment—a brief moment—he wished he'd said yes. That he'd gone out with her. Because, sure, she was tiny and pushy and talked a lot . . . but she was also soft and pretty and he wondered what it'd be like to take her in his arms and kiss her until she couldn't even string a sentence together.

But that made parts of him ache, and Hank knew he wasn't good with relationships, so he just shook his head and continued on down the long hall that ran along the back of the house and led toward the vet clinic. Once they got closer, he could hear the delighted giggles of his daughter, mixed with shrill puppy whines, and his bad mood eased a bit.

Libby was the only girl he needed in his life.

Hank opened the door and gestured inside. Becca looked at him curiously, then went into the clinic. Doc sat in his chair at his desk, the doors to the two small exam rooms closed. In his arms Doc had one tiny puppy, a bottle in its mouth, and four others were squirming on the floor on a blanket with Hank's equally squirmy little daughter.

"I . . . oooh!" Becca started to speak and then made a girlish sound of delight. "Puppies?"

"Miss Becca!" Uncle Ennis looked over at the woman in pleasure. "What brings you here?"

There was a look of pure rapture on Becca's face as she moved toward the blanket and picked up one of the squirming black-and-brown bundles on the blanket. He'd never seen a woman look like that before. The ecstasy on her face was almost uncomfortable to watch. Almost.

Except he couldn't bring himself to stop staring at her.

"I brought your groceries," Becca said, lifting a tiny puppy to her face and then closing her eyes and holding it against her cheek. "They're so little. How old are they?"

"Two weeks. The mother got run over by a car and a buddy in Ten Sleep brought them to me because he didn't have time to bottle-feed with calving going on. Knew I'd been laid up." Uncle Ennis leaned back in his chair. "Been a long time since I seen you, Becca. You're looking great. I appreciate you coming up."

"I'm helping Hannah," she murmured, her fingers tracing the tiny puppy ears as she cradled it to her chest. "My goodness, and I'm so glad I did. All my favorite people in one room." She opened her eyes and beamed down at Libby, who waved excitedly. Then she glanced over at Hank, and her face creased into a tiny frown.

Right. He supposed he deserved that. He probably needed to get back to calving, too. Caleb and Jack were busy, and there were always calves that needed to be bottle-fed, as well. He kept standing in the doorway, though, watching the woman as she swayed, holding the tiny puppy up to her cheek as if she'd never been more in love.

For some reason, he couldn't look away.

"Sorry if I'm intruding," she said after a long moment. "I was making some coffee and cleaning up your kitchen because I thought you could use the help. Should I leave? Is this a bad time?"

"Not at all!" Uncle Ennis declared, beaming at her. "I've got my hands full with watching the little one and bottle-feeding these babies every two hours. I can use all the help I can get."

"Well, I'd love to help out." She pressed a gentle kiss on the puppy's head, and Hank couldn't stop staring at those pink, full lips. She said something, smiled, and then looked at him, expectant.

He'd missed it entirely, too focused on the movements of her soft mouth. "What?"

"I asked if you guys had dinner yet. I can whip something up." She tilted her head, gazing at him for a long moment before turning to his daughter. "And I bet Miss Libby would be the best kitchen helper?"

"I would!" his daughter shrieked happily, waving the puppy in her hands around in the air like it was an airplane.

"Well then, why don't we go cook some dinner for Doc and your daddy and your uncles." Becca carefully extracted the puppy from Libby's death grip and set it gently on the blanket. "Or do you need us in here, Doc?"

"Dinner would be mighty appreciated," he said, still feeding the puppy in his arms. He glanced over at Hank. "You don't mind, do you?"

Hank thought of the frozen dinners in the freezer that tasted like trash. He thought of how hard his brothers had worked all day and what a long afternoon it had been. Not just for them, but for him, too. He'd hosed off after helping a cow with a breech birth, but he still felt like he was covered in blood and birthing fluids. There were two more cattle they needed to keep an eye on tonight, a sick heifer, and six calves in the big herd that had been abandoned by their mothers. It was a mess, and nothing sounded better than a hot dinner . . . or, heck, even fresh coffee and doughnuts, despite the late hour.

He gazed at Becca for a long moment. Stared at her mouth for maybe a little longer than an uninterested man should. Then, because everyone seemed to be waiting on an answer, he grunted and headed back out to the barn.

* * *

When he got back to the barn, all heck broke loose and he didn't have time to take another break or even think about dinner for hours. Caleb took the first shift off, cleaned up and headed into the kitchen, and then returned a short time later with a handful of doughnuts and a huge thermos of coffee and parked himself next to Hank, who was feeling the stomach of a nervous cow about to give birth for the first time.

"That one turned?" Caleb asked, his face weary.

"Don't think so."

"Good. I've had enough turned births today." He shook his head and shoved a full doughnut into his mouth. "Where's Jack?"

"Showering. Be back in an hour or so." Hank wiped his hands and gestured at the doughnuts. "Can I steal one of those?" He was starving, his stomach growling with hunger. He hadn't eaten anything since breakfast.

Caleb pulled back protectively. "Heck no. These are mine. Best thing I've eaten in months." He took a big bite out of each one while Hank scowled at him. "Go get your own."

Coffee and food sounded real good. So did sleep, but that probably wouldn't be coming his way anytime soon. He needed to check on Libby, too. And Uncle Ennis. So he got to his feet and stretched. Damn, every bone in his body seemed to hurt. "You'll be okay out here for a bit?"

"I'll text ya if shit goes sideways." And he took another bite of doughnut.

Hank thumped his brother's hat and headed out of the barn. Every step toward the house made his feet feel as if they weighed a thousand pounds, but he'd been this tired before and worked through it. There had been runs in Alaska where he'd had to walk through thick snow to get to traps in the middle of the night, or that time that the roof collapsed with a storm incoming and had to be patched before anything else. He'd worked long stretches before. Inside, there'd be no time to rest, though, because Libby would need to be put to bed, and he'd have to help Uncle Ennis around, and the laundry needed doing and there wasn't anyone else to do it.

He washed his hands and forearms in the outdoor sink, then shook off the worst of the water before heading inside. Once in the house, though, he noticed all was quiet, the lights low. Had Uncle Ennis put Libby to bed, then? The man couldn't get up the stairs with that big boot on his foot, though. Curious, he headed into the living area . . . and stopped.

Becca was still there on the couch, his daughter tucked in her arms. The TV was on, the volume muted, and she cradled the little girl against her as Libby slept, clutching her favorite book. He noticed that Libby had been changed into her favorite pink pajamas and her hair was freshly washed and fixed into two pigtails that looked much better than the pigtails he normally gave her. And before he could say anything, Becca looked over at him and smiled.

"She wanted to stay up to kiss her daddy good night," she whispered. "I hope that's all right."

Hank nodded. There was a stupid knot in his throat, but it got there sometimes when it came to his baby girl. He went to pick Libby up and she immediately put her small arms around his neck.

"Night, Daddy," she murmured, all sleepiness.

"Give me a kiss and let's get you tucked into bed, all right?" he said as he took her up the stairs to her room.

Once Libby was tucked in and he made sure she was sleeping, he closed the door halfway—never fully, because she got scared of being alone—and moved back downstairs. As he did, he passed by the laundry room and noticed that the clothes that had been stacked to overflowing in the laundry baskets were now cleaned and neatly folded. He headed into the living room and noticed Becca was on her feet, her purse on her arm as she fought back a yawn.

"You did the laundry?" he asked, since he felt like he should say something.

She nodded. "I know you guys are busy right now. It was the least I could do. The laundry's handled, but I think there's still a load in the dryer." She pointed at the kitchen. "You also had some bananas that were about to go bad so I made some banana bread. I thought it might be easy to grab on break. It's sliced up and in the fridge."

He ran a hand over his beard, a touch uncomfortable. They were busy, yeah, but he didn't like to think of how much work she'd done that night, all without a word of thanks. "Appreciated," he finally said. "You didn't have to stay so late."

Her smile was tired. "It is late, isn't it? But Libby didn't want to go to sleep until she knew you were coming in, and Doc's foot was hurting him so I made him take his pain meds and go to sleep early. I just fed the puppies, so he should sleep for another two hours at least. Besides, I don't mind." She fought back a yawn. "My first appointment tomorrow isn't until eleven, and walk-ins are slow this time of year."

"Appreciated," he said again, and then felt like a big dummy because he couldn't think of anything else to say to her. "I'll walk you to your car."

"What a gentleman." Becca chuckled, the sound gentle and just a little bit raspy, and it made him think of far too many things that didn't have anything to do with being gentlemanly. But he took her outside, opened the car door for her, and watched her drive off into the quiet night.

He didn't know what to think of her.

He couldn't stop thinking of her.

He might have eaten all the banana bread in one sitting. He wasn't entirely sure. All he knew was that he pulled it out, poured a glass of milk, and ate slice after slice as he thought about Becca. By the time the bread was gone, he still had no answers . . . but he did have a raging hard-on. His thoughts had taken a distinctly dirty route, helped along by her mouth, her chuckle, the toss of her thick dark hair . . .

It took him a few minutes of pacing before the erection subsided. He wanted to crawl back into bed, but the knowledge that both Caleb and Jack were out there working made him check in on them first. He headed out to the barn again and found both of them sitting on hay bales near a pregnant cow, and they both smirked at the sight of him.

"That was her?" Jack asked. "The one that asked you out?"

Hank scowled. "Does it matter?"

"Hell yeah, it matters. I can't believe you passed up on that. Did you see her figure?" He shook his head, marveling. "I think Alaska fucked your brain up. You should have been all over her."

Caleb just grinned. "So, you going to ask her out now?"

Now? He snorted and gestured at the cow, whose sides were heaving. She'd be going into labor any time now, if she wasn't already. "You don't think we're a little busy right now?"

Caleb waved that off. "When things slow down. You going to ask her out then?"

"Dunno." Common sense told him no, to let it go, but then he thought about her smile and that raspy chuckle, and common sense seemed very, very far away.

CHAPTER FIVE

Becca set her alarm for four in the morning and yawned her way through a drive into town. Nothing was open except for the doughnut shop, so she loaded up on a few dozen to go with all the food currently in the back of her car. The local grocery was more of a mom-and-pop sort of place, so it wouldn't be open for a few hours yet, and the guys were low on a lot of things. She figured she could help out, make a healthy breakfast for Libby and Doc and the guys, help feed the puppies, and then be in town to open her salon . . . and catch a quick nap in one of the chairs if she had to.

When she pulled up to the ranch, the sky was purple at the edge of the mountains, the sun just thinking about rising. As she got out of the car, she noticed Hank was off the porch and at her side before she could even get to the back seat of the car. He was nice, she decided, gruffness notwithstanding. And he looked . . . really tired.

She decided it was a good thing she was there this morning.

"You look like you haven't slept in four days," Becca told him brightly as she handed him the doughnut boxes and then opened the back seat of the car.

He grunted a response, then paused for a minute. "Why are you back?"

"Because you guys are swamped, Doc probably needs help with the puppies, and you probably need help with Libby." She beamed at him and then pulled out a reusable grocery bag full of stuff she'd yanked from her pantry.

Hank immediately took it from her arms.

Aw. Such a gentleman. She liked that about him. Most guys she knew wouldn't have thought to ask, and she wouldn't have thought to suggest it. But Hank took bags out of her arms before she could even say a thing, and then he was loaded up and her hands were free. "I grabbed a few things to whip up for you guys. I hope that's all right. Unless you've still got plenty of banana bread?"

He didn't answer her, and when she looked over at him, she could have sworn his cheeks were slightly red.

Maybe he didn't like bananas.

They went into the house in silence, and Hank set the groceries down on the table. She immediately started to put the food away while preheating the oven. The best thing she could do would be to make foods that they could grab easily on a quick trip into the house. Most cowboys spent all day out in the field and tended to grab food when they could anyhow, but it was worse in calving season, when cows would run off from the safety of the herd to give birth, or get sick, or any number of awful things. So . . . food that could be eaten quickly. She'd brought an entire box of protein bars and was going to make every kind of muffin she could think of. As she put on a pot of coffee, she glanced over at Hank, who was rubbing his eyes wearily as he watched her get to work. "Have the puppies been fed?"

He frowned, scratching his chin. "Don't think so, but I've been too busy to keep track."

Her heart squeezed. He looked exhausted. She was a little tired this morning, too, but she'd only had one night of little sleep and he'd probably had far too many. She moved to the table, grabbed him by his big arms, and parked him in the chair. "Stay there until the coffee's done. I'll check on your uncle."

Ten minutes later, she was pleased to see that Doc was up, feeding the puppies, and his foot was hurting him less. She gave him strict instructions to go back to bed after the feeding and headed back to the kitchen to get started on baking. Hank was still there, sipping a cup of black coffee, and so she swept right past him and got to work.

"You don't have to do this, you know," he said as she cracked a few eggs on the side of a bowl.

"Well, it's a bit late now," she joked. "Seeing as how I've got eggs in the batter already. Besides, it's a premade mix and it's just going to waste at my house. There's no one there to eat all these delicious things but me, and if I eat any more, my butt will be the size of one of the cattle." And she was having a hard enough time finding a date as it was.

Not that she usually paid particular attention, but she also knew if she put on weight, Greg would gloat about how she was falling apart without him, and she really, really didn't want to give the man anything to use against her.

"I meant coming over. Cooking."

Becca gave him a look over her shoulder. "You guys need help. Doc's helped me before, so I don't mind returning the favor. And it's not like I'm busy at home. Ever since Gr—er, my ex—moved out, I don't like being there by myself. It's too quiet. No kids, and my parents moved to Vancouver about five years ago." She shrugged. "It's just been me for a while now. Do you like blueberries? I thought I'd start with blueberry muffins."

"Why'd he move out?"

She focused her gaze on the mixture, stirring harder. She couldn't look over at him. This was . . . he was testing her, right? Becca decided to laugh it off. "Oh, come on. I know Doc loves a good story. Surely he's told you all about how Greg left me practically at the altar for the mayor? Well, she's the mayor now, but she wasn't then. They were just friends. It's complicated." She stirred harder, as if imagining Greg's smug face and all the years she'd given him, all to be jilted right before her own damn wedding that she was paying for out of pocket because his paychecks were "irregular." More like nonexistent.

"Yes."

"Yes what?" She turned and looked at him.

"Yes, I like blueberries." He drained his coffee and moved to the coffeepot to pour himself another round. "And he sounds like an idiot."

"Oh, he is." Becca slapped at the batter even harder with the hand mixer. "It was one of those 'high school sweetheart' situations. Just because he was fun and charming in school doesn't mean he was good at being a real adult. It took me far too long to figure that out."

A hand covered hers.

Becca jolted, startled. The hand touching her was enormous, tanned, and hard with calluses. It also made her tingle in a million different ways.

"Muffins, not soup," was all he said.

She snorted with amusement. "Sorry. I was just imagining Greg's head."

He chuckled—the first time she'd ever heard him laugh—and then moved away, and she couldn't decide if she was dizzy that he'd touched her or sad that he'd stopped.

Becca shook herself, then set the batter aside to grease up the muffin pan. "What about Libby's mother? Can I ask about her?"

"No."

Fair enough. She wasn't insulted. Relationships that failed were personal wounds, for all that they left scars for the world to see. That didn't stop her, though. "Speaking of Libby, who's watching her today?"

"Me."

Becca paused, a stick of butter in her hand, and glanced over at him. "You?"

"Me. Her father." He chugged more coffee.

"She's an energetic four-year-old and you're a tired man with far too much on his plate already. I could hang out with her today while you work and hopefully get some rest."

Silence met that offer.

She looked over at him, arching a brow. "So?"

"Why?"

"You really have to ask why?" She shook her head, going back to buttering the pan. "You're dead on your feet, Doc's got his hands full, and you and your brothers will probably have your hands in cow uteruses all day long." She cast him a look. "My father owned a farm, you know. I know what calving season is like. It's not really ideal for a four-year-old."

"But being with you is?"

The way he stated it was more amusement than irritation, she decided.

"I'd like to think it would be fun. I can take her to the salon with me. We'll stop and get some coloring books at the pharmacy, she can be my little assistant at the salon since it's not busy, and we'll take one problem out of your hair for the day. I can even take her up to the school and introduce her to the teachers if you like."

That got a response out of him. "Teachers? Why?"

"The summer session of preschool will be starting in another month or so. Don't you think it'd be good for Libby to get to know some of the other children in town? Make friends? It's lonely as an only child. I speak from experience." She gave him a wistful smile. "I never even had a dog."

"You want a dog? There's a whole bunch of them in Doc's office," he said dryly.

Was that a joke? She was winning him over, she knew it. Becca grinned, her heart fluttering as she looked up at him. Okay, if she trimmed that beard and the circles weren't under his eyes, he'd be stunningly handsome. She itched to work on him, if only to run her fingers through his hair and touch his face. "I'm just trying to help out, Mr. . . ." It occurred to her that she didn't know his last name. "Hank," she finished.

"Mr. Hank?"

"I don't know your last name."

"Watson."

"Mr. Watson, then."

"Hank."

"Mr. Hank," she teased. "Since you insist."

"You're impossible," he muttered. "Gimme your phone."

Her hands were buttery. Becca gestured at her purse. "It's in there. The passcode is 2343."

The big cowboy rolled his eyes. "You're too trusting." He grabbed her phone, unlocked it after a few fumbled attempts, and scowled fiercely at it as he started to flip through something. It was clear he wasn't a fan of typing on her small screen.

She tried to peek around him. "What are you doing?"

"Putting my number in. If you're taking my daughter today, I want you to be able to call."

"That's a great idea."

He tapped the screen a few more times and then gave

her a curious look as she parceled batter into each of the cups.

"What's that expression for?" she asked, and why was she having so much fun this morning despite being dead tired and arguing with a stranger? Yet, she was. She felt alive, which was weird. She was also flirting, which was equally weird.

"Your ex is still in your phone," he drawled.

"That's personal!" A hot flush stained her cheeks, and she tried to grab the phone away from him, buttery hands or not.

He held it out of her reach. "I wasn't snooping or anything. 'G' for 'Greg' is right next to 'H' for 'Hank,' you know."

Oh. Well, he didn't need to know that Greg still called her sometimes. Or that the calls normally came after nine at night on the weekend. Or that she even answered—not that she'd accepted. She knew what a booty call was and she wasn't going to be that man's personal vagina. He'd hurt her too badly for that. "Maybe I just haven't deleted him out of my phone yet."

"Want me to?" He arched one of those thick black brows at her, a silent dare in his gaze.

"Go ahead." She lifted her chin, daring him back.

Hank grunted again, tapping at the phone. "He looks like a tool."

Becca giggled at that, feeling a little better. The photo attached to Greg's info in her phone wasn't a good one, and for that, she was viciously glad. "Just put your number in already. And a picture, too."

"Why?"

She was starting to get used to his one-word comments. "Because I said so."

He grunted again, and she went back to pouring the batter. She bit the inside of her cheek to stop herself from smiling as the camera went off on the phone a moment later. "Thank you. I appreciate it."

"Now I need your number. Same reason."

She rattled it off to him as he typed into his own phone. "Look up."

Feeling suddenly shy, Becca glanced up and gave him a sheepish smile as he took a picture.

So . . . that was a thing they did.

Libby was a fantastic assistant, Becca decided.

The kid was nonstop energy, of course, but she was also nonstop fun. She talked constantly, and even when things were slow at the salon, Libby made it fun. She played paper dolls with Becca's old hairstyle magazines, cutting out women and pasting them to a poster board she'd picked up at the pharmacy when Becca had realized all the coloring books at the pharmacy were nothing Libby would like. And, sure, Libby's collage looked like something a serial killer might have done, but the little girl was having a fantastic time. When clients came in, Libby grabbed the hand broom and dustpan and swept for Becca, and her small face was so serious that Becca took a few photos and sent them to Hank throughout the day.

Not that he'd answered, of course. She didn't expect him to. She just wanted to share the cuteness.

At the end of the day, she closed the salon and stopped by the bakery for leftovers, and then they headed to the grocery store to pick up a few more things for the house. By the time they got back to the ranch, Libby was half asleep in her car seat and Becca was, too. This time, all she did was drop off the food with a promise to be back in the morning to cook it, smile at a dirty, tired Hank, and kiss Libby's cheek good night.

She went home and collapsed in bed. It had been a long day.

It was also one of the best days she'd had in a long, long time. This was what it'd be like if she was a mom, she realized. Long, exhausting hours, but filled with the happiest little girl, who made even mundane moments seem amazing. Her heart was filled with longing.

Someday, she'd have a family of her own, she hoped.

Becca closed her eyes and tucked the blankets close to her, but after a moment, she pulled her phone off the nightstand and flipped through the numbers there. He hadn't deleted Greg's information after all. He'd only pretended to.

For some reason, that made her smile. Seemed like the big cowboy was all bark and no bite. She deleted the number herself, because she was done with Greg. She didn't want anything to do with him. Not anymore. She'd already given him far too much time.

After she deleted that, she pulled up Hank's photo and gazed at it. The sight of it made her smile. His expression was stern in the picture, as if he wasn't entirely sure if he should look friendly or not. It was all mountain-man beard and black hair and dark circles under his eyes . . . but she studied his features. A good, strong nose. A nice mouth with a full lower lip. Soulful eyes. Not a receding hairline in sight.

She giggled to herself and put the phone back down on the dresser. She had his phone number and had no idea what to do with it, but . . . it was strangely nice to have.

Man, she was turning into an easy-to-please woman if a scowly picture and a phone number exchange made her feel special. But it did. Just like that brief touch on the hand earlier in the kitchen.

She suspected a lot of people didn't get to know Hank Watson . . . and it felt special to be one of the few.

CHAPTER SIX

Hank didn't go to sleep right away that night. Even though he was tired, he lay in bed and stared up at the ceiling, his phone on his belly. He wasn't going to look at Becca's picture. He wasn't. It was just a stupid picture. She was just the town busybody who'd decided to push her way into their lives to help out.

So she'd asked him out months ago. So what? It was clear she wasn't dwelling on it. And he didn't want—or need—a woman.

He didn't know why he was thinking about her.

Or the soft, shy smile on her face when he'd taken her picture. Or the way she'd flirted with him that morning.

He certainly wasn't thinking about the drowsy look in her eyes as she brought Libby home, along with a ton of groceries for him and the guys.

Hank had noticed that his brothers were now doing their best to be around when Becca was. They lingered in the kitchen when she was there, and drifted in and out of the house looking for her throughout the day.

It irritated him. He wasn't sure if they were interested in her physically, or just doing it to get under his skin, but it was working. Hank wasn't entirely sure Becca had noticed them, though. She'd seemed focused on Libby . . . and on him.

Unable to resist any longer, he reached for his phone and typed in the password. His cock got hard as he thought about how he'd boldly touched her hand, and how soft her fingers had been under his grip. He quickly opened the phonebook app and pulled up her picture.

There she was, utterly gorgeous, the long, dark hair falling over her shoulder. Even in the crappy phone photo, he'd somehow managed to capture the sparkle in her eye, the softness and gentleness of her that made him so damn crazy.

He took his cock in his hand and stroked it, staring at the photo. At Becca.

Normally, getting himself off involved no finesse, no imagination. It was the sexual equivalent of scratching an itch. Sometimes he got antsy and needed to jerk one out in the shower. It happened. He'd think of a pretty face of some actress or another and quickly "scratch the itch" in private, no relationship needed. A magazine used to do the trick until Libby had found it, and then he'd thrown it away.

He'd never jerked off to a woman he actually knew, though just barely.

But hell, just staring at Becca's picture as he stroked his length made him harder than he'd ever been. He gritted his teeth, working his cock as he gazed at her picture, imagining the feel of her soft hair sliding over his chest, what her tits would look like when she was naked . . . and the little gasps she'd make when he claimed her.

Hank had never come so hard or so fast in his life.

Afterward, he cleaned up and lay back down in bed, staring up at the ceiling. His body was replete, but his head was still churning.

He'd said no to a date. Turned her down flat.

But what if . . . what if he'd said yes? Would she be in his bed even now?

Damn. He was an idiot.

CHAPTER SEVEN

One Month Later

Becca pulled up to the Swinging C and slid her small car between the two big gray trucks parked in their usual spots. She'd come to think of this as "her" parking space, which was silly, but it made her smile to pull in every time. The predawn morning was rather beautiful, the air no longer bitingly crisp, and she'd put on a sundress and worn strappy sandals. She picked up her daily box of doughnuts—those cowboys sure did love their doughnuts—and headed inside with a paper cup of foamy latte in her hand. The bakery made all kinds of crazy coffee drinks, and since she was up this early, that deserved something involving whip and mocha, she felt.

The door to the ranch house opened before she even stepped onto the porch, and Hank was there, watching her.

He didn't greet her—never did. But he always had the door open for her, as if he was waiting on her to arrive. And that made her stomach flutter in all kinds of ways.

She gave him a flirty smile as she sidestepped into the

door, mindful of the doughnuts and coffee. Her purse was slung over her shoulder, and her tiny heels clacked on the wooden floors of the house as she went into the kitchen. Once there, she set the box of doughnuts down and immediately started to make coffee. The back of her neck prickled, and she knew Hank was standing in the doorway, watching her.

He always watched her. Every morning.

Sometimes he'd talk to her, but most times he'd just watch her. She couldn't decide if he was irked that she'd shown up again or if he didn't trust her. In her secret heart of hearts, she hoped he was noticing her like a guy should notice a woman. So maybe she swung her hips a little more as she walked, or bent over really low when she pulled something out of the fridge. Maybe her sundress showed a fair amount of cleavage.

It didn't matter. Hank never made a move, and after he'd turned her down flat? Becca wasn't about to ask again. But he could look at her and see what he'd turned down, and so she did her best to be as sexy and put together as she could even if it meant waking up far, far too early in the morning.

That was all right. She had nothing to do at night except go to bed early, anyhow.

In the last month, she'd become familiar with the ranch house, and she tugged the big bowl of eggs toward her on the counter. "You want breakfast? Or are you heading out to the barn?"

Hank grunted.

She . . . wasn't entirely sure what that response was. "Three eggs or four?"

"Four."

It was a start, at least. Becca started cracking eggs and scooped a pat of butter into the skillet. Her father had been a cowboy, and she knew they could eat, and eat, and eat. The doughnuts she brought every day were gone by the evening, and no matter how much she baked, they cleaned the fridge out within a matter of hours. So she'd make a big mess of eggs and bacon for everyone. She got to work, beating eggs and humming and . . . Hank was still behind her.

Okay, it was going to be one of those mornings. She glanced over her shoulder at him. "When does Libby's class start? Do I need to take her in for paperwork in advance?"

"Not yet."

She nodded absently.

"Uncle Ennis—Doc—gets his boot off today."

She glanced over at him. "Oh, good. I bet he's more than ready—"

"And the puppies aren't needing bottles anymore."

She paused, then turned to look at him.

Hank had his arms crossed over his chest, his expression unreadable. "Calving's slowed down, too."

Oh.

He was getting rid of her. "I see. So you're telling me you don't need any help around here anymore."

He grunted.

"That's a good thing," she said brightly, and turned back around to the eggs. A good thing, sure. Weird how that hurt her feelings, though. After all, she'd run herself ragged over the last month trying to help them out. She'd cooked more meals and baked more muffins than a damned baker. She'd done laundry, swept floors, bottle-fed puppies, and watched Libby all day long. She'd been ridiculously busy.

She'd also been having way too much fun.

It was nice to be needed, nice to be around a busy group, nice to have people that you looked after. Becca was a people pleaser at heart—one reason why she'd gotten into beauty—and with Greg out of her life, she had no one to take care of other than her clients at the salon. Her parents had moved away and so had most of her friends from high school. It had been so nice to be needed.

And now this guy was telling her to buzz off.

She swallowed hard and stared down at the bowl in front of her. "Are you telling me to get out of here?"

There was a long pause. "You're already cooking breakfast."

Well, wasn't that so nice of him. Since she was already hard at work slaving over the stove, he'd let her continue. She fought back a burst of bitterness, because Hank wasn't to blame. He'd never asked her to come and help out. It had always been Doc who'd been excited to see her. Doc had given her the money to bring doughnuts to the guys every day. Doc gave her grocery lists and hugged her for being such a "dear" and helping out. Caleb and Jack—Hank's brothers—were polite, but she never really talked to them much because they were always busy or tired. Or both.

Hank was the one she'd thought she'd warmed up, honestly. He was never super chatty . . . or even just chatty. But he lingered in the kitchen more than the others, never let her carry a full bag of groceries, and always walked her out to her car. She'd thought they'd become friends. She'd thought maybe . . .

Well, it didn't matter what she thought. He'd just told her what he was truly thinking. That she was a nuisance and they were glad to be rid of her. Fine. No more Hank . . . and no more Libby.

That last part somehow hurt the most, though. Becca had always loved children and wanted plenty of her own. In the last month, she'd spent almost every day with Libby, taking care of her because the guys were so busy and Doc was injured and had a business of his own to run. Chasing after a four-year-old was exhausting, but Libby was just the cutest, most charming little thing she'd ever seen. She loved that little girl with all her heart and loved having her around at the salon every day. She loved fixing her hair and helping her dress and loved reading books to her. It was like having a daughter of her own, even for a little while, and sometimes she (sheepishly) let herself imagine what would have happened if Hank had said yes to her date offer. Maybe someday they would've become a little family.

Ha.

"I see." She set her hands on the counter. "Do you want me to leave right now?"

Hank clenched his jaw. "Need to drive Doc in to the doctor later today."

"Of course." Of course they still needed her today. He was just letting her know that after another full day of unpaid babysitting and housekeeping, they'd have no further use for her. That was unfair, though. She wasn't really babysitting Libby—Becca would have done it anyhow, just because she adored the little girl. "I'll—"

"Miss Becca!" Libby's happy little voice lit up the kitchen. "G'morning!"

"Hey, pumpkin," Becca sang out cheerily. "You're up early."

"I wanted to have you fix my hair before we go to work today." She yawned, rubbing a small fist against her eye.

Becca chuckled and wanted to squeeze the little girl tightly. "I'm sure we can do something real pretty with your hair before we get our first customers. You know what you want done?" When Libby nodded, Becca set aside the half-beaten eggs and put her hand out. "Why don't we go feed the puppies and see if Grampa Ennis is up, hmm?"

Libby took her hand and started to lead her out of the kitchen.

Becca shot Hank a glare over her shoulder and let the child lead her out. They could wait on breakfast, the ingrates. Well, she wasn't angry at all of them. Not Doc, or Jack or Caleb. But Hank? She didn't care if Hank starved this morning.

* * *

It occurred to Hank that he hadn't handled the situation properly.

He stewed on it all day as he worked, throwing bales of hay down for the cattle and repairing fences in the mud. Their conversation was a track that ran in his mind over and over again. She'd been terribly insulted when he'd pointed out that she wasn't needed anymore. He'd meant to lead into asking her out on a date, and he'd never quite gotten there.

Now she was mad. Real mad. And mostly mad at him.

And he didn't like that much. He told himself that he shouldn't care. That he certainly didn't need to ask anyone out. If he did, he imagined he could find someone other than her, right? It didn't have to be Becca Loftis.

Never mind that he stared at her picture far more often than was seemly.

Never mind that he jerked his dick to it several times a day, and the number was increasing over time. Never mind that hearing her voice or her laughter made his entire body react.

Never mind that she loved his daughter and flirted with him.

But those things did matter . . . which was why Hank stood outside the salon like some fucking creep, staring into the windows at the woman inside as she chattered and laughed with the woman in the chair in front of her. She expertly wielded tiny scissors, her hands moving rapidly as she cut wet hair and listened to the conversation, all the while keeping an eye on Libby, who was coloring in the corner.

Libby ran up, interrupting Becca as she cut the woman's hair, displaying a picture she'd drawn, and instead of reprimanding his daughter, Becca acted like she'd just been given a gift. The woman in the chair oohed and aahed over

Libby's picture, and then Becca took Libby by the hand, ignoring the smiling customer for a moment, and went over to a wall.

It was a wall entirely covered with Libby's terrible four-year-old art. Some people thought their kids were gifted because they could scribble shit, but Hank was a practical sort. It was cute, but it was still crap. Crap was fine, because she was a kid, though. But Becca acted like each one was a treasure, and that did funny things to him.

Adria had never given two shits about her own kid, so he'd always figured his dick was bad at picking out the right women. Yet here he was, lusting over a soft, too-pretty woman who also seemed to adore his daughter. So maybe his dick wasn't that bad at this sort of thing after all.

He needed to ask her out.

She'd never offered again. Hank hoped that didn't mean she had changed her mind about things, or that she no longer found him attractive. Maybe she just wasn't the type to pry . . . he hoped.

So he stared into the window at Becca as she worked, trying to think of the right thing to say.

Apologize for this morning? Nah. It'd come across as weak. Besides, he didn't believe in starting a relationship with an apology. No, he'd have to think of something else.

Flattery? That'd be . . . awkward. He wasn't good with pretty words. Certainly wasn't good with poetry or any shit like that. 'Sides, she knew she was pretty. He was sure she didn't need to hear that from him. Should he ask if she was dating anyone? Thing was, he knew she wasn't. Doc was always teasing her about how she needed to "get back out there," whatever the hell that meant.

So . . . what, then? How did he lead the conversation toward asking her on a date?

"Daddy?" Libby ran up to the door and knocked, beaming at him. "Why are you hiding outside, Daddy?"

He could feel his face turn bright red as both Becca and the woman in the chair turned to look at him. He wasn't hiding, damn it.

Libby knocked on the door again, the bell clanging on the end of the pink ribbon like a damned gong in his ears. Hank hastily pulled the door open and scooped Libby up. "Wasn't hiding."

"Yes, you were!"

He tried his best not to scowl, especially when Becca bit her lip and turned back to her customer. "I'll be with you in just a moment, Mr. Watson," she called out.

And that was real irritating. *Mr. Watson?* Really? Was she trying to point out that she wasn't his friend? After a moment, he decided that was fine.

He wasn't interested in being Becca's friend anyhow. He wanted more from her than a buddy. Way more. Now that he'd finally decided she wasn't pranking him? He was all in.

Now he just had to convince her.

Becca continued to work on the woman's hair, casting him a curious look when he sat Libby back down at the tiny plastic desk in the corner. It was pink and unfamiliar and just the right size for his small daughter, which meant Becca had bought it just for Libby. She had a good heart, he decided. And she could cook. And she was generous.

Maybe it was time to start looking for a new mama for his daughter.

Not that he was thinking purely of Libby when he stared at Becca as she worked. If he was being honest with himself, he was more interested in Hank than in Libby. Hank and his late-night phone sessions where Becca's picture got all kinds of usage it wasn't intended for.

As the women talked and the customer paid, he looked down at Libby and noticed she had more than the usual pink glitter on her braids—she had a strand of bright pink hair tucked into each little topknot. Huh. That was new.

The bell on the door clanged and then it was just Becca and himself in the salon. Well, and Libby. Hank got to his feet even as Becca gave him a wary look and approached. Her gaze met his, and his entire body tightened with an odd sort of tension. The good kind. The kind that made his balls tighten.

"Daddy, help me color," Libby insisted.

He stepped back and touched Libby's hair and then grimaced, because the pink glitter was hell to get out of his beard and it always seemed to end up there. "You color it for me, baby girl. I have to talk to Miss Becca." Hank headed toward the chair, where Becca hovered nervously. He said nothing as he walked up, and her expression seemed to grow more uncomfortable by the moment.

"Before you chastise me," she began before he could speak, "the pink in her hair is just a temporary color and will wash out with shampoo. I was going to send a note home with her. It's not revenge for this morning." Her cheeks flushed and she nervously tucked a lock of hair behind her ear. "I keep a lot of bright colors on hand in the salon because little girls love them and sometimes a bit of bribery helps a squirmer stay still the entire time."

"That isn't why I'm here."

Becca blinked up at him. "Oh? What's going on?"

He completely forgot what he was going to use as his tactic. Apology? Weather? Something else? Hell. Eventually, he just cleared his throat. "Yes."

She paused, frowning up at him. "Yes . . . what?"

Was he sweating? The room seemed really damned hot. He wanted to wipe at his brow, but he was still wearing his cowboy hat and he was just going to get sweat everywhere if he did—or show her his own messy hair. Hat had to stay on, he decided. He licked his lips.

"You asked me if I would go out on a date with you. Changed my mind. Answer's yes."

Her mouth snapped shut. She stared at him in surprise. "I . . . oh."

That wasn't the excitement he'd expected. Wasn't she supposed to fall to his feet in blushing gratitude right about now? The look she gave him wasn't gratitude, though. Or pleasure. It was shock.

"You asked," he told her accusingly. This definitely wasn't going how he'd planned it.

"I did," Becca admitted after a long moment. "I just . . . okay. Yeah. Sure, we can go on a date." She ducked her head, her long hair falling in front of her face. "I didn't realize you were interested in me. And this morning—"

He cleared his throat. Yeah, this morning hadn't gone well. At all. "I'm . . . not good at this," he admitted.

"Dating?" She peeked up at him through her lashes, so damn pretty it made his chest ache all over again. She had a tiny smile on her lips. "You must have been pretty good at it to have been married before."

Except he hadn't been married to Libby's mother. Hank went silent. He wondered if she'd think less of him if she knew he'd been hoodwinked by a local woman who preyed upon trappers. Better to not say anything at all.

"I'm sorry. I'm prying. I know it's a sensitive topic." Her expression changed to one of regret. "I keep telling myself not to ask and I do anyhow. I apologize. When would you like to go out?"

Go out? He had to pick a date? Hank really hadn't thought that far ahead on things, but he should have. It made sense that he'd need to have some sort of plan for this. Damn it. He wasn't good at thinking on his feet. "Tomorrow," he blurted, and then figured that sounded like as good a plan as any. Calving season was slowing down to a reasonable speed anyhow.

Her eyes went wide. "Tomorrow . . . night?" When he gave a sharp nod, she thought for a moment. "It'll be Friday, and I don't have any appointments after four. I can close up a bit early. Dinner, I assume?"

Dinner sounded like a smart choice. He nodded again.

"Are we bringing Libby? Should I bring some stuff to keep her busy?"

Bring his daughter on a date? Hell no. He loved Libby. Loved her more than life itself. But the thoughts he'd been having about Becca were distinctly unchaste and he didn't want to be trying to get romantic with the pretty hairdresser with his daughter around. A four-year-old—a bored one especially—would quickly take over a date.

Besides. He knew she liked Libby. He wanted to see if she liked him enough. To see if she was having the same flirty—dirty—thoughts he was having. "Jack'll watch her."

Of course, he'd have to ask Jack, but his younger brother probably didn't have plans and Hank would offer him some money. Problem solved.

"Right. Okay." She turned her face up and gazed expectantly at him.

He nodded.

A flash of disappointment crossed her face, as if his response hadn't been what she'd expected. Did she . . . did she want him to kiss her? He wasn't sure if he was ready for that, yet. Not with Libby sitting right there. Not with that expectant look on her face.

He didn't even know if he was good at kissing. Adria had told him he was, but Adria had said a lot of stuff and then reached for his wallet, so she couldn't be trusted. So Hank nodded again, and then he felt like a damn idiot just nodding all over the place. He went and scooped up his daughter without a word, crossed the room, nodded at her again—damn it—and then left the salon without a look back.

He was going to be nervous as shit for the next twenty-four hours.

CHAPTER EIGHT

Hank groomed his beard as he stared into the mirror and tried not to sweat. He'd already changed shirts once due to his nervous sweating, and at this rate, he wouldn't have a damn shirt to wear by the time the actual date rolled around. So he concentrated on his beard, trimming a stray hair here and there because he thought maybe that would please Becca.

And for some reason, tonight he wanted to please her. It wasn't that he had expectations . . . well, hell. He kind of had some expectations, even if he told himself he shouldn't. He was hoping for a kiss, maybe. Maybe get to touch her hair. She seemed like a good-girl type, the type that would need several dates before she even considered doing anything with a guy. Not that there was anything wrong with that . . . he just didn't have experience in that sort of territory whatsoever. So he had to think like a gentleman . . . and he worried he was going to mess it up something bad.

Trapping, he knew. Wilderness survival, he knew. What

to do when a rutting moose wandered onto your property in the dead of winter? Knew how to handle that.

Take a pretty girl out to dinner and charm her?

He was way out of his depth.

"Daddy," Libby squealed as she came racing into the bathroom and clung to his legs. "Uncle Jack says you're seeing Miss Becca tonight and taking her to a movie. I want to go, too!"

A movie? It wasn't more than dinner. He hadn't thought past that. Should he have suggested a movie? Uncertain, he reached down and picked Libby up, settling her on the corner of the sink so she could watch him. "It's a grown-up movie," he told her gravely. "You wouldn't like it."

Her little face grew solemn. "Is it a movie with spider mans?"

She hated Spider-Man, which he thought was amusing. He leaned in and whispered confidentially. "Worse. It's a scary movie."

Her eyes went wide. "With ghosts?"

Uh-oh. If he even so much as brought up the g-word she'd be crawling into his bed for the next month. "Nope. Those don't exist and you know it. It's a scary movie about . . . fish."

"Fish aren't scary." She giggled.

"They are if you have to kiss them."

"No one kisses fish! Tell him, Uncle Jack!" Libby looked around him and grinned.

Hank turned, and sure enough, there was his younger brother, his own beard all neatly trimmed as if he was going on a date himself. Jack smirked and gave Hank a thoughtful look. "I don't know, Libs, your daddy's been mighty lonely up in Alaska. Maybe he was kissing fish."

His daughter's sweet squeals of laughter almost made him not mind Jack's comments. Almost. Except Jack had been making cracks all afternoon and it was wearing on

Hank's nerves. Like he needed this tonight. So he set down the beard trimmer, picked up Libby off the counter, and looked over at Jack. "This gonna be a problem?"

"Why would it be a problem?" He feigned an innocent look. "You're coming home tonight, right?"

"Of course I am. I have a daughter."

"You might get lucky—"

"I'm coming home," he growled. And that was that. "You have my cell number. Call if there's any problems or Libby gets scared."

Jack reached over and took Libby out of Hank's arms. He hauled her into the hallway and flipped her in a quick, dangerous way that made Hank's heart leap, but Libby laughed and squealed as Jack tossed her around on his shoulder like she was a sack of feed. "Maybe me and Libby will watch a fish movie ourselves, hmm?"

"Nemo!" she called happily. "Let's watch *Nemo*!"

"You go watch." Hank took one last look in the mirror and steeled himself.

He had a damned date, and he decided he was going to approach it the same way he approached everything in life. He was going to take it on with grim determination.

Everyone in the world dated, right? He could do this.

CHAPTER NINE

Becca fussed with her hair for what felt like the hundredth time in the last hour, smoothing down an errant strand. Of course she wasn't having a good hair day today. Now that she had a date? It was humid for the first time in weeks and her carefully fixed hair looked puffy and wild and slightly untamed no matter what she did to it. After wrestling with it for a while, she clipped it up and put on a pair of dangly earrings, hoping it would make her neck look longer. She put on lipstick, took off the lipstick, put on gloss, took off the gloss, and eventually put on just a light flavored gloss instead.

He might kiss her, after all, and she didn't want to get pink lipstick all over him.

That sent butterflies floating through her stomach.

The first person she'd ever kissed was Greg. The last person she'd ever kissed was Greg, and that had been two years ago. She'd never kissed anyone else and she often wondered if she was any good at it. Kissing Greg had been exhilarating at first—and wet—but over time their kisses had gone from long and passionate tongue sessions to quick, perfunctory pecks on the mouth. Maybe that was her fault, but after a while she hadn't enjoyed kissing him any longer. He'd always smelled like his dinner, or he'd been too aggressive with her mouth, and she'd always been the first one to pull back. She'd thought it was just part of the relationship changing as they'd matured.

Now she wondered if it had been a warning sign she'd deliberately ignored because she was so focused on Greg being "the one."

Sometimes she really could be so stubbornly dumb.

Still, it didn't mean she couldn't be nervous about kissing another man. Kissing was intimate, and while she'd been intimate with Greg plenty of times, she felt like she was starting over.

That was one reason why under her cute, flirty A-line pink dress, she was wearing her oldest pair of granny panties. It didn't matter how good a kisser he was; she wasn't putting out on the first date. Period. Those awful panties would remind her not to get undressed at all.

But because she wanted to be pretty, she'd also worn her tallest pair of fuck-me pumps and dangly earrings. She'd painted her nails a shell pink to match her dress, and she'd debated endlessly over perfume before deciding to skip it.

And then there was nothing to do but wait. Becca paced near the front door, doing her best not to peek out onto the storefront porch that she shared with her hair salon. She didn't want to look too eager. Too nervous. Too excited.

She was all those things, but she didn't want to *look* them. Heck, Becca wasn't even sure if she liked the man. Sometimes he made her breathless, and sometimes she wanted to choke him. He rarely said anything to her. He glared a lot. He was far too tall and hairy for her.

But she'd asked him out, and he'd finally said yes, so she

guessed they were going out, and she had *no* idea why that made her so damned nervous. After he'd turned her down, it had been easier to just think of him as a friend, and now she was thinking of him as date potential again, and it was . . . odd.

The doorbell rang, jarring her out of her thoughts, and she peeked through the curtains at the man on the porch.

Her heart fluttered again.

Okay, she *was* attracted to him. Even if she tried to convince herself otherwise, one look at Hank sent Becca's pulse to hammering. He was everything she said she wasn't attracted to—tall, rough, hairy—but, damn, he really did something to her. She gazed at the broad spread of his shoulders in the plain, dark button-down shirt. He practically bulged out of it. He wore jeans that showed off a rather tight butt, and his legs were long and strong and just . . . gosh. What would it be like to be kissed by someone like him instead of slender Greg?

Her mouth went dry at the thought.

Hank scowled at the porch and then rang the doorbell again.

Oh. Right. Here she was staring at him through the window instead of answering the door. Becca smoothed her artfully loose chignon, took a deep breath, and then opened the door. "Hey, Hank."

The big cowboy said nothing, just looked her up and down. It made her nervous . . . but it also made her squirm in a lot of good ways. "Is this okay?" she asked, gesturing at her dress. It was pale pink and sleeveless, above the knee, and it toed the line between cute and flirty and too summery.

He dragged his gaze away from her legs, paused at her boobs, and then clenched his jaw and gazed up at her face. "What?"

That was flattering. Becca found herself smiling. "Is this okay for where we're going?"

He grunted.

Becca resisted the urge to smack him in the stomach to get an answer out of him. A grunt was not a damned answer. "Where *are* we going?"

Hank gazed down at her, and she noticed his cheeks were slightly flushed and he was sweating. Was he nervous, too? If so, that was cute. To think she made a man this intimidating-looking anxious. It made her feel a bit more like a femme fatale—something she'd never been. Becca was always the sweet one, the cute one, the dependable one. Never the vixen.

Tonight, she kinda wanted to get her flirt on and see where it would take her.

"Dinner."

She gazed up at him. "I know that. I mean . . . where?"

"Steak."

Now she was the one clenching her jaw. The man was impossible. Was this how the entire dinner was going to go? Nervous or not, he had to talk to her.

Didn't he?

But it was a silent ride in his truck as he drove them two towns over. They stopped at a familiar steak house, one that she'd seen and heard about but that Greg had never taken her to. By that time in their relationship, they'd been together for so long that dates pretty much just involved getting together and having sex . . . and then she'd clean his apartment and cook for him. Yeah, she was an idiot.

She was doubly an idiot because she was thinking about her ex again while on her first date with a non-Greg man.

Hank pulled the truck up to the restaurant, and before she could get out of the cab, he was dashing around the far side to get her door. He'd done that back at her house, too, but she'd been too distracted to notice. She appreciated it now, though, and beamed at him. "Thank you, Hank."

He gave her a jerky nod, wiped his hands on his jeans,

and then went to get the door to the restaurant. He wasn't holding her hand or touching her, but it was still a thoughtful gesture. Her heels clacked on the sidewalk as she approached the front door, and as she did, she passed what must have been twenty motorcycles all piled into a row of parking spaces. Was this a biker joint? She suddenly felt very out of place in her pink dress and tall heels. But then Hank was right there, looming over her as he held the front door open, and she suddenly felt safe again.

They were seated in relative silence, Becca glancing around at the restaurant. The place was crowded, the faces unfamiliar. There was one restaurant in Painted Barrel, and if they'd gone there, she'd have known everyone in the place. Here, she felt even more out of her element.

"Do you . . ."

She looked up from her menu.

Hank rubbed his beard—had he trimmed it? "Would you like me to order for you?" he asked.

Becca leaned forward conspiratorially over her menu. "You'll have to forgive me because I haven't dated a lot, Hank. Is that a thing?" She'd heard it was back in the day, but did men still do that?

His gaze dipped to the gape of her neckline before his face flushed ever so slightly again. But a slow smile broke across his face and he leaned toward her. "Uncle Ennis—Doc—told me it was a good idea."

She bit her lip, determined not to smile. "Has Doc dated since the Cold War?"

Hank chuckled, the sound raspy and raw, and it made her innards squeeze with pleasure. "Got a point."

Feeling a little friskier, Becca winked at Hank. "I think I can manage my own order."

He pretended to peruse his menu. "Guess I won't have to worry about cutting up your steak for you, either."

A horrified giggle escaped her. "He told you to do that?"

"No, but I do it for Libby." He was smiling now, his teeth a white flash under that thick, dark beard. Oh gosh, and now her heart really was racing a mile a minute.

She kept chuckling. "I'll let you know if I need assistance."

They ordered. Hank got the biggest steak on the menu and she ordered a soup and sandwich for herself, mostly because she was probably going to be too nervous to wolf down a big slab of meat. Becca had a cocktail, and she noticed Hank drank just water. Not a drinker. That was good. They talked a little about Libby while waiting on their food, but the date still felt terribly awkward and stilted. Hank tended to answer in one-word responses unless she tried to pry more out of him, and it was exhausting.

She worried that he wasn't having a good time. That she was a crappy date. Maybe she was too chatty for him and that was a problem. So when the food was set down, she concentrated on eating, waiting for him to pick up the conversation . . . but he never did. They ate in silence, and she continued to feel more awkward by the minute.

Something told her this was going to be her last date with Hank Watson. She didn't know if she was disappointed. It was clear he didn't want to talk to her . . . but if that was the case, why had he asked her out? She toyed with her spoon in her soup, her appetite mostly gone.

"Dessert?" their waiter asked, his voice kind. She suspected he could tell their date was going badly, because he kept casting sympathetic looks in her direction.

Hank looked at her and she shook her head, and the waiter set the bill down.

"If we're leaving, I need to run to the ladies' room before we go," Becca said, getting to her feet.

Hank got to his feet, too, and nodded.

She turned and crossed the restaurant, biting back her

sigh of disappointment. Well, this was how dating went now, wasn't it? You had to date around to find the right guy. That's what all the magazines said. It was an empowered time and she didn't have to settle for the first man that crossed her path . . . except she was pretty sure she liked this one. So that was frustrating.

As she walked past the bar, her skirt snagged on something and flipped up. She felt a breeze on her butt and gasped, reaching for the back of her dress.

Everyone in the restaurant was going to see her ugly granny panties!

Except when she went to smooth her skirt down, someone else's hand was there. Becca was horrified to find that someone from the bar—a biker from the rough look of him—had grabbed her skirt and was leering at her.

"Hey there, little girl." He winked at her in a creepy way. "Where're you hurrying off to?"

Becca jerked her skirt out of his grip, humiliation staining her cheeks as the guys sitting next to the biker laughed and stared at her.

"You saw her panties," another one said, leering in her direction. "No one's getting laid tonight!"

And they all started laughing again.

She'd never been so humiliated. It felt as if the entire restaurant was full of men, all of them laughing at her. She—

A massive body clad in dark colors stepped in front of her. Before she could say anything, Hank's big hand touched her arm and he was practically shielding her from everyone's gaze. He'd stepped in front of her to confront the laughing man and was now looming over him, a deadly look in his eye.

"Don't like the way you're talking to my lady," he growled, his voice so low it was barely audible. "Sure didn't like the way you're tryin' to embarrass her."

"Pal, I'mma let you in on a secret." He laughed, drunkenly raising his glass into the air. "You ain't getting any tonight. Did you see—"

To her surprise, Hank reached over and plucked the glass from the man's hand and set it down on the bar. He leaned forward even more, inches from the man's face. Becca was frozen on the spot, unable to look away.

Hank murmured something too low to hear, and the man at the bar blanched. His buddies averted their eyes. The biker rubbed his mouth and glanced over at her. "I . . . ah, right. I'm sorry, miss. Just got carried away."

She stared at him in helpless, mute fury, not sure what else to say.

Hank turned and looked at her, waiting.

Was she supposed to give her approval? What would happen if she didn't? For a moment, she wanted to beat the biker with her purse and shout obscenities in his face for making her feel so stupid, but she was frozen in place. All she did was nod and rush to the bathroom.

She just wanted this horrible evening to end already. It had started with such promise, but everything seemed to be going wrong, all of it.

Inside the bathroom, Becca sat on the toilet for a few long minutes and wept. She was still embarrassed. That hadn't changed. She wished she'd been stronger. She wished she'd responded better. That she'd taken charge. Instead, she was hiding in the bathroom and weeping like an idiot because some jerk had harassed her. She hadn't reacted. She'd frozen, and she was mad at herself over that as much as everything else.

Becca gave herself a minute—two, max—to cry, and then she sniffed and went to the mirror to fix her makeup. She dabbed away smudged mascara, reapplied her lip gloss, and then put her hand on the door, dreading that she was going to have to walk across that crowded restaurant one more time with everyone staring at her, knowing she was wearing the ugliest panties known to humankind under her cute dress because her date wasn't going to get any.

God, how humiliating.

She took a deep breath and then opened the door and stepped into the hallway that led back out to the main area of the restaurant. In the distance, dishes were clinking in the kitchen and music was playing. It sounded normal. She didn't hear the guys at the bar, their loud laughter, or anything of that nature.

Her date waited at the entrance to the bathroom, leaning against the wall. He was an intimidating figure, made all the more terrifying by the dark scowl on his face. He straightened as she exited and touched her bare arm when she tried to brush past him.

"Wait," he murmured. "Stop."

She did, staring at the wall and at the framed picture of a butcher's diagram of beef and how it related to cattle. Huh. So that was where the T-bone came from.

Calloused fingers touched her chin. Hank gently lifted her face until her gaze met his, and he scanned her eyes, his mouth drawing to a firm, hard line at the sight of her reddened eyes. His thumb brushed over her chin, just once, and then he leaned in. "Do you have cash?"

"Cash?" She gave him a curious look. "For my half of the bill?"

"No." He leaned in closer. "For my bail money if I go beat the shit out of that guy."

Becca's eyes went wide. He was serious? As she stared up at him, she noticed the intense look on his face, the tightness at the edges of his mouth, and realized that, yes, he was very serious.

Oh. For some reason, that made her feel better. She

hadn't reacted on her own, but he was outraged on her behalf, and that somehow helped. She touched his arm. "Let's just go, okay?"

"You sure?"

She nodded.

A moment later, a big hand splayed across her back, and then Hank slowly escorted her out of the restaurant, glaring at the men as they passed the bar. Not one of them looked in Becca's direction. They all looked terrified.

And, okay, that made her feel a little better, too.

Hank calmly guided her through the parking lot and opened her door for her, helping her into the truck. He shut the door, then paused. For a long moment, she held her breath as he glanced back over at the rows of motorcycles, as if he was considering. Then he looked at her again.

She shook her head.

He nodded once and then got into the truck and started it up, and then they started the long drive back to Painted Barrel.

It was quiet in the truck cab, and Becca fidgeted with her purse and the hem of her dress, wondering if she should say anything. Eventually, curiosity got the best of her. "Would you have really—"

"Yes."

Well. All right, then. It was hard to dislike a man that was willing to go to jail for your honor. She found herself smiling in the darkness and glanced over at him again. "You really scared that guy, you know."

"Good." A ruthless smile crossed his face.

She tilted her head, watching him as he drove. "What did you say to him?"

He glanced over at her for a moment, as if debating whether to tell her. Then Hank turned back to the road once more. "Told him I had my skinning knife in my truck and

I wasn't afraid to go to prison for wearing him like a fur coat."

Becca paused. "Well . . . that's rather savage."

"That's the idea."

"Would you have—"

He snorted. "No. But he didn't know that." Hank glanced over at her again. "I'm sorry."

He was sorry? "For?"

"For not doing more."

The man had the ability to shock her, constantly. "Are you kidding me?" Her voice rose to a screechy note and she made herself calm down. "Hank, I dated a man for ten years and he never would have done that for me." If anything, Greg would have chastised her for wearing too short a dress and causing a scene, like she was the problem. "I can't thank you enough for standing up for me."

"Hated that it happened on our date."

"Yeah, well, me too."

"One thing's clear, though."

She turned to him. "What's that?"

"You have shit taste in men."

A horrified giggle escaped her. "I do not!"

"As one of those men, I can safely say your taste could be better." He grinned over at her, and for the moment, the mood between them was crackling and fun. She forgot all about the awkward dinner date and the jerks at the bar. This was the Hank she wanted to go out with. The one that made sly, sharp comments. The one that looked at her like he wanted to eat her alive. She just had to get him to show up instead of the silent, broody guy who made her feel like an idiot.

Then they were in front of her house, the pale strings of lights flickering in the salon window. She'd left her porch light on, and Main Street was surprisingly quiet for a Friday night. Hank got out of the truck and, like before, opened her door for her and escorted her to her front porch, his big hand on her back. She was acutely aware of that small touch, and for some reason, it felt wrong that the date was about to end when they'd just had a breakthrough.

She pulled her keys out and hesitated before she opened the door. "You want to come in and watch some Netflix?"

"Netflix?" he echoed.

Oh god, was he going to think she was asking him to Netflix and chill? That was code for hooking up. "It's just to watch a movie, nothing else," she blurted, and then felt her face go bright red because she'd practically shrieked that at him like a crazy woman. "I'm sorry. I'm not very good at this. I don't want you to think—"

But Hank nodded slowly. "Me either." He scratched at his hair, mussing it up, and let out a long sigh. "Here I thought calving season was hard, but it's hardest being on a date with a pretty woman."

Aw. He thought she was pretty? Becca felt herself melting at the compliment. "I've only ever dated one person, so I'm pretty rusty at this sort of thing."

"The one that didn't defend you. Right."

"But I like you," she blurted. "I think you're real sweet."

He scowled. "Sweet?"

For some reason, his grumpiness made her smile. "Sweet is good. Did you want to come in? It's okay if you say no. I promise you won't hurt my feelings."

For a moment, Hank hesitated. He shifted on his feet, clearly uncomfortable. "I don't want you to think I have ideas or anything . . ."

Ideas? Oh gosh. "Don't worry. You're not getting laid." She gestured at her skirt. "Remember? I'm wearing the ugliest panties ever."

"I liked 'em."

"They have squirrels on them."

"I like squirrels." And she could see a flash of his bright white teeth against that beard.

And gosh if that smile wasn't doing things to her insides. She was all aflutter. He saw her embarrassing panties and liked them. He'd defended her like some rough-and-tumble knight in shining armor.

Had she thought this date wasn't going well? It was going amazingly. So Becca just smiled at him and opened her door, then waited for him to join her inside.

CHAPTER TEN

She expected him to hesitate again, but this time he joined her instantly, glancing around at the inside of her small house. Because most of the bottom floor was the storefront for the salon, she had a tiny living room and an equally tiny kitchen. Her bedroom and bathroom upstairs were much bigger, but she didn't mind the small size since it was just her there. Hank seemed to eat up most of the entry hall, though, and she suspected he'd eat up most of the living room, too. Or any room he entered, really.

He stepped inside and eyed her place. It was a little . . . okay, it was super girly. Greg had lived with her off and on throughout their relationship, and she'd picked a lot of neutral things for their shared living space. Now that he was gone, she'd veered toward the other end of the spectrum. Romantic prints of paintings covered the pale purple walls—Gustav Klimt's *The Kiss*, Waterhouse's *The Lady of Shalott*, a Degas with ballerinas. She had leafy plants on her coffee tables and delicate lacy white pillows tossed over her purple sofa. Everything was ultra girly, because she liked girly things.

But Hank only looked around and then sat down on one end of her sofa as if he was surrounded by girly stuff all the time.

"Can I get you a drink? Popcorn?" she asked, setting her purse down on the counter.

"Sure."

Becca hurried over and handed him the remote to her wall-mounted television. "You pick something to stream. I'll handle the snacks." She kicked off her high heels and curled her toes in the carpet, then headed into the kitchen. Once the popcorn was in the microwave, she pulled off her dangly earrings and let her hair down. If they were going to watch a movie, she wanted to relax. Would he pick something funny? Something sexy? She wondered if he was going to send her a quiet message with his movie choice and hoped that was the case. After all, if she sat down and he'd picked *Fifty Shades of Grey*, she knew she was in for some hard-core making out.

And, oh gosh, she wanted some hard-core making out. It felt as if it had been so long since she'd been touched. Just thinking about it made her ache.

She rejoined Hank and sat on the other end of her couch, curling her legs under her as she handed him the popcorn bowl and a drink. The movie started, and she bit her lip, wondering what they were about to watch . . .

It.

They were about to watch a horror movie about a killer clown.

She turned to him. "Really?"

Hank's brows furrowed. "You said I could pick. Is this bad?"

"No, of course not," she said hastily. "I'm just surprised is all."

"I picked something I can't watch with Libby around." He gave her a sheepish look. "I can pick something else if you'd like."

"No, a horror movie is totally fine." She'd just sleep with the lights on later. No problem. Becca settled in on the couch, hugging a pillow, and started watching.

They were about five or ten minutes into the film when Hank settled his arm across the back of the couch. She was utterly aware of it, just as she was completely aware of when he slid it just a little lower, his fingertips brushing her shoulder.

So Becca adjusted her legs on the couch, shifting ever so slightly in his direction. Gosh, this was just like being a teenager again, with furtive touches and guessing whether or not each caress was intentional. Goose bumps broke out on her skin as he caressed a lock of her hair, toying with it as the movie blared on and children were lured into sewers or something awful like that. She wasn't paying attention. The movie was in front of her, but she was utterly focused on the man sitting a few feet away. She watched him out of the corner of her eye, but his gaze remained locked on the television.

Then one big hand brushed against her nape.

She shifted closer to him again, hoping he'd drag her into his lap and kiss her silly. Instead, the movie had a jump scare and she jerked, then settled back on the couch just a hint closer to him. His thumb was definitely resting on her neck, ever so slightly rubbing her with small touches that made her crazy with need.

And still he didn't grab her. Ugh. Was it because of the squirrel panties? Did the sight of them convince him that this was going to be a totally chaste date? She suddenly wished she'd worn her most scandalous panties ever, damn it. Even if she didn't want to have sex on the first date, they could kiss, right? Surely they could kiss. She leaned a little closer to him.

"You uncomfortable?"

Becca looked over at him in surprise. "No, why?"

His eyes were inscrutable in the low light of her living room. "You keep moving over."

She glanced down at the amount of sofa between them. Okay, yeah, she'd somehow managed to move over enough that there was less than a foot between them. Move back to her side, or admit what she was doing? Becca glanced over at him. He didn't look annoyed, and his hand was still ever so slightly playing with her nape.

She opted for confession. "I was hoping you'd kiss me tonight."

"Oh."

Oh? All she got was "oh"? She bit back her frown and stared at him for a long moment. He didn't move, and when the disappointment threatened to crush her, she decided she'd return to the other end of the couch and pretend like the conversation never happened. She started to get to her feet—

The moment her butt left the couch, Hank's heavy arm snagged her around the waist. He drew her backward and she tumbled into his arms, letting out a squeak in surprise. Becca turned to look at him and realized breathlessly that her face was only an inch or so away from his. They were so close that their noses were practically touching.

"Remember that part where I said I wasn't very good at this dating thing?" he murmured. "Still applies."

"Yes, but—"

She didn't get to finish her sentence. He clamped one of those big hands on the back of her neck and pulled her toward him, and then his mouth was on hers. Becca stiffened, shocked at the bristly feel of his beard against her face, but the softness of his mouth soon took over everything. He tasted sweet—like peppermint and popcorn—and she wondered if he'd been sneaking breath mints. His lips brushed over hers, nipping and kissing and exploring, and a little sigh of pleasure escaped her, her arms twining around his neck. Then his tongue was brushing against hers, and she let out a full-blown moan.

God, his mouth was amazing. Hot and insistent, he knew just how she wanted to be kissed. He didn't try to attack with his tongue. It was more of a coaxing, a flirty dance between mouths, slick and subtle and teasing all at once, and it made her ache all freaking over her body. His hand was in her hair, his other on her back, and the kisses grew hotter and more intense with every moment that passed.

He cupped her face, tilting it ever so slightly, and then began to lick at the inside of her mouth, as if he couldn't get enough. She'd never been kissed so deeply, so erotically, and her hips shifted against his thigh.

To her surprise, Hank groaned, the sound full of need, and it made her toes curl with pleasure to hear it. Oh wow. So he liked kissing her? So—

She lost track of her thoughts as he slid a hand under the hem of her skirt and caressed her thigh. Oh sweet heavens, that felt good. So good.

Whimpering, she grabbed his hand and steered it out of her skirt and to someplace new and equally bold—her breast. "Keep touching me," she whispered. "I like it."

"Becca," he groaned against her mouth. "Tell me to stop and I'll stop."

"Don't stop."

He half chuckled against her mouth and then kissed her hard once more. His big hand cupped her breast, and then he began to stroke back and forth with his thumb, caressing her nipple through the layers of her clothing.

And, oh, that was so unfair. So good, too. She moaned, rocking against his leg once more, and when he shifted his weight, his other hand locking around her back, she didn't protest. A few more kisses and maneuvering of their bodies, and then she was under him on the couch, her dress hiked up at her hips, her legs cradling him.

"Just gonna kiss you," he promised between strokes of his tongue. His hand was still on her breast, teasing her aching nipple into a rock-hard point. "Nothing more. I promise."

"Just kissing," she agreed, and tugged his shirt free from his belt. She wanted to touch him, to run her hands over those granite-like muscles. "Just kissing. Just . . . oooh." Her hands slipped under his shirt, under his undershirt, and then she touched nothing but warm, hard flesh. He felt amazing. Like a sculpture come to life. Before she'd met Hank, she'd always said she liked a dad bod—a guy with a little softness in his gut.

Nope. Apparently now she had a thing for washboard abs.

"Love these pretty tits," he rasped against her mouth, nipping at her bottom lip. "Can't stop thinking about them."

She loved hearing that. Loved knowing that he was thinking about her, obsessing over her. He'd turned her down flat when she'd asked him out. Had he been regretting it this whole time? Moaning, Becca scratched her nails along his sides and loved the ragged noise he made when she did. God, she bet quarters would bounce off his ass. She suddenly wanted to see that.

His hand left her breast and she whimpered a protest.

"No," she told him, digging her nails into his skin. "Don't stop. Don't—"

Her words died on a moan as his hand slid back under her skirt again, and he found her panties. His hand pushed between her thighs, and she was soaked. He said something sexy, something deep and growly between kisses, but she wasn't paying attention. Her focus was entirely on the hand between her legs, the thumb rubbing up and down her folds. Oh god, she'd worn the *ugliest* panties tonight. Why had she been so stupid? "You can't laugh at my panties," she told him between frenzied kisses. "No laughing."

"Panties . . . staying . . . on," he promised her, then claimed her mouth again.

She was lost in the dizzying kiss, in every delicious sweep of his tongue, and then he pushed the elastic of her panties aside and his fingers were on her folds. Becca's fists knotted in his shirt and she made a sound that was distinctly unsexy. It might have been a gurgle. She didn't know. Didn't care, either. All she knew was that Hank was dragging those thick, calloused fingers over her pussy, and if he touched her clit, he was going to make her come. She was so wet, so needy—

And then he touched her clit and she exploded. The world shattered around her and she cried out against his ear, her entire body seizing up like it wanted to fold in on itself.

Oh god, she'd never come so hard. And he just kept touching her and kissing her like he wanted to make her come *again*.

Not that it happened. Eventually the kisses slowed and became more languid, and her muscles unclenched.

He pressed another light kiss to her mouth and chuckled, his fingers stroking over her pussy one last time. "I'm sorry for what I said yesterday."

"Huh?" Becca shook her head, trying to focus on him. She was too dazed, felt too toe-curlingly amazing to try to put words together. And sounds. He kissed her slowly again . . . and then she realized she was pinned on her couch underneath a big, hairy cowboy with his hand in her ugly squirrel panties as some hideous clown killed people on the television.

This was not how she'd imagined her first date going. A hot blush seared her face.

He rubbed his nose against hers, his eyes heavy-lidded. "About you not coming back to the ranch. Yesterday morning. I tried to chase you off and that was mean of me."

"Oh." Were they talking about the ranch and not their date? "Um . . . okay."

He nipped at her upper lip, and, gosh, if his hand didn't stop stroking her pussy, she was going to start grinding against him like a shameful hussy, desperate for the next orgasm. It was his turn now, wasn't it? She supposed he was waiting for her to get up and reciprocate. Somehow, the idea didn't irritate her like it normally did with Greg.

Damn it, the last thing she wanted to think about was Greg, especially when the man on top of her felt so good, and he was still nibbling on her lips like he never intended to leave.

Hank's mouth lazily moved over hers in one last kiss, and then his hand left her pussy—and she could have cried at the loss. "You'll come by in the morning, then? With doughnuts?"

An odd request, especially after making out. "Do you . . . want me to?"

"Yeah. Gonna wanna see you."

Ooh. That made her feel warm and fuzzy. She smiled shyly. "Then, yes. I will."

He nodded. "Guess I should head home now."

"You don't . . ." She gestured at his lower half. "I can . . ."

Hank frowned at her. "No. This wasn't about getting something for myself." He almost seemed offended that she'd suggested it, and Becca wondered what she'd somehow stepped into.

"Okay. Sorry."

He sat up, raked a hand through his hair, and then got to his feet.

She sat up, too, eased her dress back down, and turned

the movie off while he headed for the door. When she stood up, her legs were wobbly. Should she follow him out? He was already in the foyer, as if he couldn't wait to leave. Strange man. Kinda hurt her feelings, really. "I had a nice time," she called out.

Hank immediately turned around and moved back to her side. He grabbed her by the arms, bent down, and planted a hot, searing kiss on her face that made her mouth feel puffy. He stared down at her for a long moment, nodded, and then turned and left.

"See you in the morning," she called softly after him as the door shut. Well, okay, there were a few mixed messages in there, but overall, the date had been rather nice. Her thighs squeezed together, reminding her of the rocket-fueled orgasm she'd just had under him. Okay. More than nice. Amazing. Her fingers brushed over her mouth and for some reason the lower half of her face felt sore. Curious, she headed upstairs to the bathroom to look in the mirror.

And gasped. The lower half of her face was bright red, her mouth swollen. Not just from the kisses, but from his beard. She leaned in and stared at her face in horror.

She had a full day booked tomorrow—Saturdays were busy at the salon. If this didn't fade, she was going to have a lot of explaining to do.

Hank couldn't stay there for one minute longer, or he was going to fling Becca down on the couch and screw her brains out. He knew she didn't want that, so he'd beat a hasty retreat out of her house and practically ran off the porch to his vehicle. He managed to drive safely out of town, but when he raked his hand through his hair, he smelled her on his fingers.

He quickly pulled over, freed his aching cock from his pants, and stroked it three times before he came all over himself. With a deep sigh, he rested his head on the back of the seat and thought about the evening.

He was terrible at dating. He knew that now, after painful hours with Becca in which he couldn't think of a thing to say to her. She kept trying to make small talk, and all he could think about was kissing her. Touching her. Tasting her. He couldn't concentrate through dinner because her hair was in this messy bun-thing and all these tendrils had escaped and kept touching her neck and he had to keep thinking about skinning and hunting and fishing to try to keep his dick from standing at attention.

Then those jerks at the bar had embarrassed her, showing the entire restaurant her panties—pink with big brown blotches on them. Squirrels, she'd said later. She'd completely frozen and he'd seen red. He was out of his seat before he could even think, and he'd wanted to hurt the man at the bar for daring to fucking *touch her*. The only reason he hadn't was because Becca had told him not to.

But he'd seen how red and puffy her eyes were when she came out of the ladies' room, and his chest had hurt. He'd wanted to fix it. He felt responsible. She hadn't wanted him to, and he was of half a mind to drive all the way back to the bar and hope that the jerk was still there . . .

And then what? Have Becca bail him out of jail in the morning? Explain to Libby that her daddy didn't know how to keep his temper in check? He stared down at his messy hands and sighed, then grabbed the package of wet wipes from the back seat of the truck. He always kept them on hand because Libby was a toddler disaster, and they were useful now to clean up the evidence that he couldn't control himself when it came to Becca Loftis.

She was just . . . so damn pretty. And sweet. And soft. He shouldn't have touched her when the movie came on, but he couldn't help it. Her hair was down, and he thought he'd sneak a quick feel of it. Just a touch, and then he'd keep his hands to himself because he needed to treat her right, treat her like a lady.

He'd mauled her anyhow. Just shoved his big brutish hand in her panties and made her come because he'd needed to like he'd needed air. Afterward, he'd felt a little guilty, but not as guilty as he should have.

Because he'd wanted to do more. So much more. But . . . more resulted in Libby the last time he'd lost his head about a woman. Becca wasn't much like Adria. She was soft-hearted and kind and gentle and she'd fall in love with him. She'd want to have a family.

And while he liked the thought of a family—and Becca in his bed—it would be here. In Wyoming. Because someone like Becca wouldn't last very long in the Alaska wilderness. It took a certain type to live in the northern reaches, and she wasn't it.

So, no, he couldn't touch her like he had tonight. Couldn't kiss her like he needed her. He sure shouldn't have wrung those little cries out of her or played with her pretty tits and . . . hell.

He grabbed more wet wipes, because he was going to need them. His cock was already hard in his pants once more.

This might be a problem. He couldn't walk around with a permanent hard-on. He had to decide if he wanted the problem of the pretty hairdresser, or if it was better to cut ties before she got too attached.

And because he was a weak man, he sniffed his hand again and jerked off one more time.

CHAPTER ELEVEN

The next morning, the redness in Becca's face had mostly disappeared. Mostly. She still looked rather suspiciously pink in the lower parts of her face, so she styled her hair to frame her face as much as possible, slathered on a bit too much makeup, and tried to pretend like it wasn't a problem.

Because really . . . as problems went? This wasn't one. She'd been kissed thoroughly on her date with a handsome man. He'd made her come so hard that she'd seen stars. And now she was going to see him again this morning. She'd slept so well last night, and she couldn't seem to stop smiling even though it was ridiculously early. Maybe she was getting used to the early-morning ranch hours, which might not be a bad thing if she was going to date a cowboy.

She picked up the doughnuts, with a bag of pink-iced doughnut holes for her little angel, Libby, and drove out to the Swinging C. She parked in her usual spot, grabbed her things out of the car, and was a little surprised that Hank wasn't waiting to take the packages from her. He was normally the first one to greet her in the morning.

That felt a little weird, especially after last night.

So she knocked, and when Doc answered the door, she gave him a brilliant smile. "Your early doughnut delivery is here!"

"Prettiest deliveryman I've ever seen," Doc teased, just like he did every time she arrived. "Come on inside. Everyone's just now stirring."

"Hank sleeping in?" she asked, then felt her face flush because, gosh, wasn't she being so obvious?

"No, he's in the barn. Bit of a calf emergency." Doc gave her a crooked grin. "You just have me this morning, and Libby."

"Oh." Well, that was disappointing, just a little. She supposed she could text him . . . or would that be too pushy? "How are the puppies?"

"Set those doughnuts down and I'll show you." He winked at her.

Hank didn't text her all morning. Or afternoon.

It was fine, of course. She told herself that over and over again, imagining the cow version of the television show *ER*. If a cow's life was on the line—or a calf's—he might not have time to text or call. She told herself that was totally normal, even if she was hugely disappointed to not hear from him. She might have had visions of showing up with doughnuts that morning, only to be swept into his arms and kissed hard.

Didn't happen.

And she couldn't dwell on it. She had clients. Her day was full and Libby was with her, so she didn't have a moment to herself. Libby was great, quietly coloring and keeping herself occupied while Becca worked and checked in on her. The new schoolteacher in town, Amy Mckinney, had showed up as a walk-in, and Becca had seated her immediately. She was nice and friendly, shy and sweet and excited about the summer session of preschool, and she'd mentioned that she wanted Libby enrolled. Becca promised to talk to Libby's father about that.

Provided she ever spoke with the man again.

No sooner had she started drying Amy's hair than Hannah came in the door. It wasn't time for her weekly appointment yet, which meant this was a gossip session disguised as a grooming emergency. Becca smothered the groan in her throat and forced a smile to her face. "Hey, Hannah. What's up?"

"Oh, my nails are looking ragged," the older woman said, wiggling her fingers as she plopped herself down in the empty salon chair next to Amy. "Thought I'd come in and see what you could do."

"Sure, give me five minutes." She smiled at Amy in the mirror and dried another section of her hair. "So, do you like Painted Barrel, Amy?"

Amy smiled. "I do. It's a great place. I—"

Hannah cleared her throat loudly and gave Becca a pointed look. "Lots of good-looking men, right?"

"I . . . I guess so?" Amy looked embarrassed. "I'm not really seeing anyone."

So she wasn't seeing Greg? Not that Becca cared, but she still felt a little stab of vindication. It wasn't that she wanted Greg to be unhappy forever . . . maybe just for about ten years to make up for all the time Becca had wasted on him. "Plenty of time for that," Becca told her. "Spend your time with your girlfriends."

"No girlfriends here," Amy began again, only to be interrupted by Hannah once more.

The older woman leaned over confidentially. "I heard you were kissing that mountain of a cowboy, Becca. It's all over town this morning."

Gah. She knew Hannah had something she'd wanted to gossip about, but hearing it out loud was still embarrassing. Becca checked her reflection quickly, certain that the beard burn was going to be bright red like a scarlet letter. Nope. Her face looked blessedly normal, thank goodness. "Who said we were kissing?"

"That's just the rumor," Hannah said innocently. "Is it true?"

"It was just a date," Becca insisted. "A first date. A very nice, chaste one." Man, she was such a liar. Her mind was still fired up with thoughts of how Hank had felt as his weight pressed her down on the couch, his hand in her panties as he'd made her come. Yeah. Not very chaste at all.

"Mmm. I've never talked to him. What's he like?"

Oh god. She was being put on the spot. "Um . . . horror movies? Steak? His daughter?" She gestured over at Libby in the corner. "It's just casual, I promise."

"Is he handsome?" Hannah asked and then gestured at her face. "Under all that garbage? Maybe you can get him to shave. It has to be hard for you, him looking like he does and you always so put together."

Amy bit her lip, her expression embarrassed. Becca felt the same way. Hannah was being pushy as heck and it was grating on Becca's nerves because she was feeling very unsure of their status. Just one tiny text would have made everything better, but did he text her? No. Call? Nope. Was she just a free babysitter and doughnut delivery service with a bit of making out on the side?

Or maybe he just thought they were super casual and she'd hear from him in a week or two. God, that would be the worst. Becca didn't know how to do casual. Not after being with Greg for ten years. She was past casual. She wanted something real. Something legit. "We're just casual right now," Becca finally lied. "It doesn't mean anything. It was just to get back on the wagon, you know? Test the waters."

Yeah, that sounded like a strong, confident answer. Now she just needed to believe it.

"Well, if you want to test the waters more, I have a wonderful nephew who lives in Topeka. He's an accountant and he's been married three times but he's still great friends with all three of his wives."

Oh boy. She forced a smile to her lips. "I'm taking it slow, but thank you, Hannah."

"I should get going," Amy said apologetically. She touched her hair. "I love this, though. It looks amazing."

Becca beamed at her. "You have gorgeous hair. It was my pleasure."

She took Amy's money and cleaned off the station after the other woman left, grateful that Hannah had given up on her line of questioning—for a few minutes anyhow. When she turned to focus on the other woman, though, she noticed that Hannah was talking to Libby, and Libby was showing her a picture. Gosh, Libby was just a delight. The little girl was adorable today in green coveralls with a tiny pink shirt underneath, and Becca had twisted her hair into two cute knots atop her head.

As she approached, she heard Libby's small voice piping up. "And this is where Daddy lives with Uncle Jack and Uncle Caleb and me." She pointed at a picture, and Becca noticed it was one of a scribbly cabin with stick figures and some triangle things in the background. Mountains, maybe?

"Is that the ranch?" Hannah asked.

"No, it's back home. Daddy says we're gonna go back there once the cows stop having babies."

It was like a punch in the gut.

Oh.

Maybe that was why Hank wasn't calling her. Calving

season was almost over. The ranch would settle on its feet once the herd wasn't needing constant supervision, and then Doc would probably bring in a few new ranch hands . . . and Hank had no intention of staying. That was probably why he hadn't enrolled Libby in preschool, either.

"Are you ready, Hannah?" Becca asked brightly. She moved to her nail station and gestured at the seat across from her.

"Why don't you draw me a cow, Libby?" Hannah said to the little girl, and when Libby started to draw again, she touched her hair gently and then moved to sit with Becca. "Cutest little thing."

"She really is."

"Good thing she didn't take after that father of hers." Hannah widened her eyes innocently. "Her mother must be dainty. You know anything about her?"

"Haven't asked. What color?" She shoved the nail polish rack forward with a little more vigor than she should have.

Hannah lingered for far too long, and by the time her nails were dry, she'd grilled Becca for information on everything. Where did they eat? What did she wear? What did he order? What did he wear? What time did they get back? What did they talk about? It was exhausting and she was relieved when Hannah finally went back to the hotel.

As Hannah walked out the door, she tittered and looked back at Becca. Sure enough, the moment Hannah left, Hank strolled in. He was wearing his cowboy hat and jeans, a checked blue-and-black shirt rolled up at the elbow.

God, he looked good.

"Daddy!" Libby flung herself up from the tiny pink desk and raced for him, the picture in her hand fluttering.

Becca looked away as he scooped his daughter up, busying herself with the broom. There was loose hair on the floor that had to be swept up, and she needed to clean her nail station. He could just take Libby and go, and that would be that. "Her bag's behind the counter, packed and ready to go," she told him. And just to prove that she had no hurt feelings, she gave him a bright smile and then started sweeping as if her life depended on it.

Hank sidled up to her, standing right over where she was sweeping and forcing her to look up at him. "Got a minute?"

Oh, so he wanted to talk now? Her annoyance flared, and in her head, she kept hearing Libby's voice saying *We're going home once the cows stop having babies.* Was he going to tell her he was leaving? Why should she care? It wasn't like they were serious. It was just one date.

And a hot make-out session on the couch.

Her feelings shouldn't have been hurt at all.

She gave him an apologetic smile and gestured at the floor. "I've really got to clean up."

"But—"

"Daddy, I have to potty," Libby proclaimed. "Number two!"

He grimaced, and she hated that she found that so damned endearing. "Mind if I let the princess here stink up your bathroom?"

Her mouth twitched in a reluctant smile. "Go over to my house. Next door. I have another haircut coming in about five minutes, so she can take all the time she needs there."

Hank nodded and gave her a searching look, as if he wasn't quite satisfied with her answer. Like he wanted to say something, and she tensed up, hoping that he would. That he'd tell her all about his day, or why he'd avoided her, or that he'd had fun last night . . . but he only nodded and took his squirmy daughter out to the porch and then opened the door to her house and stepped inside.

Becca blew out a breath and stared down at the floor.

Why was dating so stupidly hard?

CHAPTER TWELVE

She swept and mopped the floor and tidied things up, deliberately taking her time. Her final appointment for the day canceled, and she stared around her clean salon and supposed it was time to go back to her place. Hank was still there, his truck parked out front, which worried her. That meant a confrontation of some kind . . . either that or Libby had made a dreadful mess in the bathroom.

With a four-year-old, anything was possible, but Becca suspected it was a confrontation. So she steeled herself, preparing to hear the "it's not you, it's me" speech from a big, surly cowboy, and closed up shop. She locked the front and went through the side door that led to the back of her house . . .

And smelled pancakes. Heard bacon frying. That was odd. Hank was . . . cooking?

Confused, she headed into the kitchen and saw her small dining table had been taken over. One of her fat, decorative pillar candles had been lit and set in the center of the table, and Libby was at the far end, carefully folding Becca's best napkins. Hank's hat hung on a wall peg by the door as if it belonged there. A huge stack of pancakes was on the table, along with condiments and plates, and she looked over in surprise at Hank, who stood in the kitchen over the stove. He looked confident and sexy and . . . amazing.

"You're . . . cooking?"

Hank gave her a half smile. "I know how to cook. It's pretty limited, but I do know how. Hope you don't mind breakfast for dinner."

"I'm helping!" Libby waved one of the napkins at her.

"I see that," Becca murmured, moving to take the napkins from her. "And what a wonderful job you've done. Why don't we wash our hands while your daddy finishes?"

She bustled Libby upstairs to the bathroom, doing her best not to stare at Hank as he expertly flipped bacon in the pan, his stance casual and determined. He hadn't even made a mess of her kitchen, not really. Greg had cooked for her once or twice, but the ensuing disaster in the kitchen had been so dreadful that it had ended up being less exciting and more of a mess for her to clean up. When she came back down with Libby, Hank was near the table and pulled chairs out for both of them.

And she felt like she could smile for the first time that day.

"I'm sorry if I was a little short with you earlier," Becca told him as she sat down. The setup looked amazing. There was buttered toast, fresh bacon, and so many pancakes that she couldn't possibly eat all of them. He'd done this for her. She didn't even care that he was using an expensive candle designed to be used for show only. It didn't matter. He'd made her dinner.

Hank pushed in her chair and murmured in her ear. "I said I wasn't good at relationships. I'm good at pancakes."

She chuckled at that. Maybe they both weren't good at

this sort of thing. Hank was used to being on his own, and Becca was practically planning their lives together after one date. Perhaps they both needed to meet somewhere in the middle.

The pancakes were amazing. Hank had cut both hers and Libby's into a heart shape, and the remnants ended up on his plate, which she thought was cute. Everything was perfect, right down to the conversation. Libby chattered and talked to her dad nonstop, and Hank answered her between bites. She enjoyed herself, loving the interplay between the child and her father, and when dinner was done, Becca smiled at them. "Do you guys want to stay and watch a movie?"

"A different one, I hope," Hank said.

She chuckled. "I'm sure we can find something Libby appropriate."

After the table was cleared, they all three piled onto the couch—Hank in the middle—and put on a Pixar movie. Libby was rapt, her gaze glued to the screen, and Becca found watching her almost as amusing as the movie.

Not that she was paying much attention to either, because Hank's arm immediately went across the back of the couch once the movie started playing, and by the time it was halfway over, he was rubbing her shoulder and her neck as cartoon animals marched across the screen.

She should not have been turned on nearly as much as she was. It seemed wrong to close her eyes and bite back a moan as he massaged her neck, his fingers working magic over muscles she didn't even know were tight. God, this man. She'd been so frustrated with him earlier and now she couldn't even think straight she was so blissed out.

Becca was utterly disappointed by the time the movie ended. His big, delicious hand left her neck and she glanced over at him. Libby was draped over his side, her mouth open in her sleep. She was adorably sweet, as was the protective way that Hank held her close. "Looks like it's past bedtime," she whispered.

He didn't get up, though. He just glanced over at her with a thoughtful look in his eyes. "Tonight was easier," he murmured, voice low.

"Easier?"

"Easier to talk to you. Easier to be around you. I felt like a big idiot at the restaurant. Like I wasn't fancy enough for you." His mouth flattened into a hard line. "Sorry if I made you uncomfortable."

Uncomfortable? Becca shook her head, startled at the confession. "You just seemed like you didn't want to be there with me."

"There? Not really. But with you? Absolutely."

And that made her feel warm and fuzzy. "All I wanted to do was spend time with you," she confessed. "Get to know you better. I'm not interested in fancy restaurants or anything like that. I'm not going out with you for a steak. I can buy my own." Becca gave him a wry smile. "I'm going out with you because you're tall and strong, and kind and thoughtful, and you have a cute daughter that you think the world of."

He grunted, then studied her. "It's not because of the beard?"

Becca giggled. Was that a joke? Was Hank Watson joking with her? "It's not my usual, but I don't mind it."

"Tore your face up something awful last night when we kissed." His voice was low and husky, and for a moment, it felt almost as if he were kissing her again. Becca's skin prickled with awareness as he gave her a lazy smile and then touched his beard. "Gonna have to figure out how to soften this up for when I kiss you again."

She could feel her cheeks flushing. "You sound so certain."

"That I want to kiss you again? Never been more sure of

anything in my life." With his free hand—his other arm still around the sleeping Libby—he reached out and carefully traced her mouth with his thumb. "I'd do it right now except . . ."

"Except you're a human pillow." Oh, but she ached with want. She wanted him to kiss her, too.

He nodded, his expression thoughtful. "I'm not good with texts and shit like that. So if you send me those, I might not answer right away. My hands are usually pretty filthy when I'm working, so the phone stays inside most days."

"Okay."

"I work long hours, too."

She tilted her head, pretending to study him. "Are you trying to scare me off from dating you?"

"Just don't want you thinking I'm someone I ain't." His fingers brushed along her jaw and then down to her shoulder. He stared at her skin as if entranced, and she mentally willed him to drag his hand lower, to her breast. "Like I said, I'm not real good at this."

"Then lucky for you, you're a good kisser."

Even though it was dark in the room, she could have sworn his eyes grew heated. "You keep saying shit like that and I'm gonna toss you down on this couch and show you all the things my mouth is real good at."

The insides of Becca's thighs tightened with arousal. That was a bold statement, but . . . she didn't mind it. In fact, she rather liked it. "But then you'd wake Libby up."

Hank sighed heavily and glanced at his sleeping daughter, who was oblivious to their soft, heated conversation. "I know. I should be getting back soon."

"Probably." Even if it disappointed her. But he wasn't like Greg. He wore responsibility like another shirt, and that was as sexy and appealing as everything else. If she was ever in need, she had no doubt that Hank would be there instantly, whereas her ex had thought of himself first, her second. So she got to her feet and picked up his hat from the peg on the wall, along with his keys, as he gently carried his daughter out of the house and toward his truck. Becca trailed behind him, watching as he skillfully opened the truck door with one hand, cradling Libby's sleeping form with the other. He pushed the passenger seat forward and then settled his daughter in her car seat in the rear seat of the truck and carefully buckled her in.

He turned to look at Becca, and she held out the keys and hat to him. "Thank you for a lovely dinner."

"Do I get dessert?" Hank moved forward to her, his hands going to her arms.

"Dessert?"

"Just a taste," he said, and then leaned in, stooping low so he could brush his lips over hers.

And oh . . . that kiss was perfection. She moaned into his mouth as he slicked his tongue against hers. Her hands went to his shirt and she clung to him as he coaxed and tasted, nibbled and explored her mouth. She'd never been kissed like this. It was as if he couldn't get enough of her mouth, like it was endlessly fascinating to him and he had to have more, more, more. Kissing Greg had been nothing like this. Nothing at all.

She never wanted it to end.

His tongue was like heaven. His big body loomed over hers, both protective and strong. As he kissed her, the world around them disappeared until there was nothing for her except his hands on her arms, his lips on her lips, his tongue caressing her tongue . . . and the heat between her thighs.

Hank pulled away far too quickly. She could have kissed him for hours, but he gave her a rueful smile. "Told myself it'd just be a taste."

"Oh. Right." Flustered, she brushed her hair back from

her face with a shaking hand and tried to give him a smile. "Let me know when you want the whole buffet."

No sooner had the words left her mouth than she felt like an idiot. He stared at her, and then one of those slow smiles crept across his lips. He leaned in again, his fingers skating along her jaw. "Not gonna let myself feast until I have time to savor every mouthful."

And goodness, now her whole body was flushing. Becca resisted the urge to fan herself as he checked on the sleeping Libby one more time, then carefully shut the door. Hank gave her one last lingering look before he got into the cab of the truck.

She stayed on the porch, hugging her chest as she watched him drive away. It wasn't until she was back inside, tidying up the relatively small mess he'd left, that she thought about her morning ritual. Was this his way of suggesting she start coming by again?

He'd told her that they didn't need her to head over in the morning anymore . . . but he'd also returned and kissed her tonight, so was that a yes or a no? Frowning to herself, she pulled out her phone and texted him.

BECCA: I know you said you don't check this often but I'm hoping you see this. Let me know if you need me to come by in the morning or if I should sleep in.

She stared down at the phone, wondering if she should end the message with a cute emoji. A kiss? A smiley? A freaking XOXO? In the end, she went with nothing and stewed over it.

There was no answer right away. Of course not. He was probably still driving the back roads all the way back out to the ranch. Even so, she didn't want to show up and be a pest. They'd had a second date—sort of—and Hank made it clear he was interested, even if it wasn't about helping out around the ranch. And they were grown men. They'd fed themselves for years, and with calving slowing down, surely they could feed themselves again.

She wouldn't show up unless invited. Becca knew she could be a bit of a busybody and didn't want Hank to feel as if she was making a nuisance of herself.

Even so, she checked her phone repeatedly as she washed her makeup off and got into her pajamas. Her room was quiet and lonely, and she thought about the cute puppies out at the ranch. Even if this thing with Hank wasn't more than a few fun dates, she wanted company of some kind. Maybe it was time to get a puppy so she'd have someone to come home to. With that thought on her mind, she turned on the television for some background noise, picked up her book, and started to read, checking her phone again, just in case.

Her phone chirped with an incoming text after a while. Becca jerked awake—she hadn't realized she'd fallen asleep, book in hand—and looked at the screen.

GREG: Hey, I'm swinging by the house tomorrow. Want to see how you're doing and I have a few things to pick up. XOXO

Becca groaned and threw her phone to the foot of the bed.

Why was it that the only XOXO that showed up on her phone was from her rotten, no-good ex?

CHAPTER THIRTEEN

Becca didn't come by that morning.

Hank thought that was odd. Caleb and Jack grumbled about the lack of doughnuts as if they didn't know how to feed themselves. Hank ignored all of it, made Libby some peanut butter toast, and then hustled her over to Doc's office at the far end of the building.

"You mind?" he asked, setting his daughter down.

Doc looked up from the puppy he had on the scale. He smiled down at Libby as she dropped to the floor and began to play with the black-and-brown bundles, little tails wagging. "You know I don't. Did Becca not come by?"

"She's a no-show."

"Is she sick? It's not like her." Doc's face wore a look of concern. "Her father always used to joke that Becca was more tenacious than a terrier. He had a lot of dogs, you know."

"I'm sure she's fine," he said abruptly, trying not to think too hard about how he'd more or less told her to buzz off days ago. Surely she realized he didn't mean it? That he'd liked her coming around? But maybe he should have been clearer.

Hell, he *was* bad at this.

Hank kissed Libby's head and then headed out to the barn to work.

By the time the sun was setting, he practically raced inside the house, hoping to see Becca there in the kitchen. Hell, he wouldn't care if she was sitting in the living room or even in her car, just as long as she was at the ranch. But inside, all he found was Uncle Ennis with Libby and the five puppies, and Jack and Caleb scrounging through the back of the fridge looking for dinner.

Jack looked up at him as he entered, scowling. "Where's your girlfriend? I'm starving."

"She ain't a short-order cook," Hank told him, but he had to admit he liked the thought of Becca being seen as his girlfriend . . . or even just as "his." "And what's wrong with your two hands?"

"My hands have been working all day long shoveling horse shit and feeding cows. It was kinda nice to have someone cooking for us." He pulled out a jar of pickles and opened it, staring morosely down at the contents. "And now all we got is this shit."

Caleb—the quiet one—frowned at Hank. "She mad at you? What'd you do?"

"Nothing," Hank said defensively.

"You must have done something," Jack insisted, fishing a pickle out of the jar with a fork. "That girl's been up here every day for the last month even though you did your best to ignore her." He glanced over at Caleb. "You know he did something."

Caleb nodded, taking the jar of pickles from his brother.

"I didn't do anything," Hank gritted. But . . . what if he had? What if he'd missed some subtle cue? What if he was supposed to tell her that he liked her coming around all the damn time? All he'd said was that they didn't need her anymore . . . and then they'd left it at that. He started to sweat, heading up to his room to fish out his phone. He knew it was one of those things he needed to keep on him, but after living in the deep wilds of Alaska where phone service was iffy? You learned to not need it much.

But maybe he should have called her this morning. Checked in to see why she didn't come by. Hell, he was still thinking like he was in the mountains half the time, with no one to check in on but Libby. Becca was different, though. She was a town girl . . . so maybe she needed more from him. And that made him sweat—not because she might need more, but because he might have already messed things up without realizing it.

Sure enough, his phone showed a message from late last night.

BECCA: I know you said you don't check this often but I'm hoping you see this. Let me know if you need me to come by in the morning or if I should sleep in.

Well, shit. He fumbled with the tiny keypad on the phone to text her back.

HANK: hrku

HANK: here

HANK: imhrku

HANK: noimhere

Damn it, typing on the damn thing was harder than it looked. His big fingers fumbled all over the tiny digital keyboard, which was obviously made for people with hands half the size of his. Plus, he didn't know how to type all that well so it took him forever just to type that out. She was gonna think he was a Grade A moron if he tried to type an apology.

He tried calling instead, but it went to voicemail. The moment her chirpy voice picked up, he growled in frustration and hung up. Storming down the stairs, he headed into the living area and scooped Libby up, then headed for the door.

"Where are you going?" Jack called from the kitchen doorway, still eating pickles.

"Town. Gonna see Becca."

"Pick up some food, will ya?" Jack asked.

"Burger," Caleb suggested.

"You boys know how to take care of yourselves, don't you?" Doc asked, amused. He didn't get up from the couch.

The two pickle eaters stared at him for a moment. "Yeah," Jack said slowly. "But after a month of someone else cooking for me, I'd rather eat anyone's cooking but mine."

Caleb nodded. "Burger," he reiterated, and then took another bite of pickle.

Hank just glared at the two idiots and went out the door.

"Daddy, where are we going?" Libby asked, patting his arm with a small hand.

"We're gonna go visit Miss Becca," he told her in a gentle voice, changing his tone for his daughter. "You want to go say hello to her?"

"Yes!" Libby agreed emphatically. "I missed her today."

He had, too.

Becca's phone buzzed in her pocket with incoming texts, but she ignored it. Not because she was in a bad mood—she'd been too busy for that. Because her hands were gloved and covered in cherry-red dye for Mrs. Dilhauser. The woman was eighty if she was a day, but she loved her bright red hair—and she tipped well—so Becca always squeezed her in, even if it was late. Plus, she loved the woman's stories about her husband, who had passed away last fall. They'd been wildly in love for sixty years, and she adored hearing even the smallest of details about it, because she'd always wanted a love like that.

For the longest time, she'd thought it was Greg, despite how wrong they were for each other. Then after they'd broken up, she'd worried she'd be alone forever.

Now, though, she was thinking of Hank.

Of the way he kissed her. The way he held his little daughter so tenderly.

She'd missed seeing him this morning, which was stupid, and needy. Some of it was the first flush of infatuation, of course, but some of it was her problem of getting attached quickly. She was lonely, and she knew that, and just because she loved his daughter and loved kissing him, it didn't mean happy ever after was in the works. Ten years with Greg had taught her that. So she needed to slow it down. She needed to remember that a kiss was just a kiss, a date didn't mean much, and Hank was moving back to Alaska soon.

This wasn't a fairy tale, she reminded herself. She could enjoy kissing him and taking things casually. As long as her expectations were reasonable, she wouldn't get her heart broken. It was that whole "reasonable expectations" thing that was challenging for her, but Becca resolved to do better. Hank had never promised her anything, after all.

Best not to dwell on it. So she focused on Mrs. Dilhauser, on the cut and color, and by the time the woman's hair was in a fiery red puff around her face, it was getting late. She'd managed to squeeze her in at the end of the day, and now there was nothing to do except clean up and go to her empty house and do the same.

She was just closing the salon when a car pulled up in front and gave her a honk.

Ugh, she recognized that shrill little beep. That was Greg's car. It seemed he'd made good on his promise to drop by. She'd been hoping to avoid that. Mentally bracing herself, she resisted the urge to lock the door on him and instead stepped out onto the front porch to meet him. "Hi, Greg."

To her surprise, he leaned in and tried to kiss her. She sidled away, giving him a curious look. What the heck was that?

"Long time no see," Greg said, giving her his famously charming smile. It was bizarre to see it, because once upon a time she'd melted at the sight of that smile, and now it just irritated her. Greg was everything that Hank wasn't. He was trim and always dressed in a neat casual suit or a button-down. His hair always looked fantastic—or it had in the past thanks to her—and he was slick and dashing and knew he could charm his way through life.

Hank's hair always looked like it needed a trim. He scowled. He wore plaid.

Yet somehow that seemed far more appealing now, far more real. She no longer trusted Greg's easy smiles, because he smiled when he wanted something from you. And while she didn't hate the man, she still resented that he'd wasted years of her life when she'd wanted to settle down and start a family. He'd dangled marriage in front of her like a prize, made her pay for it, and then abandoned her two days before the wedding.

Okay, she was still a bit resentful.

"You didn't text me back," Greg told her, still grinning. He reached out and touched her shoulder, then rubbed her arm. "I hope it's okay I stopped by."

"Does it matter?" she said tightly.

"Becca," he said, mock groaning. "We were friends for

so long. Don't keep shutting me out. Can't we go back to being friends?"

"Not yet." She crossed her arms over her chest. "You hurt me, badly. I'm allowed to take my time to get over it."

"I just . . . miss you." He leaned in, resting his hand on the doorjamb. It meant he was also leaning perilously close to her, because she refused to budge an inch. "I miss having you in my bed. I miss being with you."

She watched him cynically. She'd fallen for this act before, when she'd given him a quiet ultimatum or two. They'd break up for two days or so, he'd confess how much he missed her, and then they'd end back up in bed together and a couple once more. He'd been so good at playing her.

Now she just felt . . . annoyed. Did he think she was still this stupid? "Dating pool run dry? You not getting laid?"

Greg drew back in surprise at her words. "Wow. That's harsh. You don't sound like you. I'm shocked."

No, it didn't sound much like her . . . but, gosh, it felt good to call him on his bullshit. "Greg, we've been broken up for two years now. Our longest breakup ever. This one's sticking. I don't care how blue your balls turn, but you're not coming back into my life."

He looked stung for a moment, then gave her another charming smile and leaned in, and for a moment she thought he was going to kiss her. Ugh. But, no, he only moved close and whispered, "You don't think I realize I made a mistake? That I realize what I lost? I—"

A car door slammed and both of them jumped.

Across the street, Becca saw Hank's big body as he glared at the two of them, storming his way around to the far side of his truck. He opened the door, gently picked up his daughter from the back seat, and then stormed toward them on the porch. He had a black scowl on his face, his expression like a thundercloud.

Oh. Had he come into town to talk to her? Something fluttered in her chest. It might be hope.

Hank scowled at Greg, one hand on his daughter's back, the other arm under her legs as he walked up to the porch of Becca's salon. Becca noticed that his glares were entirely for Greg, and when he looked at Becca, his expression turned downright protective. He loomed over Greg, stepping so close that Greg took a few steps backward. That seemed to satisfy Hank, and he put his back to the man, turning toward Becca.

"Can you take Libby inside, please?" Hank's voice was strangely pleasant.

She tilted her head at him, curious. "Is everything okay?"

"Libby wants to go inside," he said, oh so nicely again, and gave her a pointed look. "So Daddy can take care of business on the porch."

And he turned and shot Greg a look of pure hatred.

Oh.

It took Becca a moment to realize that Hank had positioned himself between her and Greg, and that his stance was one of protectiveness. His voice was sweet because he didn't want Libby to realize there was a problem, the little girl sucking her thumb and looking at Becca with sleepy eyes. Hank shot her another meaningful look and she realized he wanted her to take Libby inside because he was going to . . . do something to Greg. Beat him up? Scare him? She didn't know, but it was clear he was feeling very protective of Becca, and for some reason, she loved the hell out of it.

"Hank," she said, putting her hand on his arm. "I'm not taking Libby from you. But . . . you are going to come inside with me. Greg was just leaving."

Now Greg was the one who frowned at her. "Becca, I came to talk to you."

"I don't think I have anything to say to you."

He paused for a minute. "Don't you miss me?" There was real hurt in his tone, as if he was genuinely shocked that she didn't care for him anymore.

And for a moment, she felt guilty. Because she didn't miss him. She still felt foolish over all the years she'd spent on him. She missed her hopes and dreams of having a family and a husband she doted on. But did she miss Greg? No. She didn't miss their tepid lovemaking or the fact that he never had time for her. She didn't miss the way he always made her feel like she was the problem. He'd never cheated on her, but he'd also never made her feel particularly special.

He'd also abandoned her two days before their wedding. She couldn't forget that.

But for some reason, he was really good at making her feel guilty. Becca opened her mouth and then closed it again. She wasn't sure what to say.

For some reason, she looked up at Hank. He was watching her with a steady gaze, as if waiting to see what she wanted.

"Do you miss him?" Hank asked after a long moment.

Becca tensed, then shook her head.

"Good." He shot a vicious look at Greg and then stepped in front of her again, silently protecting her with his body. "You can leave now," he said to her ex.

"I—I came to pick up some stuff—"

"You can pick it up from the salon during the daytime. Not right now. Becca has a date with me."

She did, did she? She bit the inside of her cheek to keep from smiling.

"But—" Greg began.

"Goodbye," Hank said in a hard voice. He took a step forward, still managing to look intimidating despite the fact that he had a toddler in his arms.

Greg shot her a wounded look. "I'll call you tomorrow." He glanced at Hank one more time, then hastily left the porch, returning to his car.

She had no doubt her phone was going to be filled with angry texts from him by the morning, but she couldn't find it in her to care at the moment. Hank was here. He'd come to see her. He'd "protected" her from her ex. It made her feel surprisingly good.

Wanted.

Dear lord, how long had it been since she'd felt so *wanted*? Hank acted like she was the only woman in town and it was necessary for him to stake his claim on her. She knew that wasn't the truth, but, lord, it felt good.

Hank looked at her, waiting patiently. When she said nothing for a long moment, he leaned in. "Did I fuck up?"

Libby popped her thumb out of her mouth. "Daddy, you said a bad word."

He nodded gravely at his daughter. "I did. I'm sorry." He glanced over at Becca again, waiting.

"No, you didn't mess up." She locked the salon door and then headed over to the door to her house. "Come on inside." Even if it wasn't a date like he'd said, they probably still needed to talk.

CHAPTER FOURTEEN

Once inside the house, she was distracted by Libby, who wanted to help her make dinner. Her stomach was in knots, and the last thing she wanted to do was make a big dinner. Her phone pinged in her pocket, and pinged again with incoming texts.

"Daddy's going to make dinner," Hank declared, taking his daughter into her living room. "Why don't you sit and watch *Nemo*?"

Once the little girl was settled, her gaze rapt on the screen, Hank touched Becca's arm and steered her toward her kitchen. He searched her face, gazing down at her for so long that she wondered what he was possibly thinking. Finally, he spoke. "Hungry?"

She bit her lip. "Not really."

He grimaced. "I should probably make something anyhow. You mind pancakes again?" He went to her pantry and opened it.

"You're . . . cooking again?"

Hank glanced at her from over his shoulder. "I wasn't demanding that you cook for me and my kid, no."

Ironic, considering she'd spent the last month doing just that without a word of thanks from him. But she didn't point that out. She just silently handed him the butter as he put a skillet on the stove.

"So . . ." Hank said as he stirred the pancake mix, "that was Greg."

Ugh. Did she want to talk about Greg? To air out all her dirty laundry? To show him just how clingy a woman she was? But was it even worth trying to hide it? It'd come out no matter who he asked, and he already knew the bitter end of what had happened, as she had told him foolishly many months ago. Even Doc knew all about her sad love story. She supposed it was best for him to hear the whole thing from her. Becca sighed. "It's a long story and not a great one."

Hank leaned over past the cabinets, glancing into the living room to check on his daughter. "I've got time. Nemo and Dory don't get home for at least another hour."

Her lips twitched with amusement. "You on a first-name basis with a kid's fish movie?"

The look he gave her was solemn. "That movie is a classic . . . and no one sings in it, which means I tolerate it a lot more than most kids' movies."

She bit back a giggle at that. "Don't like it when they sing?"

He shuddered. Actually shuddered. "No."

All right, that was adorable. The thought of torturing Hank was strangely enticing. "So I shouldn't tell her that I have *F-R-O-Z-E-N* on DVD—" She cut off, breaking into laughter at the sharp look Hank cast her way. "Okay, okay." She laughed.

He leaned in close to her. "It's all fun and games until you hear 'Let It Go' sixty times a day from a four-year-old who only knows one line."

She burst into giggles. Why was this the most charming, most heartwarming thing ever? Why did it make her ache with affection for both of them?

"You're stalling," Hank told her after a moment, pushing a pat of butter around in the skillet. "If you don't want to talk about it, we don't have to."

Was she stalling? She probably was. Becca took a deep sigh, bracing herself.

"Painful?" he asked.

She nodded. It still felt like an aching, open wound sometimes. There were a lot of feelings packed into her relationship with Greg, but a lot of what was left was shame. Shame that she'd been led on and betrayed by the person she'd loved the most in the world. Shame that everyone knew about it. Shame that she hadn't been enough for him, and it was somehow her fault.

"Want to take a shot?"

A shot? "I don't have alcohol."

He nodded and pulled a small glass flask of amber liquid from a back pocket. "Brought you something." He took out a glass from her cabinet and then poured a half inch or so into the bottom. The liquid was thick and rich and looked strong as hell.

"Drink up," he told her, holding it out.

Okay, maybe she did need a shot. Becca took the glass and took a hefty swig—and choked. "Is this maple syrup?"

"Well . . . yeah." Hank gave her a sly grin. "You needed a distraction."

She sputtered, coughing. She'd just taken a shot of liquid sugar, and her mouth felt like it was utterly coated. He just grinned at her, delighted, and her coughing turned into laughter. This really was the most ridiculous situation.

Shots. Maple syrup shots.

"Something tells me there's no alcohol in that," she managed, wheezing.

"Of course not. I'm driving my daughter home later." He pointed at her fridge. "And you have nothing but heavily processed syrup. That stuff's terrible. I thought I'd bring you some real stuff."

Becca chuckled again and set down her glass. "You're a strange man."

He shrugged. "Sometimes you get bored in the long winters up north. You learn to amuse yourself." He glanced over at her again. "You feeling better?"

She was, oddly enough. With a sigh, she leaned against the counter and watched as he expertly flipped a pancake over. "Greg was my first boyfriend. I grew up with him and it seemed like I always knew him. But when I turned fourteen, he asked me out. I was delighted to be dating the cutest boy at school. My father said no." She smiled at the memory. "And that was that. He said I couldn't date until I was eighteen, because I wouldn't know my ass from a hole in the ground until then."

Hank grunted. "Smart man."

Becca laughed. "Strict man. I know those were the longest four years of my life, as I dated no one and it seemed like everyone else around me was holding hands and going on dates. Greg went out with other girls during that time, but it felt like I was all alone. Then I turned eighteen my senior year, and Greg just happened to break up with his last girlfriend at about the same time, and the next thing I knew, we were finally a couple. I was so happy. We dated until graduation, and then my father wanted me to go away to college. He hoped to sell his ranch after I graduated, and retire from ranching. He'd always wanted to move somewhere around water. It was his dream. My dream was to be Greg's wife." She grimaced at the memory. "We had a big argument. Greg was taking time off before he went to college, you see, and my father wanted me to go off to school. I wanted to stay in Painted Barrel to be near the man I loved, because I was so sure he would propose marriage." God, she had been young and stupid then.

"Did he?"

"Yeah, no. I ended up compromising with my father—I'd get an apartment in a nearby town, go to beauty school to get a cosmetology certification, and start my own business. He wasn't thrilled with it—I think he wanted me to be some high-powered suit, but that's not me. And by the time I graduated and set up my salon, Greg moved in. I think I was twenty." She shrugged. "And then within a year, he moved back out again. Said it was too much too soon, that I was clingy and stifling him."

Hank frowned.

"And maybe it was. We were both really young, so it wasn't so bad. We kept dating, but we slowed things down. And after our five-year mark of being together, I started hinting that I wanted to get married. I wanted to start a family with him. I loved him. He said he wasn't ready."

Hank flipped the pancake out of the pan and slid it onto a plate, then poured batter for another pancake. "Because he was busy with college?"

"Greg didn't go to college, actually. He kept finding excuses not to go. Or to get work. He drifted between a lot of jobs, trying to figure out who he was—"

"While you supported him, right?"

Ugh. He saw right through her. "Yeah. I figured I was making money and was happy with what I was doing, and he was still trying to figure himself out. I thought it couldn't hurt, and at some point when he decided what he wanted to be, it wouldn't matter." She raised a hand in the air. "Don't tell me how dumb I was, because I already know."

"I didn't say that."

His voice was surprisingly gentle, and that just made her ache a bit more for the young, headstrong, desperate girl she'd been. "My father and mother were a weird couple, you know? He married her because he got her pregnant and it was the right thing to do, but I don't think he ever loved her. She loved him desperately and did everything she could to get his attention, and it was never enough." Becca thought of them, shaking her head. "They're still married, and my father still acts like my mother is a burden to him. Like she's holding him back from being whoever or whatever he wanted to be. They're not happy, either of them, but I guess the Vancouver seaside helps." She smiled awkwardly.

Hank said nothing, just watched her.

"Anyhow, after a few more years of dating, I got really upset with Greg. I wanted kids. I wanted a big family. And he was still figuring out who he was, drifting from job to job. I told him I wanted to get married, and he said he wasn't ready. So I threw him out. Told him if he wasn't ready to get married, I wasn't ready to support him for the rest of my life."

He gave her an approving nod, flipping another pancake.

"That lasted about a week. Greg came back, apologized very sweetly and brought me flowers, and told me he was ready to get engaged and we could go pick out a ring."

"That you paid for?"

Becca sighed. "That I paid for, yeah."

He made a noise that wasn't approval but indicated he was listening.

She went on. "So we were engaged, but every time I tried to set a date, he wasn't ready. It was a bad time, he was trying to get his real estate license, all kinds of things. That went on for a few years, and I kicked him out again. He came back within a day and we set a date. And then as the date got closer and closer, he started acting weird."

"Weird?"

"Weird like he spent a lot of nights out with the guys, or he'd go and spend hours talking to Sage, a friend of ours from school who also never left town."

A low growl escaped his throat. "He was cheating on you."

"I'm not sure that he was." Becca crossed her arms and leaned against the counter, watching him work. It was a pleasure to see his slight movements, the way he expertly made pancakes, all without a single hint that she should take over for him. "Sage is the nicest girl, and she'd had a crush on Greg ever since we were kids. The entire town knew about it. Anyhow, I'm sure Greg liked the attention. He just showed no interest in anything wedding or family and would find an excuse to leave the moment I wanted to talk about anything. I should have seen it for what it was, but I was very stubborn and positive I was finally going to get my wedding. We could figure everything else out after we crossed that finish line, you know?" She shook her head. "But then Sage started dating someone and didn't have time to be Greg's buddy, and I think that made him panic. I think he liked the idea of having his cake and eating it, too, and he liked being the center of Sage's world as well as having me. When Sage moved on, he freaked out. She was never pushy like his awful fiancée, you see." She grimaced at the memory. "And to be fair to Greg, I was being pushy."

Hank gave her a disbelieving look. "You're defending him?"

She took the spatula and flipped the pancake before it could burn, since his attention was now focused solely on her. "Not at all. I just know what I was like. I was very, very, very focused on getting married. A bridezilla, you might say. At any rate, Greg decided he was in love with Sage and broke up with me two days before the wedding." Her voice took on a bitter note. "After I'd paid for everything. The church, the reception, the catering, the honeymoon, matching wedding bands, all of it. He humiliated me in front of everyone, because the whole town was invited. It's all anyone's been able to talk about ever since. I closed my shop for days, went on the honeymoon by myself, cried buckets, and came home early." She shook her head. "I don't think I wanted Greg as much as I wanted this picture in my mind of what my life should be like. I wanted a family. I wanted children. Maybe some of that was loneliness, because even when I was with Greg, I still felt like I was alone. Like he never really got me."

"You were alone. He didn't get you," Hank growled. "The man's a user."

"He is. He'd rather get by in life with a pretty smile than a day's work." Becca sighed ruefully. "And I still would have married him, so that makes me an idiot."

"And now?" He took the spatula back from her.

This felt good, working together, making dinner together and talking. It was easy. It felt right. It wasn't hard or awkward, like the date had been. "Now I think I'm mostly just resentful of how he wasted my time and how pigheaded I was. I don't miss him. That was two years ago, and every so often he tries to reconnect. I'm not sure if it's guilt or habit for him, but I'm done." She shook her head. "I still want a family. I still want love . . . but now I'm thinking maybe I'll just get a dog." She chuckled, as if her sad joke was funny.

He didn't laugh.

She kind of wished he would. Sympathetic laughter she could deal with. "So . . . that's my story. The whole, psycho, clingy lot of it."

Hank shot her a look. "I didn't say that."

"You didn't have to. I fully acknowledge that I'm the type that gets attached fast." Becca bit her lip. "I'm trying to do better."

"Maybe you weren't the problem," he said slowly. "Maybe he should have made his ideas about your relationship clearer so you knew he wasn't ready to settle down. Maybe he didn't say anything because he wanted you to keep supporting him. Or maybe he was the problem and not you."

That was nice of him to say, even if it wasn't true. "Oh, come on. If you were dating someone for a few years and they got fixated on getting married? What—"

"I'd say yes." He flipped a pancake. "If we've been dating for years I must see something in that person I love, so, yes."

She was stunned by his quick answer. "Is that what happened with you and Libby's mom?"

The look he gave her was uneasy.

"I won't judge you," Becca said softly. "Even if it's terrible. I shared my ugly, embarrassing past. Can't you share yours?" She bumped his hip with hers in a flirty way. "Maybe you need a shot, too."

That made him chuckle. "I guess that's fair." He handed her the spatula.

She took it while he poured himself a small amount of maple syrup, and she grimaced in memory at the cloyingly sweet taste as he downed it. Then he sighed, looked at her, and sighed again. It was clear he didn't want to talk about it. At all.

Which made her all the more curious.

Hank glanced in the living room again to check on Libby, then turned back to her. "My land is north of Fairbanks, just outside a place called Foxtail. Not a big population. Very remote. Once a month, someone flies in some supplies, but for the most part, when you needed stuff, you drove down to Fairbanks for about a week. Sold your furs, restocked your pantry, let off some steam. Adria lived in town, and apparently her way of making a living was to pick a particular man, hook up with him for a few days when he was flush with money, and get him to pay for things. When that ran out, she'd find a new guy." His jaw clenched. "I didn't know this about her until it was too late.

Went back to town about a year later and she handed me Libby. Said she was mine, and she couldn't be bothered raising a kid. It'd ruin her lifestyle. So I took Libby home and that was that."

Becca was silent. Shocked, a little. The story had been short, but she suspected there was a wealth of hurt and embarrassment in his tale, too. He didn't know he'd been used by this Adria woman until it was too late, and she could only imagine how he'd felt at the discovery. And then to find out he had a baby with her? After being shamed by her? He was a good man, because it was clear his little girl was his world. "So you and Adria were never a couple?"

He snorted and gave her a wry look. "We were for about a week. Then I ran out of money and she ran out of interest."

"Has there ever been anyone else?" she couldn't help but ask.

"Just one."

"Oh?"

Hank nodded. "She got the gum out of my daughter's hair one night."

She melted at those sweet words. Totally melted. "You said no when I asked you out, though."

"Thought it was a joke, honestly. Pretty things like you don't ask out guys like me."

Now she was blushing. "I admit I did have an ulterior motive. I asked you out because I figured if I dated someone else, maybe people would stop throwing Greg in my face."

He stiffened. "And I was the first one that came along?"

Uh-oh, was he thinking she was just like his ex? "Actually, I liked how good you were with your daughter. You were the first guy that appealed to me in a long, long time. Still are."

"Even though I wasn't very nice to you for a while? Told you not to come by the ranch?"

Becca smiled. The mountain of pancakes was mostly done, so she pulled a few plates out of the cabinet and looked over at him. "I figured I was being a nuisance. Did I mention that I'm headstrong? I'm also a bit of a control freak. I think that's why I was set on having my own salon—I like being in charge. So it hurt my feelings a little that you told me to leave, but I also figured I deserved it."

"I shouldn't have said that," he told her, plucking the plates out of her hands. "You helped out a lot, and I know watching Libby is a full-time job on its own."

She hesitated, feeling shy. "I like her. And I like you." Their fingers brushed as she let him take the plates, and for some reason that felt more electric than anything she'd ever done with Greg. "Is it true you're moving back to Alaska soon?"

Hank shot her a curious look. "Who said that?"

"Libby. Is it not true?"

He was silent for a long moment, holding on to the plates. "That's the plan."

"Oh." For some reason, she found that crushing. Here she thought they were truly bonding, getting somewhere, and she was getting attached . . . only for him to be planning to go back to Alaska. He was going to be leaving her behind. "I see."

"Does that change things? You and me?" He stared at her with intent, dark eyes.

Becca thought for a moment. Her lips parted. She fought back her disappointment and tried to look at it logically. Did it really change anything? They'd been dancing around officially dating, but nothing had been declared other than they liked each other. Nothing had been promised. It was just her nature to think that a date or two led to more. But . . . did it have to? Couldn't she just like him and enjoy being with him and take it day by day? "I guess we can be casual, right? Have fun with this thing until you leave?"

He nodded once, but the heat in his eyes made her feel like this thing was anything but casual.

"We'll just take it one day at a time." She smiled at him.

"One kiss at a time," he agreed.

And, god, wasn't she the most impatient of women, because just hearing that made her want to kiss him right then and there.

CHAPTER FIFTEEN

Later that evening, after Libby had watched two animated movies and Hank had held Becca on the sofa and kissed her neck until she was trembling, Hank took his daughter home and tucked her into bed. It was past midnight, and he knew he shouldn't have kept Libby up so late, but he also couldn't help himself. Every time he told himself he needed to go home, he needed to call it a night, Becca would look over at him with that shy, half-flirty look on her face and bite her lip, and he'd be a goner. Next time he'd pay more attention to the clock, he decided.

Next time maybe he wouldn't get so utterly enthralled by a pair of lips.

He pulled the blankets up to Libby's chin and tucked them close around her.

"Daddy?" She opened sleepy eyes to look at him.

"Yes, baby?"

"Did you kiss Miss Becca?"

"Yeah, I did." No sense in lying about it, because he planned on doing it a lot.

"You should marry her," his daughter declared sleepily. "So she can be my mommy."

"We're going back to Alaska, remember?"

She nodded and rolled over, going to sleep, but the conversation bothered him even after he went to his own room.

Becca had asked if he was going back to Alaska. The moment he'd said yes, she'd said they would keep it casual. What the hell was that? She always said she didn't know how to be casual and yet she was suggesting it? He'd been about to suggest that maybe she could move back with him when she threw that "casual" bomb.

Hank didn't know what to do about it.

The smartest, safest thing would be to back off entirely. Keep his head down and his lips to himself.

Even so . . . he didn't want to. For the first time, he'd met someone that fascinated him. Someone that he wanted to talk to and that he wanted to hear talk, even if it was about nothing at all. He wanted her smiles, her laughs, he wanted to drink in the way she casually tossed her hair over her shoulder as she bent to work. He wanted more than casual.

But . . . he lived in the backwoods of Alaska and he planned on going back there. There wasn't a place for a hairdresser there, much less a hair salon. She'd have to give up her business to go rough it in a cabin with him.

Hell. Why did even thinking about it feel like a mistake? He wasn't changing his life just because he'd kissed a pretty woman a few times.

Maybe she was right to suggest this thing between them was casual . . . even if he didn't like the idea.

Becca was in a good mood the next day. The weather was beautiful, which meant that everyone came out of the woodwork to get their hair cut, oddly enough. It always happened like that, not that she was complaining. It was

Monday, and strangely, she was getting so many walk-ins, even though Mondays were usually the slowest. When business was booming, you took advantage of that. Besides, she didn't mind. She didn't have anything going on until later, when Hank finished his day's work.

She wondered if he'd come over tonight. Probably. She'd have to stop by the grocery store when she had a lull between clients and pick up a few things, maybe a couple of steaks and some corn dogs for Libby. She knew the little girl loved corn dogs and could live on them, even if it wasn't Becca's first choice for a nutritious meal. She just knew that as much as she loved that Hank cooked for her, she wasn't sure she wanted pancakes again.

Then they could settle in and watch a movie. A kids' movie.

Which meant she could kiss Hank for at least ninety minutes while Libby was occupied.

"You seem happy," the man in her chair said as she ran the shaver over his neck. "You keep smiling to yourself. Did you have a big weekend?"

"Small one, really," she confessed. Didn't mean it wasn't great.

"The small ones are good, too," he told her with a grin. "You have a beautiful smile. You seeing anyone?"

"I . . . um, yes. Thank you." Becca's face felt hot as she turned off the clippers and then dusted his neck. He was one of the newer cowboys that worked out at Sage Cooper-Clements's ranch. For the first time, she looked at him, noting that he had nice eyes and a handsome smile . . . but he wasn't Hank. "I am seeing someone, sorry."

"Just bad luck on my part," he told her with a wink as she took the cape off him. "If it ever changes, you let me know. Can I come in for a trim in about two weeks?"

"Of course." She chatted with him, made the appointment in her phone, and tried not to feel too weird about it.

Men asked women out all the time. It was something that wasn't a big deal; it really wasn't.

Even so, she couldn't help but giggle to herself. Her phone dinged with a text not a moment later, too.

GREG: Hey. Sorry about the other night.

GREG: My hair's getting a little shaggy. I don't suppose you could squeeze me in for a trim and we can talk? I wouldn't mind seeing you again. :)

The door opened to the salon, and she shoved her phone into the pocket of her apron, trying not to grimace. It was Amy, the schoolteacher, an apologetic look on her face. "Is this a bad time? I saw you were open."

"It's fine, come on in." She patted the chair. "I was just snarling at a text from my ex."

"I know what that's like," Amy said with a chuckle. "You do lashes, right?"

"I do!" It was one of her new favorite things, actually. "Your eyes are already beautiful, though. I doubt you need them."

Amy gave her a rueful look. "Isn't it your job to talk me into things instead of out of them? I don't know. I just . . ." She sighed and stared at her reflection in the mirror. "Need a change. I feel blah. Unpretty." She hesitated a moment. "Alone."

"Normally I'd say that I can sympathize," Becca began, settling a pink cape over Amy's shoulders. "But I seem to be overflowing with men lately. It's the strangest thing. The last guy asked me out, and my ex is texting me, and I'm already seeing someone." She shook her head. "Is there a full moon? I've been utterly single for two years now and no one had the slightest bit of interest. Now I'm starting to get weirded out."

"It's because you're unavailable," Amy told her, wiggling her eyebrows. "Men want what other men have. That, and you have the cutest sparkle in your eye. You just look so happy."

She felt happy. For the first time in a long time, she felt like there was something to look forward to at the end of each day. "Maybe that's it."

"At least you're not going to be lonely," Amy said helpfully. "I just moved here and I feel like a pariah. Everyone knows each other, and then there's me, sitting on the sidelines. I need to figure out how to make friends."

"Well," Becca began, leaning on the back of the salon chair and meeting Amy's gaze in the mirror, "I can do your lashes, but that'll take two hours and you really, really don't need them. Or I can give you a blowout, and then we can go and get coffee at the bakery and talk about men or the lack thereof?"

Amy beamed. "I would love that!"

CHAPTER SIXTEEN

It had been years since Becca had gone out for coffee with a girlfriend and just chatted. Not that she didn't talk the ears off everyone that came into the salon, but this felt different, more personal, and it was so much fun. She'd forgotten just what it was like to have girlfriends. All of hers had moved away after high school, and when she wasn't working at the salon, she'd usually been spending time with Greg.

She'd let herself fall into a rut. Maybe it was time to be more social again.

Becca and Amy sat with their coffees at a small table at the bakery and laughed and chatted until Becca saw Hank's big red truck pull up. They made plans for the following weekend and exchanged phone numbers, and it felt . . . good. Felt right.

She greeted Hank as he headed for the salon. He was another thing that felt right. He was wearing cowboy boots and a dark shirt and hat, and, damn, he looked good. She noticed there was no Libby with him. "I guess we're not watching *Finding Nemo* tonight?"

"Only if it puts you in the mood." He stooped down to kiss her, an action she always found heart melting. "Thought I'd take you out to dinner."

"Oh?" He laced his fingers through hers, holding her close as she beamed up at him. "Is that why you look so fancy tonight?"

His eyebrows went up. "I look fancy?"

"For you, yes."

For some reason, her response seemed to bother him. "Do you not like my beard?"

That was odd. "I never asked you to shave. I think you're handsome either way."

Hank just rubbed it thoughtfully. "I don't look like your ex."

"No, you don't. And that's a good thing." She held on to his arm. "So where are we going?"

He gestured down the end of Main Street, where Wade's saloon was open. It was the only restaurant in town, so it didn't surprise her, but it would also be the first time they'd officially gone out in front of the town, and it felt like a big step.

"Are you sure?" Becca asked him. "Everyone will know we're dating."

He stopped and gave her a long, slow look. "Is that a problem?"

"Not for me. I just wasn't sure how casual you wanted to take things."

For some reason, he scowled at her. "Let's just go eat." His hand clasped hers tightly as he pulled her toward the tavern.

Okay, something was clearly bothering him. Strange. Maybe it was something with Libby? Should she ask? Becca studied his face, but he didn't seem particularly upset. Cranky, maybe, but upset, no. Maybe he had a bad day at work—lord knew that if she had to spend her time in cow poop all day it'd make her surly. She squeezed his hand. "I'm glad to see you."

Hank paused on the sidewalk and gazed down at her. He scrutinized her for a long moment, his gaze practically looking her up and down. "You're honestly the best thing I've seen today . . . after Libby," he added. "Feel obligated to say that."

She chuckled. "I'll take it, you know."

His thumb brushed over the back of her hand in a caress that sent goose bumps all through her body. "Missed seeing you this morning. I know it's not realistic to have you dragging yourself up to the ranch at the crack of dawn, but it doesn't mean I don't miss you."

"You just miss breakfast," she teased, her heart racing. This man knew how to make her feel wanted; that was for sure.

"Did I mention breakfast? All I mentioned was you. I'd be just as happy if you were there and the fridge was empty." He shrugged. "The others, not so much."

Becca laughed, because Caleb and Jack only spoke to her when there was food involved. They were definitely stomach-led men. "Any time you need me to come by and help out, you know I'll be there."

"But what if I just need you?"

There he was, making her all breathless again. "That, too," she whispered.

He glanced at the bar at the end of the street and sighed heavily. "At this rate I'm not going to be interested in dinner at all."

Heck, at this rate, neither was she. Becca turned her face up to him hopefully, imagining for a moment that he'd take her by the hand and drag her back to her place and to the couch for a heavy make-out session and some petting.

Gosh, she'd been thinking about the petting constantly in the last few days. She loved having Libby over, but when they watched a movie with her sitting in front of them on the floor, all they did was kiss and furtively touch hands. She still thought about that first night they went out, though, and how he'd made her come so hard.

She was dying for a repeat. *Dying.*

But he only squeezed her hand. "Come on."

Becca bit back her whimper of protest and followed his lead.

Once inside the bar, she felt the intense scrutiny of what felt like all of Painted Barrel, population 200 and some change. It wasn't the entire town, of course; it just *felt* like it. She'd been in Wade's bar plenty of times; it was the only real food joint in their small town other than the bakery, so it tended to be crowded even with people who had no interest in drinking. She pointed at one of the round tables toward the back of the crowded bar, and Hank put a hand on her back and steered her toward it, then pulled her chair out for her.

It was his usual manner—he always did this for her—but with everyone in town staring at them, she felt utterly conspicuous. They were probably going to be watched all through dinner, and wasn't that awkward? She hoped Hank didn't notice. She hoped it wouldn't bother him, either. She knew the townsfolk well and was on good terms with most everyone, but Hank was a stranger to them. He'd get a lot of stares and attention, and she suspected that was something he wasn't a big fan of.

Sure enough, the moment they sat, she could see people watching them and whispering. Smiling, too, but mostly staring. She glanced at Hank and noticed his nostrils flared as he picked up his menu.

"We can go somewhere else if you're not comfortable, Hank," she whispered to him.

"It's fine." He put the menu down a split second later and slid his chair closer to hers, then put his arm on the back of her chair. It was a possessive gesture, one meant to show that she belonged to him, and Becca loved it. It also made her incredibly aware of his big hand just brushing against the tips of her hair and the small of her back.

Becca pretended to study her menu a bit more, though she knew it by heart she'd been there so often. "Is Doc watching Libby today?"

"Nope." He leaned in. "Caleb and Jack are having an uncle slumber party with her. I'm told there will be lots of princess movies and she's going to give them princess beards. I'm going to owe them big."

Becca stifled a laugh, glancing up at him. "That's really cute and nice of them."

He just leaned in closer. "It's a slumber party, so I can stay out late." And he touched a lock of her hair, curling it around his finger.

Oh, she liked that idea. She liked it a lot. Becca looked up at him, breathless. He was close enough that their chairs were practically parked side by side, hips touching, and it made dinner feel intimate even if they were in a restaurant full of strangers. She wanted to lean in and touch him, to give him a kiss just so she could feel his lips on hers, but she wasn't sure how he'd feel about public affection.

Damn, it was hard being in the early stages of dating someone. Thrilling, but hard. "Late is nice," she managed, a blush on her cheeks. That meant more than just kisses when they got done with dinner. She was suddenly ready to go back home and—

A man passed by the table. Tipped his hat at her and winked.

Becca stared at him for a moment, trying to place him, and then remembered—it was the cowboy from Sage's ranch that she'd given a trim earlier that day. It shouldn't have been surprising to run into him, but she could feel her blush elevating.

At her side, Hank tensed, his body going rigid. "Who's that?"

"One of my customers. He, ah, asked me on a date. I told him I was with someone." She bit her lip. Hank started to get up from his chair, a black scowl on his face, and she grabbed his hand. "Where are you going?"

"To kick his ass."

"Hank, no, don't. Please." She clung to his hand, forcing him to look at her. "Let's just have dinner, okay?"

He thumped back into his seat, glaring at the back of the man at the far end of the saloon. "Did he make you uncomfortable?" Hank looked at her. "Harass you?"

She shook her head. "I think he was just flirting. It's fine. I'm not interested." She tried to make a joke of things, to lighten the tension. "I told him I was with you, but I didn't mention that we were casual. I didn't want to give him hope."

Hank's gaze turned piercing. "What does casual mean to you?"

That was a curious question. Didn't it mean the same for everyone? Not exclusively dating? Taking things day by day? "I . . . I don't know," she confessed, not wanting to put something out there that might hurt his feelings. "I guess we need to figure that out together."

He studied her for a long moment and then nodded, his arm returning to the back of her chair. She could feel him subtly pull it closer to him, as if he needed to drag her close and hover over her protectively. It was a little ridiculous, sure, but it also felt really good to be so wanted. She didn't mind in the slightest.

They ate, and it was a nice dinner even if things felt a little awkward between them. The cowboy winking at her had made Hank go silent, which she wasn't a fan of. She preferred when he talked. But he touched her all through the meal, rubbing her shoulder, holding her hand, and listening to her as she talked about her day. He stole a fry or two from her plate, and he was attentive and sweet. So as dates went, she couldn't complain. She much preferred their dates when they were alone together rather than in public, though. She'd never felt strange about being in public before, but now she was utterly aware of just how much attention was on them. With Greg, she'd wanted the attention. Maybe she'd wanted it because she wasn't getting it from him, so she needed the acknowledgment that they were the town sweethearts. Who knew. All she knew now was that every time someone gave them an odd look—as if they were a mismatch—she bristled just a little bit inside and scooted just a hair closer to him.

She casually mentioned dessert, and Hank ordered it and then insisted she eat almost all of the chocolate cake herself. Furthermore, Hank didn't let her pay for dinner. He picked up her cash and handed it back to her, ignoring her protests, and that made her feel good, too. By the time they got up and left the saloon, she linked her fingers with his and her body was humming, thinking about Libby's sleepover.

She hoped she was going to have a sleepover of her own.

The thought made Becca breathless with anticipation . . . and a little bit of fear, too. She'd only ever slept with Greg. This would be new for her—for both of them, if what Hank had told her was true. And she loved Hank's kisses and his touches, and she was craving more, but she was a little nervous at the same time. What if the rest of it wasn't any good? What if she couldn't come and he thought she was frigid? She came with Greg, but not often, and usually ended up faking it just to make him feel rewarded. After a while, it was always faking, and that didn't help their fraying relationship stay together when it splintered each time.

She wasn't going to fake it this time, she told herself. If he couldn't make her come, well then, they'd figure something out. Maybe she'd get one of those Hitachi wand things everyone always talked about in women's magazines. She was open to something like that. She was open to lots of things, as long as they felt good and they were together in all of it. Heck, she didn't mind if all he wanted to do was kiss and cuddle tonight.

Okay, maybe she'd mind that a little bit. It was just that she wanted to go a little further, do a little more. See where this thing between them could lead. And she hoped he did, too.

Her heart was fluttering in her chest as they headed back down Main toward her salon-slash-home. She noticed that his truck was still parked in front and wondered if she should ask him to move it to someplace less obvious . . . then decided it didn't matter. People would know they were dating. She didn't care what they thought beyond that. She was an adult. Heck, she was almost thirty and single—she could do what she wanted. Becca turned to Hank as she got to her doorstep and gave him a slight smile. "Want to come in?"

He just arched a brow at her. "Unless you'd rather me touch you out here on the porch?"

Okay, now she was visualizing him touching her on the porch, and that should not have been near as much of a turn-on as it was. My goodness. "Inside is fine," Becca told him, her insides quivering. He'd said touch. Not kiss. Touch. Maybe they'd take things further tonight . . . god, that sounded so good. She was more than ready. Her libido had felt long dead, and now it was flaring to life again just being around him. Biting her lip, she unlocked her door and then stepped inside. "What do you—"

Hank shut the door behind her and leaned against it, pulling her into his arms and interrupting her thoughts. A little moan escaped her as he dragged her forward until she straddled his big thigh, and his hand went to her waist. "Been waiting all night for a chance to be alone with you."

"Just all night? I feel like I've been waiting days," she teased, a trembling note in her voice as she lifted her arms and put them around his neck. "What did you have in mind now that we're alone?"

"Nothing involving a kids' movie."

She chuckled at that. Thank goodness. "You had something dirtier in mind?"

"I have lots of dirty things going through my mind when it comes to you, Becca Loftis." The look he gave her was intense, his expression downright devouring.

Her entire body prickled with awareness and her nipples felt hard against the front of her sweater. "I'm going to need details."

"Details . . . or a demonstration?" His hands slid lower, went to her ass, and lifted her up just a fraction, dragging her up his thigh and making her private, throbbing spots rub against his leg in the most obvious—and delicious—fashion.

"Both?" She slid a hand to the front of his chest, played with one of the buttons on his shirt. She'd wanted him to throw her down on the floor and start kissing the hell out of her, but oh man, this flirty conversation was fun. It was making her all turned on without a single deliberate touch. She'd never been so aroused . . . maybe ever. Maybe it had something to do with the fact that when Hank talked about picking her up or dragging her around, he could do it. He was strong and powerful, and that was such an aphrodisiac. He made her feel small and helpless, and while she didn't care for that outside of a relationship, in the bedroom? It was hot as heck.

"I can do both," he murmured, studying her. "But I think we need to figure out you and me first."

She blinked at him. It was hard to concentrate on his

words when his big hand was splayed across her backside and she could grind against his thigh with a twitch of her hips. He had her like this, and they were sharing flirty words, and now . . . now he wanted to set relationship boundaries?

Was he determined to make her scream with frustration?

"What's wrong with you and me?"

"I . . ." He frowned to himself. "Forget it. It's not important."

"What?" she pressed.

Hank shook his head. "Just forget I said anything. I'd rather talk about kissing you everywhere than start an argument."

Argument? The last thing she wanted was that. She was definitely on board with the "kissing you everywhere" part, though. She hesitated, but when he didn't continue, she supposed she should let it lie. They could talk later, maybe, after they'd both kissed so long and hard that they were dopey with endorphins.

Kissed . . . or other things. Becca had never gotten off the pill, and tonight she was utterly grateful for that. If he wanted to take things all the way—and, gosh, she hoped he did—she was more than ready. So she plucked at the button on his shirt, undoing it. "Then should we move this to the couch?"

"Too far away." He grabbed her ass tighter and then carried her—carried her!—over to her kitchen table. She made a sound of surprised protest when he sat her down, and then he captured her mouth in a kiss, leaning over her as she sat on the table. Becca clung to him, wrapping her legs around his hips and running her hands up and down his big chest. God, had she forgotten just how utterly enormous Hank was? Because touching him like this reminded her that he was carved of solid marble, nothing but hot skin and thick muscle, and it did all kinds of crazy things to her. She'd have bet that there wasn't an inch of fat on him anywhere . . . and she wanted to find that out for herself.

Tonight . . . she was going to, she decided. Tonight she was going to get her mouth all over him and do a little exploring. That sounded downright delicious.

Hank seemed to have the same idea she did. He nipped at her lip and kissed her sweetly, his tongue playing erotic little games with hers as he slid her long tunic dress up her hips and found the waist of her leggings, tugging them downward. When she had a long day at the salon, she dressed for comfort more than style, so she was wearing a cute skater dress and dark leggings, along with a pair of platform wedges. Greg had always told her it made her look shorter, so she wore things like this in defiance of his memory.

"You're so fucking pretty," Hank growled in her ear as he nipped at her earlobe. "Been driving me crazy all day, thinking about touching you."

That confession made her tremble. "Oh?"

"Been wanting to get my hands on you," he told her, his teeth grazing her neck. His beard scratched at her skin, but instead of bothering her, it just turned her on all the more. "Undress these curves of yours and just taste you all over. I'm going to do that tonight."

"You are?" She could scarcely breathe, lost in the erotic picture he was painting.

"Hell yeah. Gonna kiss you everywhere you'll let me. I might not have a ton of experience at doing it right, but I won't give up until you come." He cupped her chin and made her look into his eyes, trapping her with his gaze. "If that's what you want."

Was he asking for permission to kiss her everywhere? Dear lord, did he possibly think she'd say no? "Of course I want that. Why—"

"Because I'm a big dirty mountain man . . . or a cowboy, I guess. And you're so sweet and pretty." He traced his thumb over the curve of her lower lip, and her nipples felt like diamonds. "Never dreamed I'd touch someone like you."

"Hank, I've been waiting for this," she told him, cupping his neck. "You're not a big dirty anything to me. You're my boyfriend . . . and I want you to be my lover." The words sounded corny the moment they came out, but they also felt astonishingly bold. She'd never demanded that a man touch her before. "Kiss me. Kiss me everywhere you want, because I plan on doing the same to you."

He gave a pleased, low growl in his throat and tore her leggings down her thighs in one swift move.

She gasped, but his mouth was right there to kiss her, and this time it wasn't a playful kiss, but one of the deeper, drugging kisses that made her lose track of reality. They traded hot, fevered caresses, his tongue making her feel as if it was licking her lower than just her mouth. She throbbed with awareness, her body full of need. She wanted this. She wanted this so much.

Hank's hands slid to her waist and he gripped her hips, then pushed under the skirt of her tunic again. As his mouth claimed hers, he found the band of her panties and dragged them down, just a little.

"Squirrels?" he asked between strokes of his tongue.

"Wh-what?" Becca couldn't think, not with his mouth devouring hers.

"Got squirrels on these?" He teased a finger in the band.

She managed to shake her head. They weren't her sexiest pair, but that didn't matter, because they were coming off, and his attention was far more focused on her mouth than her clothing. "No squirrels."

"You know what should be on them?"

"What?" she asked, breathless.

"My lips."

Becca whimpered as he knelt on the floor, pushing her thighs apart. Her leggings were bunched at her calves, her shoes still on, and it was a glorious form of torture as he carefully pulled one shoe off her foot, and then the other. He eased the leggings off her, then oh so carefully slid one thigh over his shoulder and hauled her forward.

Her hands went to the table and she braced herself, leaning back, staring down at him in rapt fascination. Part of her wanted to be shy, to close her legs and suggest they go slower, but the rest of her was screaming for his mouth to be on her skin. She wanted him. He wanted to do this. Why stop him?

Even so, as he began to kiss up her thigh, she worried. Her body twitched with each brush of his mouth on her sensitive skin, right up until he kissed her mound. "Hank," she whispered, then paused. She was shy about this sort of thing, weirdly enough. She'd had sex with Greg regularly in the beginning of their relationship, but he'd never shown any enthusiasm for going down on her. After a while, she'd stopped suggesting it and wondered if she was ugly down there, or if there was something else repulsive about the act itself. Greg's junk wasn't the prettiest thing to have in her face, but she'd always been happy to make him happy.

He looked up at her as she said his name, his eyes dark with lust. "You gonna tell me to stop?"

"I just . . . you don't have to—"

He made an irritated sound in the back of his throat and, in the next moment, buried his face against her flesh, eliciting a squeak from her. "You think I don't want to touch you here? Are you insane?" This time, he stopped playing with the band of her panties and began to pull them down even as he pressed his mouth against her mound. He paused only to let the silk fabric of her panties pass his lips, and then he was pressing kisses on the neatly trimmed strip of her curls.

"Been thinking about doing this to you since that first night." He looked up at her. "You tell me if I do something you don't like and I'll stop."

"Oh, I like it," Becca protested. "It's just that—"

He flung her panties aside and then practically dove between her thighs, silencing her interruption. She leaned back once more, bracing her hands on the table and trying not to squirm.

Oh god. His mouth on her was . . . a lot. She closed her eyes, her mind overwhelmed with sensation. It wasn't just the tickle of his lips or the slide of his tongue against her folds; it was the prickle of his beard inside her thighs, and his grip on her butt. Each of those things was enough to make her needy, but all of them together, and she felt like she'd collapse—except she was already sitting on top of her own dining table.

"Damn, Becca," he breathed. "Didn't know you'd taste this good."

"Y-you're welcome?" She didn't know what else to say. A ticklish squeal escaped her as he ran a finger up and down the seam of her pussy, then swept it deeper, touching her from clit down to core. "Oh . . . Hank . . ."

"You can touch me," he growled out, not lifting his head from under her skirt. "I'm not gonna stop."

She put a tentative hand on his thick, dark hair, and then fisted it, sucking in a breath when his tongue brushed over her clit.

"Oh, sweet Jesus, that was good." He did it again, and then he seemed to push his face deeper, working her pussy with long, deep strokes of his tongue, and she felt like she was crumbling. She slid lower on the table, her hand in his hair, as he continued to work her with strong, hard licks that made her thighs twitch and everything inside her tremble.

"Love this," he murmured between licks. "Love your taste."

Oh god, he really did seem to like it, because he didn't let up in the slightest, even when her legs started to jerk. Her body tightened, and she started to grind against his mouth, as if unable to stop herself.

"Tell me what you need," he commanded when she pushed against his mouth. "Tell me what'll make you come hard, baby."

Baby? Heck, she nearly came just then. But then he brushed a finger up and down her wet folds, dragging it over her as if trying to figure out the key to unlocking her. He pushed into her with one thick finger, and she moaned, hips arching as he began to slowly thrust in and out with that finger.

"More?" he asked, his breath hot on her wet skin a moment before he licked her again.

"My clit," she told him, and then blushed when he immediately sucked it into his mouth and began to work it with his tongue. "Just . . . steady. Don't stop."

She wanted to give him more instructions, but then his tongue found the underside of her clit and began to tap in a steady motion in rhythm with the finger pumping into her, and then she felt it. That hot, deep spiral began in her belly, everything slowly tightening. If she could let that build, it'd be a hard, body-shaking orgasm deep from within—the best kind. She just had to relax and let it happen.

His tongue flicked against her clit, over and over. It felt so good, yet she started to feel guilty when that orgasm didn't come busting right out of the gate. Instead, it kept slowly building, taking its sweet time to crest, and she started to worry that he'd lose interest or change something. "Keep going, please. Oh, please. I know I'm taking a while, but it's so good."

He growled again and lifted his head, and she could have cried at the pause. "I'm not stopping 'til you come all over my face, baby."

And then he lowered his head and picked up the same aggravating, intoxicating rhythm as before, the one that was oh so slowly sending her over the edge.

Becca whimpered, clinging to Hank's head with both hands now as he worked her clit, never letting up, letting the moments build and build. And then suddenly she was there, her entire body feeling as if it was collapsing on itself, her insides shuddering as she came hard. A little cry escaped her, and then she pushed at him as the orgasm quaked through her, trying to get him to ease up. He didn't, though, and it kept ripping through her, tearing her apart with such intense bliss that she felt like she was going to fall right off the table.

When he finally lifted his head and pressed a ticklish, bearded kiss on the inside of her thigh, Becca felt like a puddle of mush. "I liked that."

Such a simple statement. But that was Hank. He didn't like to use more words if he didn't have to. A little giggle escaped her and then she smoothed the hair she'd rumpled—and fisted—with shaking fingers. "That was amazing. I'm sorry it took so long—"

He shook his head, cutting her off. "Never apologize. I just wanted to make sure I wasn't doing it wrong."

She let out a dreamy sigh and fell back on the table. "God, no. You couldn't have done it more right if you'd tried."

"Good." Like she was a child, he scooped her up off the table and carried her. She thought he'd stop by the sofa, but to her surprise, he went up the stairs and all the way to her bedroom, gently laying her down on her back. Then he lay next to her and curled his big body against hers. She was the small spoon, and, oh, this was almost as nice as the orgasm. She loved cuddling.

Almost as nice. That orgasm had been pretty amazing.

She hugged Hank's arm to her waist, not complaining

when he slid it up to her breasts and cupped one. That had probably been the best orgasm she'd ever had. Did she tell him? Or would that seem insincere? Becca didn't know. He'd asked her what she'd liked, and he'd taken his sweet time, making sure that it was good for her, and he hadn't even come yet. Heck, she could feel the hot brand of his dick in his jeans, pressing against her backside.

But he wasn't rushing her. Instead, he just held her close and toyed with her hair, his hand possessively on her breast. She wished he'd kiss her neck again, but their size differences made that impossible in this position, so she just smiled and snuggled back against him. "Just for the record, that was amazing."

Hank's low chuckle teased the top of her head. "Good. My first time. Glad I got it right."

"You . . . never did that before?"

"Nah." He paused, silent for a long moment. "Adria just wanted to have sex real quick like and then have me go to sleep. Couldn't figure out why. Now I know it's because she wanted to go through my wallet, but at the time I just thought maybe she wasn't into me touching her. That my hands were too rough or something."

"I like your rough hands," Becca admitted, since they were being open and honest. It was easier when you weren't looking at the other person's face to confess things like that . . . and the fact that he'd just made her come so hard helped the words ease out of her, too. "I like them all over me." And she squeezed the hand resting on her breast.

One rough finger moved back and forth, teasing the tip of her breast, and she had to bite back a moan. "Kinda like 'em all over you, too. You're so soft." His voice was full of wonder. "Everywhere."

That made her blush. It was also turning her on again, and she thought about turning around and pushing him onto his back so she could go down on him, but his fingers were teasing her nipple so perfectly she was going to be selfish for a moment longer.

She arched against his touch, rubbing shamelessly against his hand. "What about you, though?"

"What about me?"

There was a wariness in his tone that hurt her. Like somehow, deep inside, he was expecting Becca to be using him the same way Adria used him. That if he didn't get too invested, didn't let her do the touching, then he'd be in control of the way he felt.

Well, screw that. If she was going in deep, so was he.

So Becca sat up, letting her hair fall over her shoulder, and looked down at Hank with her most sultry expression. "When do you get off?"

"Every night in the shower," he admitted baldly, drinking her up with his gaze. "Thinking about you."

And just like that, she was all turned on again. She crawled over him on the bed, feeling sexier than she ever had, and leaned down to kiss his mouth lightly. "Then maybe it's time I get to touch you."

"You don't have to—"

Becca put a fingertip to his lips, quieting him. "You think you're the only one with an imagination, Mr. Watson?"

The hungry look he gave her was aching with need. "Baby—"

"Shhh." She tapped her fingertip over his mouth again. "I want to explore you a little. Unless it'd make you uncomfortable?"

He clenched his jaw, then mutely shook his head.

Biting her lip, she teased another button open on his shirt, and then leaned in to kiss the small bit of flesh exposed. He was wearing an undershirt beneath his button-up, but above the fabric, she could see a bit of thick chest hair. He was brawny and raw in all ways, her Hank, right down to his chest.

God, she'd never been so turned on by the sight of a hairy chest in her life. But this right now? This was absolutely doing it for her. Becca made a humming noise of pleasure in her throat, then slid one leg over his thigh until she was straddling him again, and slowly unbuttoned his shirt the rest of the way and pulled it free.

He immediately sat up and pulled the shirt over his head, then flung the clothing aside and lay back down.

"Oh wow," she breathed, gazing down at the muscled expanse before her. There wasn't an inch of Hank that wasn't rock hard, tanned, and ever-so-slightly hairy. She'd never been into a man with so much hair before, but it just made him seem a little more savage and untamed than a smooth chest would have, and she loved it. Becca leaned in, curling her fingers in the crisp hair, and then let her hand trail down his chest, her fingertips moving through the creases of his muscles. The man had freaking obliques, for goodness' sakes, the vee disappearing into the waist of his jeans. He was literally hard everywhere.

Everywhere.

Her gaze slid down to the thick bulge inside his jeans. It was just as enormous as the rest of him, if the outline that met her gaze was to be believed. And, oh mercy, she was having fun with this. He was like a package that kept on giving. With a little humming noise, Becca reached for his belt and worked it free, then pulled it through the loops and flung it aside. Hank was breathing hard, his hands clenched at the sides of the bed, almost as if he were afraid to touch her.

Like he might want that too much.

Becca took his hand in hers once more and kissed his palm. It was rough and weathered, just like the rest of him, but it was also a turn-on. She knew what those calluses felt like against the insides of her thighs, against the slickness of her folds, and she loved the way they felt. With another quick kiss to his palm, she placed it on her breast and rubbed it against his hand. "Touch me while I touch you."

He groaned like a man in pain. "Becca, baby . . ."

"I'm not going to stop unless you tell me you absolutely don't want my mouth on your cock," she teased him, wriggling as he found her nipple and began to coax it with his fingers. That was all it took for her core to feel hollow and needy and aching once more. "That you don't want my tongue all over you, tasting you like you tasted me."

"You know I want that," he rasped.

"Then touch me and take that pained expression off your face."

Hank grimaced. "Not pained." His fingers stroked over her nipple again. "Just . . . concentrating so it doesn't get too good too fast."

Ah. Now, that, she understood. "You tell me if I need to ease up, then." Her hand smoothed down over the bulge of his cock. Oh yeah, that was all him. Good lord, the man was built in every way. They made them big in Alaska, it seemed. "This is . . . impressive."

"It's because you're so small." His hand slid down her side, then went under her skirt and caressed her bare ass.

He made her sound like she was pocket-size instead of just short. "Not too small to take you in my mouth," she murmured, and slid his zipper down carefully, just in case he wasn't wearing underwear.

And . . . he wasn't. That somehow didn't surprise Becca. Hank wasn't the type for fuss. Maybe this monster in his jeans didn't fit right in the underwear he'd worn in the past. All she knew was that she didn't care, because it meant one less barrier between them. She eased his pants down his hips slightly, and he lifted his hips to tug them down further to help her along.

Then his equipment was free and Becca got her first

long look at the man in all his glory. Emphasis on glory, she decided, because he was impressively large. He was bigger than she'd ever seen—not that she'd had much experience—and instead of a slender wand, his dick was impossibly thick, a vein trailing up one side. The prominent head was a deep purple, drops of pre-cum already wetting his skin, and the entire package rested in a surprisingly tidy nest of dark hair between his lightly furred thighs.

Becca made a noise of pleasure in her throat and slid her hands down his thighs, framing his privates with her hands. "That is . . . wow."

"Too much?" She could feel him tensing, as if he was a problem.

She shook her head. "I don't think I'd ever use that term. Maybe . . . a 'mouthful.'" She grinned at him. "You're perfect, Hank."

He gave her a sharp nod, and her heart pinged in her chest. For a man that had a child, he was acting very shy, and she reminded herself that his one week of sexual experiences hadn't been great.

So she needed to make this amazing. He deserved to have better memories for his spank bank.

Becca leaned in and curled her fingers around his girth, testing him. Nope, her fingertips didn't meet—but she did have small hands. Even so, it was fascinating to squeeze him and feel the tension and heat in that big, thick shaft. "This is making my mouth water," she confessed. "I might not be able to hold off."

His big hand squeezed her butt tightly, as if those words were just as erotic as a touch. "Do it."

Oh, she would. She planned on it. Becca moved forward, squeezed him again, and then gave the head of his cock a long, slow lick.

Hank groaned as if pained.

She hummed in her throat again, loving the way his hips twitched and jerked as she touched him, and leaned forward to lick him once more. He was ever so slightly salty with pre-cum, and she licked up the drops and teased the head of his cock with small circles. Her tongue played over his skin, toying, even as she squeezed and gently worked the base of his shaft.

His hand was gripping her ass so tight it was a wonder he didn't shatter. She suspected he didn't even realize how tense his body was, but she could feel it. He practically vibrated on the bed, a look of grim determination on his face, and she remembered what he'd said about concentrating.

As if it was a problem if he came quickly.

In fact, Becca decided that was her goal. She took him into her mouth, working him slowly deeper with lots of licking and coaxing. He didn't fit nearly as well as she'd hoped, but that didn't matter as long as she used her tongue to the best of her ability. She concentrated instead on licking and nibbling and working his base with slow, steady pumps of her hand. She murmured his name over and over, and told him how good he tasted and how much she liked it.

"Becca," he rasped. "Need—"

"Do you want to come on my face or in my mouth?" she asked, flipping her hair back to gaze over at him. "You decide."

He groaned as if in pain, and then his hips jerked and he was coming all over her hand. She squeezed him, working his length as he released. She waited for him to lie back and exhale, to catch his breath, before she got off the bed and retrieved a towel. Then she wiped her hands and gently cleaned him up. "Hank—"

The big guy grabbed her and pulled her down against him in the bed. This time, he curled around her with them face-to-face, and she smiled happily up at him.

"You might be the best thing that's ever happened to

me," he murmured, thought for a moment, and then added, "Second-best thing."

The first-best thing was obviously Libby. As a father, it made sense, and she knew he loved his daughter beyond reason. Second best to that? She'd take it.

CHAPTER SEVENTEEN

One Week Later

Hank checked the shoes on his horse, using a pick to work caked mud free from the hooves. He'd been quiet all morning, fighting back yawns.

Even so, it was a good morning. He'd been out late with Becca. They'd driven into Casper to catch a movie—horror, his favorite—then promptly ignored the movie and made out the entire time. They'd managed to make it back to her house and get upstairs before the clothes came off. She'd sucked his dick so hard that he'd seen stars, and he'd gone down on her for what felt like hours. He'd made sure she'd come twice before taking a breather, and when they finally went to sleep, it was with his hand between her thighs, possessively holding her against him. He'd woken up incredibly early to be home in time to start the day's chores, but he knew his brothers were bound to say something.

They always said something.

Caleb was the first one to speak. He leaned against the

stall door, watching Hank as he worked, and then politely coughed. "Late night?"

Hank looked up at his brother and glared.

A moment later, Jack was there, his expression a little more gleeful. "Didn't see you in your bed last night."

"Why were you checking?"

"I slept on the couch. You know, because of all the uncle sleepovers we've been having." Jack grinned, looking like the cat that ate the canary. "We've been watching your kid. Least you can do is spill a little of the beans."

He wasn't wrong; they had been watching Libby more often. Not every night, because he wasn't a shithead, but once or twice during the week, he wanted to have alone time with Becca, so he'd bribed his brothers to watch his little girl. "I paid you for that, too. Couple of hundred." He worked a chunk of mud free. "You're the most expensive babysitter ever."

"It's because we have to watch *Frozen* seventy times in a night," Jack said. "Hazard pay."

Caleb snorted. He watched Hank work for a moment longer and then tilted his head, regarding his brother. "You might wanna slow things down. Don't wanna give her ideas."

That made him straighten. He knew his brothers were just looking to get under his skin, but he was irritated at how effective those particular words were. "Give her ideas? Like what?"

"Uncle Ennis says that she's the marrying type. Chased her old boyfriend all over town and tried to get him to marry her until he got smart and bailed a few days before the wedding." Jack wiggled his eyebrows. "She might decide to lasso you next. Best be careful around that one. She sounds like a man-eater."

"Doc said that, huh?" Hank commented, voice dry. He doubted that very much. Oh, there was probably a grain of truth somewhere in there, mixed in with Jack's exaggerations. "That's not what she's like."

"You sure?" Caleb asked, his expression thoughtful. "You're over there every night."

He scowled at his brothers. "She's a good cook."

"That's because she wants a husband."

They had it all wrong. Hadn't Becca told him she wanted to keep things casual? And even though they were together every night, all over each other, they'd never gone beyond heavy petting and oral. It wasn't because he was afraid of kids; that was for sure.

It was because that whole "casual" word haunted him every damned night.

Casual.

She wanted to be casual.

It drove him nuts. "Casual" was bullshit. What did that mean? That she wanted to go out with those guys that winked and flirted with her? That she wanted to keep her options open even though she was dating Hank?

He was obsessed with the word "casual," and not in a good way. He was also obsessed with Becca, but that part he didn't mind.

"Should we get tuxes?" Jack asked, teasing. "For the inevitable wedding?"

Hank turned and growled at his brother, alarming the horse. He immediately put a hand on Trixie's neck, trying to calm her skittish movements. "You don't know what you're talking about."

"I think I do," Jack said boldly, pretending to rub his short beard. Out of the three of them, he was the only one that cut his close to his jaw. Said it was to show off his baby face, but Jack was also never serious. "I think we're just days away from you deciding you want a cute little bride to take back to Alaska with you once we finish up here."

His nostrils flared. Hank knew he was going to upset the horse again, so he calmly left the stall and shut it behind him, then glared at Jack. "You're wrong."

Hank's tone must have gotten through his brother's thick skull. Jack exchanged a look with Caleb and they trailed after him as he headed deeper into the barn. "What crawled up your ass?"

"Nothing," Hank said gruffly.

"Something," Caleb added, and waited.

He turned around and stared at his brothers, sighing deeply. They weren't going to leave him alone until he confessed, and part of him wanted to. He wanted to get it out in the open so someone else could share his pain. So someone else would know what he'd been stewing over for the last week of bliss—and inward agony. After a moment's hesitation, he admitted, "She knows I'm going back to Alaska so she wants to be casual."

They stared at him.

Hank turned and left, and to his irritation, both of his brothers followed behind.

"Casual?" Jack asked. "What the hell does that mean?"

He threw his hands up. "Fuck if I know. It means . . . casual. I guess that we aren't a thing. Not a real thing."

"And you're okay with that?" Caleb asked.

Hank snarled at him over his shoulder. "Does it look like I'm okay with that?"

"So don't go back to Alaska," Caleb said quietly.

Both Jack and Hank turned to look at him as if he was crazy.

Caleb just shrugged.

"No," Jack said, rubbing his hands together. "You need a plan. You need to make her so in love with you that she can't bear to be apart from you. I think you're already halfway there, but you need to seal the deal." He grinned. "Then when you go back to Alaska, she'll be begging to come with you and cook for us."

"'Us'?" Hank said flatly.

"Well, I sure don't want to do the cooking." Jack grinned.

"It might be nice to have a woman around. She can help out with Libby and she can make sure your mood is better." He elbowed his brother.

Hank didn't elbow him back. He just shook his head, feeling rather defeated. "She has a business here, Jack. What's she gonna do in a cabin in the middle of nowhere Alaska with just me and my two dumbass brothers? Paint our nails? Give the bears perms?"

Caleb snorted.

"Which is why you gotta romance the hell out of her," Jack continued. "Make it so none of that shit matters."

Strangely enough, Jack had a point. What if he could convince Becca that the perfect answer was going back to Alaska to be with him and Libby? He crossed his arms and gazed at his brother, curious. "What do you suggest?"

Jack lifted his shoulders in a shrug. "No clue. I'm no ladies' man. Take her someplace and romance her. Surprise her in the middle of the day with a date or something."

In the middle of the day? He frowned. "We both work. She has a business. She can't just up and leave."

"She cuts hair, Hank. It ain't as if she's saving lives." Jack rolled his eyes.

"Just because it's hair doesn't mean it's not a worthwhile job." He pointed at his brother, irritated at his casual attitude. "She got all that gum out of Libby's hair so I didn't have to cut it like you suggested. She's responsible and she cares about her clients." Every time he went to her place, she was squeezing someone in at the last minute or fixing a trim, just because she knew it was important to her clients. Becca worked long hours and he didn't want Jack talking down about her.

"Okay, well . . ." Jack crossed his arms, thinking. "If you can't steal her away, maybe take her to a big dinner. A nice steak."

"Already did that."

"Ask her friends," Caleb suggested.

They both turned to look at him.

"Ask her friends," their normally silent brother repeated. "They'll know what she likes."

He had a point. Hank rubbed his beard thoughtfully. "She does have coffee with the new schoolteacher on Saturdays."

Jack gestured. "There you go. Go talk to the schoolteacher."

"Right now?"

"What are you waiting for? For her to decide she wants to be casual permanent-like?"

Ugh. Just the thought made him want to tear his beard out. "No."

"Then, go." Jack gave him a shove. "And take Caleb with you since he seems to be the idea man."

"Me?" Caleb echoed. "Why me?"

"Because he clearly can't do this on his own." Jack shook his head. "If the word 'casual' comes up again, you put a stop to it, since this fool clearly won't." He gestured at a scowling Hank. "I'll get the hay unspooled and start feeding the cattle. You two hurry in to town, talk to the teacher, and then come back and tell me what she said so we can plan this out."

Hank narrowed his eyes at Jack. "Why are you so gung ho about this?"

He just patted his stomach. "I miss the breakfast doughnuts."

Figured.

An hour later, Hank and Caleb parked in front of Painted Barrel's elementary school. The sign out front read HAVE A GREAT SUMMER!! And Hank bit back a curse. "It's summer break. School's not in."

Caleb nudged him with an elbow, then unbuckled his seat belt. "Might still be there. Summer school."

Right. Becca was always bugging him to get Libby signed up for that. Pre-K. Said Libby would benefit from having friends her age. He thought of his independent little girl and wondered. She never seemed lonely. Maybe she was one of those kids that didn't need anyone but family. Heck, Hank and his brothers had grown up just the three of them with Dad and Mom out in the wilderness . . . except Libby didn't have brothers.

He'd think on it.

They got out of the car and put their cowboy hats on, and Hank felt real weird walking into the school. Like he shouldn't be there. The moment they walked in, he saw the office to the right and headed there. A woman sat at the desk, fussing with her computer, and gave him an impatient look when he cleared his throat.

"Can I help you?"

"I'm looking for a teacher."

Caleb bit back a snort of amusement, and it took everything Hank had not to kick his brother.

"You don't say," the woman replied in a dry voice. "Are you here to enroll someone for the fall? Or for the summer session?"

His thoughts raced. What was the teacher's name? All he knew was that she had great hair—Becca always commented on it—and she was about Becca's age. "Uh, maybe? I want to talk to the teacher first."

"What grade?" The woman tried to hide her impatience behind a smile.

"My daughter's four."

"Pre-K?" She nodded and pulled out a folder, then held a stack of papers out to Hank. "You'll want to enroll her soon. Classes start in a week. Here's the paperwork—we'll need that back quickly—and supplies and the list of things your daughter needs before she can join the class."

"I want to talk to the teacher first," he repeated. If it wasn't that particular teacher, maybe she'd know which one had good hair and was Becca's age. It wasn't a big school, so there couldn't be that many teachers. The building was small and cozy, the brick outside faded with age.

The woman stood up and pointed down the hall. "Miss Mckinney is probably still in her classroom, though she might be heading out for lunch soon. If she's here, she'll be in room 202. If not, you'll have to come back some other time or email her to arrange a meeting."

He nodded, grabbed a smirking Caleb by the arm, and dragged him down the hall, looking for room 202.

They found the door, and to Hank's relief, a nice-seeming young woman sat behind a desk covered in colorful cutouts. Pictures of apples and big block letters decorated the wall, along with posters of kittens and puppies and other happy things. She stood up as they entered the room, a welcoming smile on her face. Her clothing was modest, with a long, tan pencil skirt and a pale blouse. He tried to figure out if she had nice hair, but it was pulled back in a long ponytail and didn't seem nearly as nice as Becca's tumbling waves . . . but maybe he was biased.

"Hi there. I'm Miss Mckinney. Are you parents . . ." She looked at them with a question in her eyes, waiting.

He took off his hat, feeling awkward. "I'm Hank and—"

"Oh, Hank!" She clasped her hands together, delighted. "Libby's father? Becca's told me so much about you. You must be here to enroll her in pre-K for the summer! I'm so glad."

"Unless you can teach her how to shoot a gun or skin a fox, I don't think Libby needs additional learning, but thank you," Hank said, feeling curiously protective of his daughter. Why did everyone assume Libby needed school? Did they think he wasn't a good father to her?

She cleared her throat politely. "Well, no, pre-K is about being social more than anything else. It gets small children used to the school environment, and we try to instill a sense of fun in learning. It sets a good foundation for their future, or at least I like to think so." The teacher smiled brilliantly at him.

From behind him, Caleb made a choked sound.

Miss Mckinney looked over at Caleb, a curious expression on her face. "Do you have a child, too? I'm sorry, I don't remember Becca saying anything else . . ." She trailed off, gazing at him.

Hank waited for Caleb to respond, but his brother had gone mute. He nudged him, and when that still didn't make Caleb speak up, he answered for him. "Brother."

"Oh. Of course." Miss Mckinney's smile grew wider. "Becca did say you had a wonderful family network for looking after Libby. That's so great. I can't wait to meet her."

"I came here to talk about Becca, not Libby," Hank interrupted.

"Becca? Is she okay?" Her brow creased in concern.

"She's fine. I need to woo her."

"Woo . . . her?" The teacher's gaze flicked from Hank to his brother, then back to Hank again. "I'm sorry. I'm confused. I thought you were already dating."

"We are, but she keeps saying it's casual. I need to convince her that it's not."

"Oh." She still looked a bit confused. "I'm probably not a great person to ask for advice, but I'll do what I can. What do you need to know?"

Hank watched her closely. "What do couples do together?"

"Therapy?" she teased.

Caleb gave a braying laugh, the sound overly loud and echoing off the walls.

They both turned to look at him. Hank scowled at his brother and then turned back to the teacher. "I need ideas for something that will make her feel special. Let her know that I'm in this for the long haul."

Because he was, wasn't he? The more he thought about it, the more right it felt. Becca was perfect for him. She was soft where he was hard, sweet and understanding where he was impatient, and she loved his daughter. She loved Hank's kisses, and when she came, she made the most beautiful sounds that he'd ever heard. Yeah, he was in it for the long haul, all right.

Now he just had to convince her that she was, too.

"Well . . ." The teacher paused, thinking. She clasped her hands together and tapped them under her chin. "I mean . . . if it was me, I'd love a big gesture."

"A big gesture?" Behind him, Hank could have sworn that Caleb leaned in.

"Yes. Not that flowers or dates aren't great. They are. But it's easy to run to the corner store and grab a bouquet of flowers, you know? Easy to make it seem like you put in effort when you really didn't. A big gesture requires commitment, though. It requires planning. It shows that you know her enough to really understand her and what she likes, and it tells her that you've been taking the time out from your schedule to do this for her because she's a priority for you, not an afterthought." She gave him a rueful smile. "Just speaking from personal experience."

"Sounds like," he muttered, and Caleb nudged him from behind. He ignored that. "So . . . a big gesture."

"Thought and effort are always appreciated," she said with a little shrug.

She had a point. "What sort of big gesture, then?"

"You know her best. You have to decide." Miss Mckinney beamed at him. "Becca talks so highly of you that I'm sure you'll think of something perfect."

Something perfect. Hell. He was going to have to give this some thought. But he nodded at her. "Well, I appreciate your time. Thank you, Miss Mckinney."

"Please, call me Amy." She smiled at both of them, her expression gentle. "And I really would love to meet Libby. We have a wonderful group of six children signed up for pre-K this summer, and I'd love for her to get some playmates her age. And it's only half a day, so you don't have to worry about her being gone for too long."

"I . . . I'll think about it."

She gave a happy little clap, and he could have sworn that Caleb practically swooned behind him. "Please do," she said excitedly, oblivious to his brother's reaction.

Hank nodded and mumbled something about having a nice day, then hauled Caleb out of the classroom with him. He dragged his brother down the hall and out into the parking lot. Once they were there, he scowled at the man and gave him a strange look. "What's gotten into your ass?"

"Nothing." Caleb glanced back at the school, then at Hank. "You think she noticed me?"

"She couldn't have missed you. You made weird noises and laughed like a donkey."

He groaned. "I didn't, did I?"

"You did."

"Damn." Caleb ran a hand down his face. "I just saw her and . . . my brain froze. I've never seen a more beautiful woman in my life. Have you?"

Hank couldn't even remember what she looked like. Ponytail. Lots of beige. "I . . . guess?" His tastes went to short, curvy women who didn't know how to stay out of his business and who had a fondness for cutting hair.

Caleb's face grew solemn. "I'm going to marry that woman, Hank."

Huh. His brother never made declarations like that. Not Caleb. Jack was the blowhard. Caleb was the quiet, thoughtful one. If he was that in love with the teacher after five minutes, then that was that. "Can your true love hold off for a bit? I need help figuring out what sort of big gesture I'm going to do for Becca." He had ideas, but he needed to pull a few things together first. "Come on."

CHAPTER EIGHTEEN

"You're humming," Hannah pointed out as Becca blow-dried her curls. "That's the first time I've heard you humming in over a year."

"Am I? I guess I am." She grinned, turning the chair ever so slightly so she could round-brush the next section of Hannah's hair. "I'm just in a good mood."

"Because of that big lumberjack?"

"He's a cowboy, thank you very much," Becca teased. Though at times, Hank did rather look like a lumberjack. "And it might be because of him. He's coming over tonight."

"I heard he comes over every night."

She mock shook the brush at Hannah's reflection like a chastising finger. She should have known that the hotel owner would be keeping tabs on what Becca did every night. Hannah loved nothing more than to watch everyone in town. Said it was better than reality TV. Maybe it should have been irritating, but she was too happy to care. Hank came over every night, and most of the time he had Libby with him.

Every once in a while, he didn't. And those nights, he tended to stay until just before dawn.

She loved Libby . . . but those nights were secretly her favorite. Not because the little girl wasn't around, but because on those nights, Hank parked Becca on every piece of furniture in the house and they made out like teenagers. Tonight promised to be more of the same, so she just smiled sweetly at Hannah. "Date night. You know how it goes. How's Clyde, by the way?"

Hannah giggled like a schoolgirl. "That old fart. He told me I get more beautiful every year. I told him it was time for a visit to the eye doctor." She sighed. "He's a good man, though. Helping out up at Price Ranch. You know that Annie's pregnant again?"

"Is she? Dustin must be so excited." Becca smiled. This was gossip she loved hearing. She wanted to hear about babies and happy families.

"Oh yes. So many sweet little ones up there at that ranch. Does my heart good. They're like grandchildren to me." She beamed at Becca. "Just like yours will be."

Awkward. But sweet, in a way. "You have a big heart, Hannah."

"I just hope that lumberjack—excuse me, cowboy—of yours sees that you have a big one, too, and it needs snatching up."

Becca chuckled. After well over a year of Hannah constantly dropping hints at Becca, she could take a "subtle" nudge like that easily. "Actually he said he's got a surprise for me."

"A ring?" She gasped. "So fast?"

"I . . . no, I don't think it's a ring." Becca furrowed her brows. It wasn't . . . was it? They were casual. Even so, her heart skipped a beat. "I think he's just trying to surprise me. Maybe for my birthday?" Though it wasn't for another five months. "Or his birthday?"

"Well, if it's jewelry, I need all the details first thing in the morning."

"If it's jewelry, you'll hear me screaming with delight," Becca added wryly.

"So you'd say yes, then?"

Would she? They were still getting to know each other, but what she knew of him, she adored. It felt very different from her last relationship, when there were quirks and irritations that she cheerfully ignored because she had a goal in mind and was trying to shape Greg into that person. This wasn't about shaping Hank into the perfect groom at all. She just . . . liked being with him. Loved being in his arms. Loved his smile, loved hearing him talk. Loved his darling little girl. She didn't want to rush anything, but at the same time . . . she didn't want to wait around another ten years and hope for the best.

But that might sound desperate. Becca Loftis, getting married after a short period of dating to the next guy that asked her out? She had to be careful what she said to Hannah. So she just smiled and went with, "Provided there was a long engagement so we could get to know each other better? Sure."

Hannah was clearly disappointed in her answer. "Thought you'd be done with long engagements, but to each their own."

Ouch.

She hurried up and finished Hannah's hair, easing off on the conversation to try to edge the woman toward the door. Once she was gone, she headed to the back room, pretending to stock up on shampoo. Instead, she closed the door behind her and leaned against it, closing her eyes.

Thought you'd be done with long engagements.

She knew Hannah hadn't meant to cut so deeply, but that one was going to be leaving a mark for quite some time.

As if she'd been the one to want a long engagement last

time! Becca couldn't remember how many times she'd begged Greg to pick a date. Told him that she'd have been perfectly happy running off to one of those elopement cabins that were all the rage in the mountains. That she'd have been happy with the quickest of ceremonies as long as there was a ring on her finger and a future with the man she loved.

Instead, all she'd gotten was ten years of stress and heartbreak, and now a reputation that she was the one that stalled and had cold feet—thanks to Greg's slick lies. It made her sick. Her hands trembled as she clutched at the small sink in the back room.

She was happy, wasn't she? Why did she let crap like that get to her?

The bell chimed on the door, indicating she had a client. Biting back a groan at their timing, Becca wet her fingertips and smoothed her hair, then pinched her arm to distract herself from the tears that threatened to fall. She was fine. She was.

With a brilliant smile on her face, she left the back room, prepared to meet a customer . . .

And saw Hank instead.

With a wiggling bundle in his arms, a red bow around its neck.

"Hank?" Becca stared at the puppy in his arms. It whined and tried to break free the moment it saw her, and she reached her arms out. "What the heck?"

He handed her the puppy. She knew this particular little girl. She was one of the puppies that Doc had been hand-feeding for the last month or so. She'd gone from a teeny sausage of a pup to the roly-poly black-and-brown squirming bundle that Hank presented her with, all floppy ears and big liquid brown eyes. The moment the puppy was in her arms, the rascal started licking Becca's chin, and Becca couldn't help but giggle.

It was her favorite puppy. She'd only ever told Doc and

Libby that she had a favorite among all the cute little dogs, but this one was it.

"This is a two-part gift," her boyfriend said, his voice grave. "Is it okay?"

"Of course it's okay!" She laughed as the puppy barked and nipped at her chin, as if agitated by her giggles. She cradled her in her arms, fascinated at the sweet face that was now hers. "I just . . . why?"

"You said you were lonely at night." Hank watched her intently. "I don't like that, so I brought you a friend."

She smiled at him, her eyes misting with silly tears. Hadn't she always wanted a dog? Her father had ranch dogs when she was a child, but she wasn't allowed to play with them. He thought she'd distract them. She'd begged Greg for them to get a dog when he'd moved in with her, and after he'd left . . . it just hadn't occurred to her. Of course she could have a dog. She was an adult.

Even so, this was the best, most thoughtful present ever. Ever. It beat the heck out of a bouquet of flowers or a bracelet. Anyone could get those, but Hank didn't want her to be lonely, and he'd gotten her her favorite of the litter deliberately.

It was the little things that made her melt, and she was definitely melting into a puddle right about now.

Smiling, she rubbed the puppy's ears. The little girl didn't have a name, but maybe Hank could help with that. "She's wonderful. Thank you so much. You're the best boyfriend ever."

Hank leaned down and gave her a quick kiss. "I'm glad it was a good call."

The puppy started to chew on the ribbon, her head tilting as she tried to get to the bow, so Becca carefully removed it from her neck and set her down to explore. "It's the best call . . . Did you say a two-part gift?"

He nodded.

"You know my birthday isn't until December, right?" She didn't know what she'd done to deserve all this.

"It's not a birthday present. And part two is coming just as soon as I get the guts."

Guts? She sucked in a breath. Surely . . . surely this wasn't what she thought? Her heart fluttered in her chest, and Becca wasn't sure if it was excitement or anxiety. What if he proposed and then just strung her along for years like Greg did? After all, he wasn't staying in Wyoming. He—

"I think the puppy just pissed on the floor."

His chagrined words broke her out of her freak-out spiral. Becca whirled, and sure enough, her new little buddy was popping a squat right in the corner. "Poor baby." She grabbed paper towels out of the back and mopped up quickly. "She probably needs a walk."

Hank pulled a leash out of his pocket and offered it to her.

She clipped it onto the tiny, adorable collar on the equally tiny, adorable neck, scooped her up, then looked at Hank. "Or do we need to do gift number two first?"

He waved a hand. "It can wait."

She exhaled—had she been holding her breath? God, why was she so nervous? Becca watched Hank out of the corner of her eye as they went outside and let the puppy explore the grassy medians. Was he distracted? He kept rubbing his beard, a faraway expression on his face. She wondered what he was thinking.

"I need a name for her," she told Hank. "Did Libby have any ideas?"

His smile was rueful. "She called her Alaska."

Oh. Okay, that was a weird coincidence—she hoped—but it was kind of a cute name. "Alaska it is." She scooped up the puppy when she lay down in the grass, and gestured to the salon. "Should we go back inside?"

Did he look pale? Oh god, was this bad news? But Hank nodded. "Sure."

Her heart pounded as he put a hand to her back and they returned to the salon. The moment the door shut behind them, Hank moved aside and headed for one of her salon chairs. He sat down and gave Becca a long, long look.

Okay, now she was really confused. She folded a few towels into a makeshift bed behind the counter and set Alaska down, then moved to Hank's side. "What is it?"

One big hand gestured at his brushy beard. "It's this. Cut it all off."

Becca frowned. "What do you mean?"

"This is for you. I'm gonna cut it off." He smiled, but it looked more nervous than excited. "It's part of my big gesture to show you how much you mean to me."

Was that what this was? Becca melted, reaching up and touching his face. She caressed his jaw—and his beard. "Oh, Hank, you don't have to cut your beard off to impress me. I would never ask that. I like your beard. I like you. You don't have to change a thing."

He gazed up at her thoughtfully, his expression turning heated. His arm went around her waist and he caressed her butt through the skirt of her dress. "I don't like how it tears you up. Your pretty skin gets all red and raw when I'm done kissing you. Both your face and your thighs." He stroked his knuckles along her jawline. "Don't like to think I'm hurting you."

"I like your beard," Becca stated again, blushing. She especially liked it below the waist. "And let me show you a little something." She moved to her counter, picking through the bottles of product before she came upon the one she needed. Becca returned to him and showed him the bottle of beard oil. "This will help a little."

"I . . . see." He sounded so reluctant that she wanted to laugh.

"You put a bit of oil on your hands"—she demonstrated—"then rub it into your beard and massage it into the skin." She leaned close, so close that she was practically straddling him as she worked her fingers through his beard, then rubbed his jaw. His body tensed under hers, and Becca was getting ever so slightly aroused just from this. Touching him was a turn-on, always. "What do you think?"

He scowled at her. "I think I don't like the idea of you doing this to your customers."

She arched a brow at him. "You think I crawl all over all my clients just to rub a bit of oil into their beards? This is just for you." She stroked her fingers through his beard again. "Don't you think this feels softer? Sexier?"

He groaned and tugged her closer, his hands cupping her butt. "I like the way this part feels." Hank gazed at her thoughtfully. "You sure you don't want me to cut it off for you? I will."

"I like you just as you are," Becca admitted. "If you like the beard, I like the beard. Besides, I think it's sexy." She rubbed the tip of her nose against his. "All of you is sexy."

"Becca," he groaned, closing his eyes. "Before we get too distracted, we—we need to talk."

She leaned back, eyeing him with worry. "Well, that didn't sound good. Talk about what? Is this why you came bearing gifts?" She was immediately suspicious . . . and a little hurt. This had happened in her last relationship, too. Whenever Greg had wanted to apologize for something or to tell her something he knew would upset her, he'd tried to sweeten the bad news with flowers or a nice "surprise" dinner out. It had gotten to the point that she'd started to dread whenever Greg showed up with flowers, because it meant her day was about to go downhill.

"I can't keep doing this," Hank began.

She jumped out of his lap instantly, stung. What the hell? "You're breaking up with me?"

"What? No, I didn't say that." Hank lurched to his feet.

Becca rushed away from him, grabbing a hand towel

and wiping the oil from her palms. "You came here with gifts so you can break the bad news to me easily, is that it?" She laughed bitterly. "I guess it's a good thing we never made it past casual, right?"

He practically snarled, the sound surprising in its utter frustration. "That's the problem, Becca. You keep saying that we're casual like it's something we both decided on, but every time I hear that word, I want to scream."

Surprise flooded through her. She turned to look at him, confused she hadn't just misheard him. "You don't want to be casual?"

"Have I ever said that I did?"

She blinked. Tried to think. "I thought . . . I thought we agreed that we'd be casual since you were going back to Alaska."

"Am I in Alaska, baby?" He got up from the chair and moved toward her. Stalked, really, like she was his prey and he was a predator on the hunt. It was . . . really damned sexy.

She shivered. "No."

"I don't like casual," he said, approaching her. "In fact, I hate casual. I hate the thought of anyone thinking you don't belong to me. I hate the thought of someone else touching you. I hate the thought of you and me not being a thing. Of it not being important. Because it's sure as hell important to me." Hank gestured at the puppy. "That's why I wanted to do something big for you, show you how much I cared. Because I can't do this casual shit, I really can't. I'm not a casual man."

Joy swelled inside her, and Becca clutched at her chest, as if a touch could contain the pounding of her heart. "I don't want to be casual, either. I've never wanted that."

Hank gave her an exasperated look. "Then why the hell did you say it?"

"Because I thought that was what you wanted! I know I

can get clingy. I worry I latch on entirely too fast for a normal relationship. I wasn't sure if you wanted that."

"I'm fine with fast." His words were low, sweet music to her ears. "Real fine with it."

"I am, too," she told him, and then added, "I'm on the pill."

His brows went up. "We moving that fast, then?"

"Why not? I want you, and you want me . . ." she said boldly, and then her bravado failed her. "Don't you?"

Hank's look grew utterly intense. "You know I do."

She wanted to ask him about Alaska. Wanted to ask him what happened to her—to them—when he moved back. But that was months away, wasn't it? And he'd pointed out that he was here right now. This wasn't a marriage proposal. This was being exclusive with someone and seeing how things shook out.

Alaska was far off in the distance.

Hopefully.

So she bit her lip and gave him a smile. He moved toward her, closing the distance between them, and she sidestepped, scooping up the puppy. "Lock the door to the salon, please," Becca whispered. "I'll take this little girl next door and get her settled so you and I can be alone."

His mouth curved in a hint of a smile, and he gave her a look that devoured her. "Hurry, then."

Oh, she would. She all but dashed through the connecting door into the house and headed for the kitchen. She didn't have puppy food, but she did have some leftover chicken from yesterday, and she cooed and made kissy noises at the wiggly baby in her arms as she pulled it out of the fridge. Five minutes later, it was chopped up and in a bowl on the floor in the bathroom, along with fresh water and a nest comprised of a couple of shirts that smelled like her and a thick blanket. That ought to hold the little girl for a bit . . . she hoped. She was new to puppy parenting, but she couldn't wait to learn all about her little girl.

"Tomorrow morning, we'll go to the pet store after work and get you all kinds of goodies, okay?" She promised Alaska, stroking her soft fur as she gobbled down the chopped chicken. "A bed, some dog food, and all the good stuff. Maybe Dad would like to come with us."

"Dad?" came the voice from the hall. "Am I a dad to a puppy now?"

"You might be," Becca said, straightening. She washed her hands and then carefully closed the bathroom door while the puppy was eating, escaping into the hall. "You think it's okay to leave her alone in there for a bit?"

"Unless you want to show her what Mom and Dad do in the privacy of their room."

Maybe it was a better idea not to have the puppy watching them together. At least . . . not their first time. She wanted it to be all about her and Hank, nothing more. "We'll just keep an ear out to see if she cries, then." Her pulse was fluttering in her chest as he moved closer, then leaned one hand against the doorjamb, practically standing over her and pinning her to the wall. Her nipples hardened in response and she was incredibly aware of his nearness. "So . . . Libby?"

"Uncle sleepover," Hank murmured, reaching down and toying with a lock of her hair that danced over her shoulder. "Had to pay Jack and Caleb double their usual rate for watching her tonight. I think they're getting tired of babysitting."

"Oh. We can always set her up in the guest room," Becca said, thinking. "It'll be like she has a room of her own. We can get a nightlight and some stuffed animals and a baby monitor—does she need a baby monitor?—and make it feel like home . . ." She trailed off as he brushed his fingers under her jaw, then ran his thumb over her lower lip.

"Let's worry about all of that in the morning. Is the puppy situated?" When she nodded, he slid his hands to her waist and then hefted her into his arms. She gave a little cry of alarm and flung her arms around his neck to steady herself. "Then we're going into the bedroom and we're not coming out until I've made you scream my name. Twice."

Now, that sounded like her kind of challenge. Becca shivered with anticipation, stroking her fingers over his neck as he hauled her into the bedroom. She was so glad she'd made her bed and cleaned up this morning . . . and even more glad that since she'd started dating Hank, she'd thrown away the squirrel undies. Today she was wearing a matching pink set that made her feel pretty and flirty . . . because she'd secretly hoped he'd get a chance to see them.

Not that he'd paid much attention to her panties this last week. It was more about what was under them.

Hank set her gently down on the bed and stared at her, his gaze locked on her as he reached over and took one boot off, then the other. He was starting with undressing, which meant that things were going to get heated fast. That was totally fine with her. She felt like this week had been one long bout of foreplay, and she was more than ready to take things to their natural completion. Heck, she was practically quivering with need. Hadn't she thought about this for days on end? Dreamed about what it would feel like to have his big body covering hers as he claimed her for himself? They'd been enjoying each other this week—oh boy, had she ever enjoyed herself—but this felt good. It felt right.

It felt like it was about time. But then again, Becca was an impatient sort.

He tossed aside his boots and pulled his socks off, then moved his hands to his waist. Slowly. Far too slowly. Biting back her frustration, she reached for his belt, trying to unbuckle him faster. He batted her hands aside gently and continued his slow undressing, to the point that she glared at him as he slung his belt aside with all the speed of a snail.

He wanted to be like that? Fine, two could play that game. Becca got up from the bed and kept her gaze locked on him as she reached behind her for the zipper to her sundress. She eased it down and the straps fell forward on her shoulders, the bodice sagging. She shimmied and held it to her breasts as she slid her arms out of the straps, and then turned away as she let the dress fall to the floor. Then she was in only her pink lacy bra and panties and her sandals.

And the sandals were quickly discarded.

Hank groaned and reached for her, but this time she was the one that pushed his hands aside, casting him a coy, playful look over her shoulder. "Naked, please."

"Tease," he muttered, but she heard the impatient rustle of clothing as he stripped down behind her. She sauntered to the far side of the bed, only to be snatched at the waist by her big, strong cowboy.

With a yelp, Becca bounced on the bed and giggled as Hank flung himself down next to her. Hank was so serious most of the time, so when he showed a bit of playfulness, it just made her melt. He tugged on her leg and flipped her onto her back, and then she was gazing up at him, breathless, as he grinned down at her.

The man was naked. Finally.

A pleased sigh escaped her, and Becca slid her hand over his chest. "You're the best boyfriend."

"I'd better be the only boyfriend," he mock growled, and lowered his head. She thought he was going to kiss her, but he slid lower, nipping at her neck, and the now-softened bristles of his beard tickled her skin. A little moan escaped her, and she squirmed underneath him as he nipped again, moving slowly but steadily lower. His big hand reached behind her back, unfastened the clasp of her bra, and then tugged it off her.

Her nipples were tight and aching with anticipation as he moved down her collarbones, his hand warm as he caressed her arm. His big body was over her, but he kept his weight carefully propped up so as not to crush her. She wanted that crush, weirdly enough. She wanted him to sink down on her with that heavy, delicious weight so she could revel in the feel of all of him on top of her. It was an oddly specific craving, but she'd been unable to think of anything else for days now.

Well, okay, that wasn't entirely true. She thought about a lot of things when it came to Hank. Like the tickle of his beard on the insides of her thighs. The way he knew how to go down on her and make her come so hard. The way he didn't mind if she took a little longer to climax, because it gave him more time to taste her. The way his big, heavy cock felt in her grip—or against her lips. His reactions when she touched him.

She was obsessed. Happily so.

Hank's mouth moved lower, and his hand moved to her breast even as his lips closed over her other nipple. He teased her with his lips, then gave her a gentle scrape with his teeth that made her senses reel. A moan escaped her, loud against the quiet sounds of their breathing.

"Love the way you taste, baby," he told her between licks and nips. "Love these pretty breasts." He palmed one and toyed with the tip, rubbing the pad of his thumb back and forth over it in the way that drove her absolutely insane. He spent an exquisite amount of time on her breasts, lovingly tasting and caressing each mound, making sure to give each breast equal amounts of attention. When his mouth lingered too long on the left, he'd lift his head, blow lightly on the wet nipple, and then switch to the other side.

It was the most delicious kind of agony, and Becca was squirming, panting, and utterly lost by the time he began to kiss lower. She arched against him in silent suggestion, but he only put a hand on her belly and gently pushed her back down to the bed.

She made a sound of protest, her hands going to his hair, and she gave him a little push in the direction she wanted.

His teeth scraped at her bellybutton, and she felt him chuckle against her skin. "Pushy, pushy."

"I need you," she whispered. "I need you so badly."

"I'm gonna give you everything," he promised, kissing lower. "Don't worry."

Oh, she wasn't worried. It was that hungry impatience that was driving her insane with need. Even so, she knew he'd make it good for her. Knew that by the time he was done, she'd be practically lifting off the bed with her orgasm. Knew that he'd make her come over and over again if that was what she wanted. He'd never rushed her. Not once, not ever.

But it was hard to slow down and enjoy the sensations when all she wanted was more, more, more. She was hungry for him—no, ravenous. And when his tongue dipped below the waist of her panties, a gasp broke from her. "Oh god, Hank."

"Right here." His breath fanned over her sex. "Not going anywhere. Not anytime soon. I promise."

Becca moaned. She wanted him to go down on her, but she also wanted him deep inside, filling up all the spots that were clenching with an empty ache.

All the sounds she was making just seemed to slow him down, though. He took his sweet time toying with the waistband of her lacy panties, pressing hot kisses along her skin just above the band and then nipping at her through the fabric. His mouth went to one hip and then he slowly kissed his way back over to the other hip again, all while she undulated and rocked and whimpered as if she were dying.

Just when she was about to go mad, his rough fingers went to her waistband and he began to slowly tug it down.

"Fuck, baby, these panties are soaked. Look at how wet you are. How ready. You're making my mouth water." His beard brushed over her thighs a second before the fabric of her panties did. "Kinda makes me want to pull them back up and just tongue you through the fabric for a while—"

"No!" she cried out, and tried to pull them from his grip.

He chuckled, all slow and in control, just as he always was. "So hungry for my mouth."

He had no idea. Becca bit down on her lip as he slowly, exquisitely dragged her panties down the lengths of her thighs and then her calves. She wanted to fling her legs wide open in invitation as he settled his big shoulders between her legs. He ran his fingers along the insides of her thighs, sliding from knee to apex, and by the time he got to her mound, she was breathless once more. She loved the feel of his big hand as he gently pushed her thighs apart—she'd been waiting for that. Waiting for that small touch that told her that he was in control. That this was all handled . . . and that it was his idea. Maybe she was still shy when it came to oral and didn't want to be a bother, and that was why she waited for him to open her up like a flower.

"Gonna taste you now, baby," Hank told her, his beard tickling against her thighs and making her squirm. "Been waiting for this all day long."

Oh damn, so had she. Becca closed her eyes and curled her fingers in his thick hair, waiting, her body utterly primed, for his mouth to descend.

When it finally did, she practically came right there.

And then his mouth was on her, and it was so good. It always shocked her just how good his mouth felt on her sex. Like he'd been taking classes or something. Because the way he touched her? The way he knew instinctively how to drive her crazy with lips and tongue? It was far too good. He was perfectly aligned with what her body needed—more than that, he listened to her subtle signals and cared about making her come and come hard. That was the best thing about being in bed with Hank: he paid attention. It wasn't good for him unless it was good for her, and he was patient enough to wait until she got there, too. They'd fooled around constantly for the last week, and while it was getting easier for her to let go and lose control with him, it still wasn't fast or easy. Her mind started to work, her brain piling up with worries, and then the orgasm would slip a bit further away. It was just how she was. But Hank was patient and unwavering, and he loved to touch her and taste her, and he always, always made sure she came hard before he got his own. Sometimes she'd stroke his cock for him while they kissed until he came on her hands. Sometimes he'd do it to himself while he had his mouth buried between her thighs.

Today, though, he was going to come inside her, and that was the most exciting thing of all.

Becca shivered when his lips played across her sensitive flesh. She was already hot and slick, ready for him, and he made a small sound of appreciation as he tasted her. He brushed gentle kisses over her folds, then began to lick and nibble and tease, knowing that it'd make her squirm. When she murmured a protest, his big hand went to the inside of her thigh and held her down as he used his other to pull her folds apart so he could suck on her clit. It sent electrical currents all through her, and for a moment, Becca thought she was going to come right away. Her hips arched, but the orgasm fled the moment she thought about it—like it always did—and so she squirmed and panted and moved restlessly against his mouth until it started to rise again. This time, he kept up his steady chain of touches, the flick of his tongue against the underside of her clit constant and speeding up until a low scream burst from her—and her release rocked through her body.

Hank made a pleased sound in his throat, licking her

sensitive flesh until she began to twitch with every stroke of his tongue. He pressed a few more kisses to the insides of her thighs and her mound, and then lifted his head to gaze up at her. "I could stay here all night, you know."

Oh, she knew he could.

Becca stroked her fingers through his hair. "I want you on me, Hank. I want you in me. Please."

He growled low, pressed another hard kiss to the inside of her thigh, and then surged up. He moved over her, his big hips settling between her spread thighs, and she eagerly lifted her legs to encircle him.

Hank kissed her, his mouth tender despite the urgency of his kisses. He tasted like her body, and it added an erotic, sultry edge to their caresses, and it didn't take long before Becca was moaning against his mouth. She arched against him suggestively, waiting for him to move, to claim her. Instead, all he did was kiss her. "Hank, please."

"Could kiss you forever," he told her, and gazed down at her so seriously and for so long that she blushed. He made it seem like every moment with her was a gift . . . was it any surprise that she was falling for the man?

The moment the thought occurred to her, it filled her with panic.

Falling. For Hank. Of course she was. She was someone who fell into love quickly. She knew that. And how could she not fall for Hank? He was nothing that she'd thought she'd ever wanted but had ended up being everything she'd dreamed of. He was gentle despite his hulking size. Considerate. Thoughtful. A good father. An amazing lover. And he made her feel so . . . special.

The "I love you" hovered on her lips, but she pushed it back, settling for something far more carnal. "Take me, Hank."

He gave her another slow, thorough kiss, nipping at her lower lip. His hand slid down to her thigh and he adjusted it against his hip, shifting his weight. She felt the head of his cock press against her core, where she was slippery and hot and aching and hollow.

"Tell me if I do something you don't like," he whispered between kisses. "Or if it's too much."

"It won't be," she promised him. She wasn't a virgin. It'd be fine.

Even so, when he pushed forward, Becca was a little surprised at how . . . big he felt. Of course he was big. Hank was a huge guy, all over. She'd known from handling his cock in the last few days during their make-out sessions that he was thick, but as he slowly pushed into her, she couldn't decide if it felt like too much . . . or if it was amazing. A little gasp escaped her and he froze over her, worried.

"Keep going," she encouraged, raising her hips in suggestion. "Don't stop."

"Becca—"

She kissed him fiercely, this time being the aggressor, and he let out a ragged groan even as he surged deep into her. She clung to him as he settled his weight atop her, working ever so slightly deeper with little movements of his hips. It felt as if he was touching her womb, he was so deep inside her, and maybe it had been a long time since she'd had sex, but she'd never felt so . . . full.

"You okay?" he asked between nips on her mouth. It was like he couldn't stop touching her, stop kissing her.

Becca could feel the tension in his big body. He practically vibrated over her, tense as a bowstring.

He didn't move, though, just remained frozen atop her, and so she stroked her hands up and down his sides, caressing him. She reminded herself that his memories of sex were probably not the greatest—the release had probably been good but everything after that had been tainted, so she didn't care if she came again or not, because she just wanted it to be good for him. "You feel amazing," she told him softly. "You're so big inside me it feels as if you're hitting all the spots that have ached for so long."

Hank groaned, pressing his forehead to hers. She could feel his big body shudder.

"You can't hurt me," she promised. "You feel good. You feel so good. Move as much as you want, as hard as you want." She touched his face gently and then moved her hand down to his hip, then to his ass, and caressed the hard muscle there. "I want all of it."

"Might not . . . last long," he gritted out. "You feel so fucking good."

"Then that just gives us more time to do this again," Becca promised him. "Just do what feels good, what feels right."

He sucked in a deep breath between gritted teeth, and then his hips jerked. It was a short, hard thrust, and the sensation sent pleasure skittering all through her. He was so big she seemed to feel it everywhere, and he seemed to touch parts of her that had never been hit before. Her hands tightened on him.

"Can you do that again?" she whispered, her body clenching. "That felt really, really good."

He claimed her mouth in a rough kiss, and pumped into her again, his body fierce. She moaned into his mouth and then he was on her like a wild animal, thrusting deep and hard over and over again, as if unable to stop himself. As if his body had lost all control and he just had to release.

It felt amazing. Becca dug her nails into his shoulders and moaned, arching up against him to meet each thrust with her body. The elusive orgasm was beginning to spiral through her belly again, encouraged by something deep inside her that Hank's cock rubbed against with every stroke, and she started to whimper with his movements. "Keep going," she managed. "Oh god, that feels so good. Oh, Hank—"

He growled again, leaning in and biting her neck and then sucking on the skin hard as he jackhammered into her.

She came again, much to her surprise—no, she exploded. Everything was suddenly pleasure and release and a little scream escaped her as her entire body clenched up in the wake of yet another release. That was all it took for Hank to come, too, and his teeth dug into her shoulder as his release shuddered out of him, their bodies quaking at nearly the same time. He continued to move erratically over her, as if unable to stop, and then slowly exhaled deep, clutching her against him. He didn't collapse on top of her—much to her disappointment—but immediately pulled away and flipped onto his back, panting.

Becca was a cuddler, though. She followed him over and pillowed her head on his shoulder. "Should I leave you alone? Do you need a moment?"

He snorted and tugged her against him. "No. You stay right here."

She closed her eyes, pleased. She'd clean up in a minute—as he no doubt would, too—but for now she just enjoyed the blissful pleasure of curling up against her lover.

Her lover.

The man she loved.

She'd stress about that later. For now, she closed her eyes and breathed in his scent and thought the world was pretty perfect.

CHAPTER NINETEEN

It was still dark outside when Hank woke up. Becca, not surprisingly, was still asleep. He was used to the early mornings and instantly getting up and starting the day, but he lay in bed and watched the woman at his side—his woman—sleep. She was a messy sleeper, he decided, kind of like his daughter. She sprawled in the bed, her long hair everywhere, and her hands were on his side, her leg tossed over his. It was like she had to touch him even as she slept. Not that he minded—he liked that, just like he liked that she slept with her mouth slightly parted and every so often mumbled in her sleep. It was cute.

It was a shame he'd have to wake her up.

He let Becca sleep for a moment longer, eyeing her naked body and waiting for his morning wood to subside. He could wake her up and roll her over, push between her thighs and claim her like he had many times last night . . . but then he'd never leave her bed. Already he felt addicted. So he reached over and caressed her bare backside, and then rubbed it until she awoke and squinted at him in confusion.

"What is it?" she mumbled, scrubbing a hand across her eyes like his daughter did. "What's wrong?"

"Nothing's wrong. It's time to get up."

She peered at him through the curtain of her thick hair. "What?"

"Time to get up. We're going fishing." He gave her bouncy ass a light smack, and the way it jiggled just made his dick get all hard again. Hell, he needed to stop touching her before he got completely distracted. Reluctantly, he pulled his hand away. "I told Libby we'd go fishing with her today."

"Oh." She yawned and sat up. "Well, okay. If she's waiting for us . . ."

"She is," he lied. Libby probably wasn't up yet, but he knew the best time to go fishing was bright and early. They could nap later, anyhow.

A short time later, they'd both showered and she'd taken Alaska out for her first walk of the day and fed her. They drove out to the ranch, and the moment his truck pulled up, his little daughter was on the porch, wearing her favorite overalls.

"Daddy!" she cried, holding her fishing rod. "Come on!"

He laughed, his heart aching with joy at the sight of her. God, he loved that little girl more than life itself. He got Becca's door for her, and while she retrieved the puppy, he went to his daughter and swung her into his arms, planting a kiss on her head. "Were you good while I was gone?"

"Yes, but next time you have a sleepover with Miss Becca, I want to go, too." She scowled at him.

He grinned. "We'll see."

Hank checked in with his brothers while Becca chatted with Doc about the puppy and he gave her a bag of puppy food. Then they packed their fishing gear into the car. Becca pulled together a quick picnic lunch and grabbed a blanket while they retrieved the worms Libby had hunted up the night before with her uncles, and then they were off.

It wasn't a far drive to one of the nearby lakes, and when they pulled up, the scenery was breathtaking. Kinda reminded him of home, he decided, with the mountains and trees and the wildflowers blooming amid the grasses. The lake wasn't very big, a small, weathered dock on the far side that made Hank's parental instincts flare in alarm. They'd be standing on the shore to fish, he decided, and while he readied the poles, Becca laid out the blanket and Libby chased the puppy. Then the fishing rods were ready, and Libby put a worm on her own hook, much to Becca's surprise. Hank was proud, though. His little girl was capable and smart, and not easily grossed out. She was a wilderness kid and she knew how to handle herself.

She was also a noisy kid, keeping up a constant stream of conversation as she watched her bobber in the water. She told Becca all about hunting for worms the night before, and how she'd helped Hank pick out Alaska, and which puppy was her favorite and why. She talked about other times they'd gone fishing and she asked again and again about the sleepover. All the talking was probably scaring away the fish, but Hank couldn't find it in him to mind. Libby was having a great time, and Becca was, too. She curled up on her side on the blanket, watching them both and petting the sleeping puppy curled up against her. There was a look of such contentment on her face that it filled his heart with longing.

This was how it should be, he realized. His woman at his side. His daughter, too. Everyone happy and enjoying the day in the great outdoors. This was his family.

This was everything he'd ever wanted . . . and he couldn't picture anyone else he'd rather share it with.

"Daddy!" Libby shrieked, shaking him out of his reverie. "I have a bite!"

Sure enough, the bobber went under and jerked again, nearly hauling his little girl into the water. He reached over and put his hand on the rod and helped her steady it, ensuring that it wouldn't pull her in. "Remember what I showed you on how to bring it in?"

He was the proudest papa alive when minutes later, she brought in a fish the size of his hand, and Libby danced with joy. Becca took pictures with her cell phone and then Libby showed the fish to the puppy before she decided the fish needed to go back into the water. He had a daddy fish, she decided, like in *Finding Nemo*, and his family would be looking for him.

"Something tells me dinner isn't going to be fish," Becca murmured as Libby sent the fish back into the lake and waved goodbye to it.

"Something tells me I should make her watch *Frozen* more often than *Nemo*," he grumbled. "That was perfectly good eating."

Becca just chuckled and reached over to squeeze his knee. He put his hand over hers and rubbed her soft skin, and the world felt . . . right. He glanced down at Becca, feeling utterly content. "Hope you don't mind if this is how we spend the morning."

She smiled softly at him and squeezed his hand. "I don't mind at all. My first appointment isn't until one." She turned to watch Libby playing at the edge of the shore and then gave him a thoughtful look. "Hank . . ."

"Yeah?"

"You said you wanted to do a big gesture for me, right?" She bit her lip and gazed up at him. "What if you enrolled Libby in pre-K? Just for the summer? It'd give her a chance to be with other kids her age, learn what school is like . . . I think she'd really enjoy it."

It was on the tip of his tongue to tell her that school wasn't necessary. That he was gonna be taking his daughter back to Alaska soon enough, which meant he'd be home-schooling her and teaching her things that were useful in the wild, like how to sharpen a knife when out in the wild or how to check over your snowmobile to ensure it wouldn't break down on you out in the field. But Becca looked up at him with such earnest eyes that he didn't have the heart to tell her no. It meant so much to her.

And wasn't that everything he'd ever wanted for Libby? Not just for him but for his daughter? A mother that actually cared about what was best for her? Becca had never acted like his daughter was a nuisance to have around. She just always made room for her, even if it encroached on their private time together.

He hated the thought of sending Libby off to a stupid school all day. Thought it was pointless. But the teacher had said that Becca would appreciate a big gesture, and that he'd know what it was because he knew Becca.

So he sighed and gave her hand a squeeze. "I'll fill out the paperwork tonight."

She bit her lip, smiling slyly at him. "Bring it over to my house and I'll help."

Something told him that paperwork wouldn't be the only thing happening that evening. Hank grinned.

Days passed and they settled into a routine. Hank spent his days on the ranch, working alongside his brothers. Once the day's chores were done, he drove into town and headed for Becca's salon. They had dinner together at her house—and he cooked if she had an appointment that ran late and took the puppy out for walks.

He'd gotten the puppy for her so she'd have company on lonely nights, but for some reason, he was the one lonely at night. So he spent every night at her place and just woke up bright and early to go back to the ranch for another day of work. They made a room for Libby at Becca's house, and Libby loved sleepovers. They'd all play a game together—usually slapjack or I spy or something easily doable with a four-year-old, and then they'd tuck in Libby together and then go to bed early themselves. Not that there was much sleeping getting done. It was a challenge to remain quiet enough throughout sex so they wouldn't wake up Libby down the hall, but that was part of the fun. Becca and Libby woke up extra early to have breakfast with him, and he kissed both his girls goodbye as he headed out in the morning. Libby spent the day with Becca, "helping" in the salon and chatting with customers as if she'd always been there. That weekend, Becca took her into Casper for some new school clothes, and Libby had loved her cute, frilly little dresses so much she hadn't wanted to take any of them off. She'd slept in them, too, curled up with little Alaska in her bed, and her room got ever pinker and girlier because Becca couldn't resist buying Libby girly things. She loved spoiling his daughter.

Hank had never been so damned happy. Life felt pretty damned perfect. Was Wyoming the same as Alaska? No, it wasn't. There were far too many people around, even in this small town, and everyone wanted to know your business. People started recognizing him as Becca's boyfriend and would stop him in the street and ask how they were doing, or if Becca could squeeze someone in later that afternoon for a highlight.

Like he knew what a highlight was.

It wasn't the wild, untamed wilderness of northern Alaska, that was for sure. There were no moose, no foxes hiding in the bushes, no rivers brimming with salmon and crusted with ice from the mountains. There was scenery, and it was nice, but there were ranches and cattle and he stayed in a cozy little house with a bedroom for Libby and a bedroom for him and Becca, and it wasn't quite the same as his rough-hewn cabin he'd shared with his brothers. No, it wasn't quite the same at all . . . but that didn't make it bad.

With Becca around, nothing seemed quite so bad.

Just her smile brightened his day. Her laughter was addictive, and he was starting to need the warm clasp of her body like the way he needed air. It was so different than it had been with Adria—he realized that now. Being with Adria had scratched an itch, but it hadn't satisfied the lonely parts of his soul, parts that he hadn't realized were there until Becca curled up against him and gave a bone-deep sigh after sex. For the first time ever, he felt connected to a woman. Like they were on the same page, mentally, physically, and emotionally.

Like they wanted the same things in life.

It was funny—before he'd started dating Becca, he'd never thought he'd end up with a woman. Thought he'd live his life out alone in Alaska, turning into a grizzled old mountain man alongside his brothers. Now, he was starting to see a different life in the future, one involving growing old with a woman who worked as hard as she loved, who claimed she was needy even if she had an independent streak, and who adored his daughter as hard as she adored him . . . and her dog.

It had only been a few weeks, but Hank also suspected that when things lined up perfectly and the world showed you the right person? It didn't matter if it was three days or three years. You just knew.

And with Becca . . . he just knew. She was his as surely as he was hers.

He hadn't told her that yet, of course. His woman had some hang-ups about relationships, courtesy of the last jackass, who'd left her dangling for ten years. The man was a moron, Hank decided, because he should have had Becca married and claimed as his within months of first dating her. That was Hank's plan, anyhow. He had to move a little slower than he wanted, though, because she worried people in town would think she was "rebounding," or that she wasn't with Hank for the right reasons.

Like he cared what anyone else thought.

That had never bothered him before. Even this morning, as he headed into the ranch, he braced himself for another round of teasing from his knucklehead brothers. They loved to rib him about his relationship with Becca, but he didn't care. He was with a good woman and they were just jealous, alone in their own lonely beds.

When he pulled up to the ranch house, he headed inside to get coffee. His brothers were in the kitchen, sitting with Doc. All of them looked over at him and smirked as he came in.

"You look tired," Jack told him boldly. "Late night?"

"Early morning," was all Hank said. He moved to the coffeepot and poured himself a cup.

"No doughnuts?" Caleb asked, tone mournful. "Damn."

"He was too busy," Jack teased. "Probably took all of his strength just to get out of that bed."

"Now, now," Uncle Ennis said mildly. "Becca's a nice girl and your brother's an adult. Let's leave things alone, shall we?" He lifted his coffee cup to his lips and took a sip, then added, "But you do look like hell."

Caleb and Jack snickered.

Hank made a face at them and gulped his coffee. So he hadn't been getting much sleep lately. Didn't matter. Other things were more important . . . like spending time with Becca. Watching movies with Becca. Sliding between Becca's thighs and staying there for hours while she tugged at his hair and made all those sexy whimpers like she was dying to be noisy and couldn't because she didn't want to wake up Libby. "I can always take a nap here," he drawled, draining his coffee and then pouring himself another cup.

"If you're tired, you can take a nap," Uncle Ennis declared. "Never let it be said I ran my employees into the ground. Where's Libby this morning?" His uncle loved the little girl almost as much as Hank did.

"With Becca," Hank told him. "She's helping out at the salon and then they're getting some shoes for school tomorrow."

"School?" Jack straightened, disgusted.

Caleb's brows went up.

"Pre-K," Hank explained. "For learning how to be friends and shit." It sounded like crap to him, but Becca was excited for Libby, and Libby was excited, so he was trying to be excited, too.

"I think it's good," Uncle Ennis declared with a nod. "That little girl needs friends her age."

"But why?" Jack wanted to know. He frowned at Hank. "Why's she need to make friends here? We're not staying."

He had a point, but Hank didn't say anything. It was just for the summer. The session was eight weeks, according to the paperwork Becca had made him read. Didn't seem like that long a time, and he wasn't ready to head back just yet. The cabin would be falling to pieces and needing all kinds of repairs, and their equipment in storage was going to need tune-ups and work done if they didn't use them before the cold weather hit, but he found he wasn't in a rush. Not right now.

"When are you going back?" Uncle Ennis asked, curious.

"Calving's done," Jack said. "We can train up whoever you need first, of course, but . . . soon? We need to get back to Foxtail before the snows hit."

He wasn't wrong. They'd need time to get supplies, get their gear in working order, and repair anything out of order. Living outside of Foxtail wasn't an easy life, that was for sure, and you had to be prepared.

Caleb leaned back in his chair, his arms crossed over his chest. "Don't think I'm going back this year."

Jack threw up his hands and rolled his eyes. "Here we go."

Caleb shrugged.

"It's because of that woman, isn't it?" Jack pestered him. "The one you won't shut up about?"

Caleb just stared off into the distance, but there was a hint of red on his cheeks.

Hank watched his brother in surprise. A woman? Caleb? And he wouldn't shut up about her? He tried to think of women his brother had met . . . and only came up with one. "Not that schoolteacher?"

Caleb turned redder. He jerked to his feet and put his mug in the sink, then silently headed out to the barn.

Jack just gave Hank a look of disgust. "This is your fault, you know."

"How is this my fault?"

His brother jerked to his feet and shook his head. "You're changing everything. You know we were just supposed to come down here for a year or so, stock up on some cash for supplies, help out Uncle Ennis, and then head back north. Now Caleb's pining away for some schoolteacher he ain't never said one word to, and you're all over the local hairdresser, and I'm starting to think we're never going back to Alaska." He gave Hank a look of disgust. "Do you even want to go back home?"

"Of course," he said automatically, a scowl on his face. "The plan hasn't changed." He just . . . hadn't thought about the plan much lately. It hadn't seemed all that important.

"So you're leaving here with me in a few months? Once Uncle Ennis gets a few new hands and we get them all situated?"

Hank glanced over at his uncle, who mildly sipped his coffee, clearly trying to stay neutral. Was he going to leave in a few months? He hadn't thought hard about it—hadn't thought about it at all in a while, really. "If Libby's done with school," he began.

Jack made a noise of disgust. He grabbed his hat off the hook on the wall and turned to glare at Hank. "Is that what you want or is that what *she* wants?"

"Libby?"

"Becca," Jack spat. "All of this is you changing just to make some woman happy and—"

"Watch yourself," Hank said quietly.

Jack made a sound of disgust and turned and walked out to the barn.

Hank stayed behind. Sipped his coffee like there was nothing wrong. Inside, though, he was stewing. He was furious at his brother for trying to divide him and Becca. For trying to make it seem like Hank was ruining their lives. Becca didn't have a mean, divisive bone in her body. All she wanted was to take care of Hank and Libby, and all he wanted was to return the favor. Jack was just stewing.

He was jealous.

That was all. He set down his coffee cup and turned on his heel, heading for the door that led toward the barn.

Uncle Ennis cleared his throat.

Hank turned. "What?"

"Do I need to look into hiring some new hands?" He lifted his coffee cup, gazing down at the crossword paper on the table. "I can check with Jason over at Sage's ranch. Just give me the word and I'll put out some feelers."

Hank . . . didn't have an answer. He stood, waiting, expecting the right answer to fall to his lips at some point. Yes, they'd be leaving soon, hire away. No, they were staying for at least another winter. He kept waiting . . .

And all he could see was Becca's face. Her eyes flashing with welcome as he came through the door. Her soft arms as she reached for him and pulled him close. The way her hair fell over her face as she straddled him and rode him in bed. The way she curled up with his daughter to read a bedtime story.

He had no answer for his uncle.

That pissed him off. Now he was in as foul a mood as Jack. With a low snarl, he stormed out of the house without giving anyone an answer.

CHAPTER TWENTY

Even though he thought about the argument with Jack all throughout the day and into the night, Hank didn't say anything to Becca. No sense in upsetting her. The next morning, Libby was as excited as could be. She wore a brand-new pink-and-white gingham dress with a matching white-and-pink T-shirt underneath the bib. She had cute little pink sparkly sandals, and Becca braided her hair into two pigtails and beamed at her.

"You are so adorable, Libby. Miss Mckinney is going to be so excited to see you!"

Libby squirmed with excitement all through breakfast, and that made Hank feel better about taking his daughter in to school. Perhaps Becca was right. Perhaps this was the right thing for her after all. Libby could stand to be around some other kids. Becca loved having her around, and Uncle Ennis adored her, but when she was cranky, it was hard to juggle both her and the day's work. It'd give everyone a break to have the little girl in school, and she'd get a few new friends.

So once breakfast was over, they both kissed Becca goodbye, and Libby hugged Alaska. Then they got into Hank's truck and he drove her over to the school. There were a few other parents heading in with their children, but the moment they pulled up to the school, instead of wiggling with excitement, Libby got quiet.

"You ready?" Hank asked as he turned the truck off. "Won't this be fun?"

Libby popped her thumb in her mouth and started to suck it, her eyes wide.

"It'll be fun," he reassured her again.

He got her out of the car and tried not to notice how she clung to him, one hand tight on his shirt as she sucked her thumb frantically. He took her to the classroom where he'd met the teacher once before, and inside was chaos. Instead of the quiet classroom from before, the room seemed to be filled with parents, all talking over one another as children ran around the room screaming. Miss Mckinney immediately headed in his direction, a beaming smile on her face. She wore a bright green dress and her hair was pulled back in a bun, glasses on her face, and she looked very much like a teacher.

Hank had no idea why Caleb was so in love with her.

"Hello there! You must be Libby," Miss Mckinney said, beaming at the two of them before her gaze focused on Libby. "Miss Becca has told me so much about you. I can't wait for you to be in my class."

His bold, fearless daughter made a sound of distress, sucked her thumb harder, and then buried her face against his neck.

The teacher just smiled. "Everyone has a bit of nerves on the first day. It's totally fine. Just let me know when she's ready and I'll take her."

He nodded.

The teacher moved away to greet one of the other parents, and Hank was alone with his daughter. She clung to him like a burr, quiet, and he gave her back an awkward pat. "It's gonna be okay, Libs. You'll like it here."

She shook her head and burrowed closer. "Daddy, I want to go home."

"It's just school," he promised her. "You're gonna play games and have fun with the other kids and then, before you know it, I'll be here to pick you up, okay?" The paperwork had warned that some kids got shy on the first day of school, but was it supposed to feel like he was ripping his own guts out when he dropped his kid off?

Slowly, he managed to extricate her from his shirt, but Libby's thumb popped right back into her mouth. She held his finger tight and looked around the room, nervous.

He crouched low and gave her a hug. "It's gonna be okay. You'll have fun. Trust Daddy."

She looked at him, nodded slowly, and when the teacher put her hand out, Libby went to her reluctantly. Miss Mckinney gave him a wave and a thumbs-up, indicating that it was handled, as she took Libby away into the class.

His chest hurt as he watched his daughter leave. When did she get so damn big? She was just a baby. His baby. She still sucked her thumb and wet the bed when she had bad dreams. She wasn't big enough for school.

He swallowed hard and forced himself to walk out of the classroom and back out to his truck. Once there, he stared at the dash for a bit, glancing at the clock over and over again. He needed this morning to go by fast so he could get Libby back. Work wasn't gonna happen. He was far too distracted. Instead of heading back to the ranch for a few hours of work like he was supposed to, Hank turned and headed down Main Street, then parked in front of the salon and went inside.

Becca was there, a book clutched to her chest as a redheaded lady chatted with her. The woman was heavily freckled and had a baby in one arm and Alaska in the other. She beamed at Hank as he entered and reluctantly set the puppy down.

"That's the best book on training tips for a dog, but if you need help, you just give me a call. I'm happy to be of assistance. I don't think you'll have issues with this little sweetie, though."

"I appreciate it, Annie," Becca said, beaming. She touched the baby's hand and wiggled it. "And Morgan."

"Well, we have to stop by Sage's office and pay the water bill," the redhead said, heading for the door. The puppy started to follow her and Hank scooped it up as they passed by. "Talk to you later, Becca. Thank you again!"

"Bye," Becca called cheerily and moved to Hank's side. She set the book down and took the puppy from him, giving it a quick kiss before noticing the look on Hank's face. "Oh my god, is everything okay?"

He shook his head. What could he say? That he was freaking out over sending his kid to school? It seemed a silly thing to get upset over. Becca had reassured him a dozen times that Libby would love it, and in his heart, he was sure it was fine.

It was fine. It was all fine.

He still grabbed Becca and dragged her close, holding her against him as he tried to ignore the churning in his gut.

It was fine.

Just fine.

It was just preschool.

Despite Becca's loving attention, Hank was utterly distracted all morning. He lurked around the salon, pretending to fix the hinges on the door since they squeaked every time it was opened. He watched the clock like a hawk, counting down the minutes until he could see Libby's happy face again. Every dad went through this, right? He reassured himself that this was normal, that he wasn't being obsessive or overprotective. Libby had to go out in society at some point, and pre-K was a good place to start.

Except . . . she really didn't have to do any of that shit if they were in Alaska. And wasn't she happy there? She loved to fish and check traps. She loved to carry small logs of wood to the woodpile. She loved the outdoors. Loved being at his side constantly. It was just the whole ranching thing that made things difficult. A four-year-old couldn't be at his side constantly when he was moving the cattle into a different pen, or fixing fences, or on horseback. It'd be fine when she was older, but right now she was little and fearless.

When it came time for him to go, he gave Becca a quick kiss and sprinted out the door, practically tearing through Painted Barrel's quiet streets to return to the school. He could hear a child crying as he entered the school, the sound a loud, shrill wail of utter misery—and he knew it was his daughter.

Hank burst into the pre-K classroom, startling the parents and the teacher, who was kneeling next to his miserable daughter. Libby's face was bright red from crying, her hair a mess of wild tendrils. She was crying so hard that hiccups shook her, and when she saw him, she reached her arms into the air just like she had when she was a baby.

And his heart hurt even worse than before.

"Mr. Watson, it's good to see you," Miss Mckinney began as he shoved past her to scoop up his daughter. "Libby had a challenging first day—"

"No," he said firmly.

"No?"

"Last day," he told her. He wasn't doing this shit to his daughter again. He put a hand to Libby's head and held her close as he turned to scowl at the teacher. "She doesn't need this shit. She's not coming back."

"Mr. Watson," the teacher began again, her brows furrowed. The smile remained on her face. "I promise you, it'll be all right. Lots of children—"

"No," he said firmly again, and turned his back on her. Protectively hugging his daughter against him, he stormed out to his car. "I've got you, Libby. You don't ever have to go back to that awful place."

She shuddered and hiccuped, snuggling against him, and he was filled with a protective urge to just get in his damn car and drive her all the way back to Alaska, back to the remote cabin where no visitors ever came by and his kid didn't have to worry about "socializing" or any of that crap. She didn't have to change a damn thing about who she was.

She was perfect, and he was going to lose his shit on the first person that suggested otherwise.

Hank paced back and forth in the parking lot, reluctant to let his daughter go. Just seeing the school made him agitated, though, and he decided to walk back to Becca's salon. He'd let Becca soothe both of them, let her fuss over Libby's misery and his, too, and when they both felt better, he'd come back and retrieve his truck. With that plan in mind, Hank hugged his daughter against him and stormed down the sidewalks of the small town, glaring at anyone that passed by.

He didn't want to be Friendly Hank today, or Town Hank. He wanted to be Alaska Hank, because no one fucked with that guy. No one made his daughter cry.

No one.

Becca came rushing out of the salon the moment he turned down the street, her eyes wide. "Hank? What's going on? Amy told me that you swooped into the class and that you weren't going to bring Libby back? What happened?" Her face was the picture of worry, her gaze going from Libby, who sniffled against his neck, to Hank. "Libby, are you okay, princess?"

Libby reached her arms out to Becca, and Hank reluctantly let her go. Becca held her close, giving him a concerned look as she rubbed Libby's head. "Did you have a bad day, sweetheart? What happened?"

"She's not going back," Hank said grimly. "She's not going to school. Ever. In fact, she's not going to any school, period. She doesn't need it. My father homeschooled me and my brothers and it was fine for us. I'm gonna do the same for Libby."

She gave him a strange look. "After just one day? Don't you think you're overreacting?"

Overreacting? It hit him like a blow to the gut. Libby was his daughter. Didn't Becca realize he'd do anything to protect her from harm? Didn't she know that nothing made him feel weaker than hearing his daughter cry and being unable to do anything about it? "She doesn't need that shit," he told her again, trying to be patient. "School is useless back in the wild. There's no school there."

Becca froze. She stopped stroking Libby's back and stared at him for a long, long moment. "So . . . you're going back?"

He knew what she was asking. Of course he did. Foxtail and Alaska had been on his mind all day. He kept thinking about how much simpler things were there. How much easier. Life here in Wyoming was far more complicated, and the responsibilities were different, and he wasn't sure he liked that. He wasn't sure it was right for him and his daughter. So he put his hands on his hips and straightened his shoulders defiantly, almost daring her to argue with him. "Going back just as soon as I can."

She licked her lips, and he could have sworn he saw her hand tremble on Libby's hair as his daughter cuddled against her. "What about us, Hank?"

Well, there was an easy answer for that. "You come with us."

Becca stared up at him. "To Foxtail?"

He nodded.

She looked over at her business, then at him. "Is it a big town?"

"Foxtail is. Couple hundred. But I don't live directly in there. I'm about an hour away, more or less."

Her face was pale. "More or less?"

"Everyone's kinda spread out. There's a couple houses clustered together along the road, but most of us are off on our land. You'd like it. The mountains are beautiful."

She didn't look as if she liked the idea, though. In fact, she looked . . . kinda hurt. "And where would I set up my salon? Are there enough people to warrant a business like mine?"

Hank was silent. Most of the people that lived around Foxtail were trappers or men that enjoyed living off the grid. There were a few women, but none like Becca. They were just as rough-and-tumble as the men there, and there sure wasn't demand for a business like hers.

"So I'm supposed to give up my business—my life—to follow you to Foxtail," she said patiently. There was such hurt in her tone that he would have preferred her screaming instead of this cold disappointment. "What am I supposed to do all day?"

"I haven't figured that part out yet." She could cook for him and Libby and his brothers, but even just thinking that seemed dismissive. Being up in the north would change her, too. She'd go from soft, gentle Becca to a woman with calloused hands and a roughened attitude to go with the land. She'd have to give up her friends and her business, her love of frothy coffees and shopping and Netflix and running hot water. Their cabin was pretty rudimentary, powered by a solar grid, and what that bit of energy didn't provide, manpower did.

She shook her head slowly. Kissed Libby on the forehead, and handed his silent, teary-eyed daughter back to him.

He said nothing. He didn't like where this was going. There was a resigned look on her face that made his gut go cold.

"I love you," Becca said softly to him. "I love you, and I love Libby."

She loved him? Pure joy burst in his chest, and he felt like grabbing her and kissing the hell out of her—except he had his sniffling daughter in his arms. A smile curved his mouth. She loved him. Everything was going to be okay.

Becca's expression didn't lighten, though. "I love you, but I can't go to Alaska with you. I can't leave behind everything that I am for a life I'm not sure I even want." She shook her head slowly. "I love you, but just because it's what you want doesn't mean that it's what I want."

He stiffened. His joy was quickly replaced with irritation. "You make it sound like it's the end of the world—"

"Maybe it isn't for you, but it is for me. I'd go from being my own person to someone wholly dependent on you. I'd need you for everything, and I wouldn't have an income—"

"That doesn't matter—"

"To you it doesn't matter," Becca interjected, cutting him off. "But to me, it does. I know to you I'm just cutting people's hair and painting nails all day long, but I have an identity here. I'm part of a community. I run a successful business. I bought my own home. I'm happy." She gave him a sweet, melancholy smile. "And I'd be none of those things if I went to Alaska with you and sat around the house."

He wanted to point out that it wasn't a house, it was a cabin, but it seemed like the wrong time. "So what are you telling me?" he asked defensively, hugging his daughter close to his chest like she was a shield, like she could protect him from Becca's words, which cut deeper than any knife.

Becca just shook her head. "I'm just telling you where I stand. I love you. I love Libby. I love both of you. But Alaska isn't in my future, and I guess . . . neither are you." Her eyes sparkled with tears and she swiped at her cheeks. "I'm sorry."

So this was it, then. She was breaking up with him, all because she wanted to stay and play with people's hair instead of go to Alaska with him. Be at his side through everything. "Don't be," he told her harshly, and he walked away, back toward the school, back toward the truck he'd abandoned there.

He was angry. Not hurt, he decided, but pissed.

Becca was breaking up with him? Over a stupid cabin in Alaska? Didn't she understand that Libby came first? That he'd never do something that made his daughter miserable? She loved him, but he guessed those were just words, easy to say when they'd end up meaning nothing.

Words were cheap. Incredibly cheap.

Maybe she was doing him a favor, turning her back on him when he needed her most. He was seeing who she truly was.

Even though he told himself that, part of him ached with regret and despair.

Actually, not just part of him. All of him. His entire soul felt like ice.

As if she hadn't just rejected the love of her life, Becca calmly went inside her shop, shut the door, and locked it. She had an appointment in about fifteen minutes, but she calmly texted her next appointment and asked to reschedule. Then she scooped up a wiggly, happy Alaska, went upstairs to her bedroom, and collapsed into bed.

She thought she would cry. Burst into tears and sob all day long. There weren't any tears yet, though. Maybe it hadn't sunk in that she couldn't have a life with Hank. Maybe the disappointment was too crushing, too new.

She felt dead inside. She was calm, though. So, so calm, unlike how it had been with Greg. When Greg had broken up with her just two days before the wedding, she'd lost her mind. She'd screamed and raged, thrown things at him, and had the biggest temper tantrum ever. She'd sobbed until her eyes felt permanently swollen, and she'd been so angry. So disappointed, because he'd robbed her of a life that she thought she deserved. Not wanted, *deserved.* She'd waited him out for all those years and had nothing to show for it.

Looking back? With this new heartbreak slowly tearing her apart inside? She hadn't ever truly been in love with Greg. Oh, maybe she had when she was a teenager, but over the years it had turned into something that was comfortable and easy, and something she'd expected to go her way. It was safe to be with Greg, even if whatever passion they'd had for each other had long since turned into familiarity and just a hint of contempt.

This was different.

This was soul crushing and deep. This made her feel hollow with the ache inside her, as if she'd never smile again. She loved Hank. Loved Libby. Wanted nothing more than for them to be a family.

But Hank didn't care enough about what she wanted. He hadn't confessed his love back. Didn't care enough to suggest that they work it out and that he stay in town. So it wasn't meant to be.

It. Wasn't. Meant. To. Be.

Every word gutted her. Made the pain double in her chest until she was moaning with misery. Alaska licked her face, little tail wriggling, and Becca realized she was crying after all, silent tears sliding down her cheeks only to be licked away by the puppy.

He'd suggested she go to Alaska with him as if that was the answer to everything. It wasn't, though. It was the wrong answer, and the surest way to kill her spirit. Without a job, without a purpose, Becca would just be a burden. She'd be dependent on Hank to show her how to do the smallest of things, because she wasn't a camper and didn't know the first thing about roughing it. Not that it was camping, of course, but it sounded awfully close.

Hank didn't understand. If she gave up her business, gave up all pretense of working and being independent, she'd end up just like her mother—completely trapped in a miserable marriage. She'd be utterly controlled by Hank's whims and unable to support herself. Her life would be the children alone and she'd have no identity outside of mother. And while that worked for a lot of people, Becca had seen how miserable it made her own mother and she was terrified of falling down the same path. Of having her husband decide what she should wear or how she should fix her hair, because he was the one paying the bills. She'd be at his mercy.

Hank was a good guy. A wonderful guy. Kind and caring. Loving to his daughter and to Becca. He was everything she'd ever dreamed of in a partner . . . except for this stubborn insistence on going back to Alaska.

Could he be happy here? With her? If not here, then some other city somewhere else? It wasn't that she wasn't willing to relocate—she'd go anywhere if they could be equal partners. She could start a new business somewhere else if that was what he wanted to do . . .

But his insistence on moving back to Alaska meant that

what Becca wanted didn't matter. That hurt so badly that she thought she'd die from the pain.

Little Alaska—god, she wished she'd never picked that name—whined and licked her face, squirming until Becca hugged her close and cuddled the puppy to her chest. "We'll get through this, little baby. I promise. It'll only hurt for about a year or two." Her voice choked on the words. She snuggled the puppy for a bit, letting the soft fur and wiggly body distract her. Even if Hank had broken her heart, Alaska really was the best gift. Maybe she needed a new name, though. "How do you feel about Jennifer?" she asked, stroking the soft, floppy ears. "Do you feel like a Jenny?"

The puppy ignored her.

"Alaska?" she said tentatively.

The ears pricked and the tail thumped, her attention focused on Becca.

Well, crap. Alaska it was. Becca sighed and pulled her phone close with one hand, the other tucked around her puppy. Maybe he'd call her and confess that he'd changed his mind. That it had been a mistake. He'd overreacted, upset because his daughter was upset. That was reasonable.

She wanted him to call and say he wasn't going back to Foxtail after all.

She stared and stared at the phone, but it remained silent.

No texts.

No calls.

No nothing.

CHAPTER TWENTY-ONE

Becca stayed in bed for the rest of the night, eating ice cream doused in chocolate syrup to drown her sorrows and watching romantic comedies that made her bawl every time the hero did something sweet for the heroine. She fell asleep with the television on, puppy in her arms, and somehow she got through the first day of her breakup without completely shattering.

Hank didn't call or text, and she started to realize that this truly was a done thing between them. That there was no more Hank and Becca. It hurt, and she would grieve it and move on as best she could.

So she got dressed, walked the puppy, fixed her hair, and brushed her teeth. She stared down at the birth control she'd forgotten to take last night and then chucked the entire package into the garbage. The next time she had sex with someone, it was going to be her forever partner. No more of this waiting for a family. If her soul mate wasn't ready, then they weren't soul mates.

Of course, that just made her hurt worse, because Hank was so good with his daughter. He'd love more kids, she knew, and he'd be just as attentive a dad to them as he was to Libby. He'd been perfect for her.

Except she'd declared her love and declared that she wasn't moving, and that had killed everything.

Feeling wooden, Becca finished getting ready and opened her salon as if it was any other normal day. Her day was full thanks to the appointments she'd pushed from yesterday to today, and she found herself a bit too busy to focus on her grieving. If someone commented on her red eyes and nose, she blamed allergies. If someone asked about Hank and their dating, she quickly changed the subject, asking about grandchildren or the ranch, or anything else to distract. And she somehow got through the day without crumbling.

Mostly.

Becca was just sitting down to take a quick break between clients when the door to the salon opened and Amy peeked in. Her friend was dressed in a peach dress with a nipped waist and a swingy skirt that made her look lean and beautiful, setting off her dark ponytail. She wore a look of concern on her face as she slipped inside. "Knock-knock. Got a moment?"

"Of course," Becca said, forcing a smile to her face. She was getting pretty good at faking it, even though her cheeks hurt. "Come on in."

Amy hurried inside, shutting the door behind her, and then bit her lip. "I couldn't help but notice that Hank's little girl wasn't in class today. I know she struggled yesterday. Is everything all right? I was going to call and check in, but since you and I are friends . . ." She trailed off and gave Becca a curious look.

"Oh. Yeah." Becca cleared her throat, trying to rid herself of the knot that was growing. "Hank has decided that his daughter doesn't need preschool. Or any school. He's taking her back to Alaska." She managed to say it quite calmly, and then ruined her facade by starting to cry.

"Oh, honey." Amy's voice was full of sympathy as she moved to Becca's side and pulled her close in a hug. "I feel responsible. Like it's my fault she had a bad day—"

"It's not you," Becca said between sobs. It wasn't. The day at school had just brought the whole topic to the surface. It had to come out at some point, and it would have never been easy to discuss. In a way, it was good that it had come out early, before Becca had tossed more of her life away on another man who didn't want to give her his forever.

So she cried and told Amy all about it, and her friend made sympathetic noises and called him a jerk and promised to come over later that night with popcorn and wine and a chick flick. Then Amy had to leave again, and Becca's next client came in, and somehow she managed to make it through the rest of the day.

And through the evening, watching movies with Amy and drinking wine. They finished early because Amy had school in the morning, and Becca checked her phone again before bedtime, downing her last glass of wine in irritation as the stupid phone remained silent. Well, she was just as stubborn as Hank. If he didn't want to talk, she didn't want to talk, either.

She'd told him she loved him. She'd also told him she wouldn't go to Alaska. If he didn't want to make it work, that was on him.

It still hurt, though.

Days passed, and her heart continued to ache like an open wound. She'd occasionally see a big, tall man around town with a dark beard and her heart would skip a beat . . . only to realize it was one of his brothers. They never failed to pass by her salon and peer into the windows, as if checking up on her. So she made sure to laugh a little harder than she felt, tried to seem a bit more joyous than she really was, and basically acted like she was having the best time in her life when she was secretly dying inside.

Becca missed him, though. She missed Hank's big presence, his steadfast protectiveness, and his quiet calm. She missed his capable hands and his scratchy beard and everything about him. She missed Libby, too. She missed the little girl's sweet laughter and her constant questions, and the array of drawings pinned on one wall of the salon reminded her of just how much she'd miss the little one when they were truly gone to Alaska.

She knew they hadn't gone yet. The rumor mill chugged constantly in Painted Barrel, and word was that Doc up at the Swinging C was looking for more experienced ranch hands but hadn't found any yet. She supposed she should have been glad about that, but it just made her pain linger, like slowly peeling off a Band-Aid. She wanted to rip it free, to get the pain over with in one quick, searing bolt, and then move on with her life.

Of course, life didn't work out that way. It never did. After all, Greg had never left Painted Barrel, and so she'd had to deal with his presence constantly in her face after the Wedding That Wasn't. And she'd gotten through that.

She'd get through this, too.

It was as if thinking about Greg brought him out of the woodwork. The next day, he walked into her salon with a bouquet of daisies and a smile on her face, and she didn't know whether to laugh or to cry. She kinda felt like doing both.

"Becca! How's my favorite girl?" He threw his arms wide, indicating he wanted a hug, as he strolled into her salon.

Ugh. How was his favorite girl? *Sick of your shit,* she wanted to say, and a laugh bubbled up in her throat. She was so tired of pretending to be just fine, just fine. With Greg here in her face—with flowers, no less—she couldn't decide if this was some sick brand of karma playing out or if she was just going to be tortured to death by the universe.

"Hi, Greg." She went into his arms and let him hug her, and the scent of his cologne was in her face, and for a moment she felt weirdly comforted. He patted her back and rubbed her shoulders, making soft, comforting noises. "Thanks," she said after a moment and pulled away. This time, her smile was a little easier, a little more genuine. It had been nice to be hugged, even if it was by Greg, of all people.

"Heard the bad news," he told her in a grave voice and held the flowers out to her. "For you."

"Bad news, huh?"

"Oh yeah, it's all over town about how the big cowboy dumped you."

She winced at that. Was that what people were saying? "Mm."

"You know I never found you too clingy," he told her magnanimously. "You're just very affectionate."

Great. This was what she needed to make her day even worse. Becca wanted to just run away and hide. Instead, she went to the back room to get a vase, and Alaska looked up from her spot on her puppy bed. The tiny black tail wagged with excitement to see her, and it brought a real smile to Becca's face. She put the flowers in a vase and then scooped up her little companion, kissing his ear softly.

The look on Greg's face was nothing short of horror when she returned. "When did you get a dog?"

"It was a gift." The best one she'd ever gotten.

"Can you send it back?" He looked disgusted. "They're so unclean. Tell me you didn't kiss it or let it lick your face."

Becca kissed Alaska's ear again, just for good measure.

Greg's lip curled like he was seeing something obscene. "I swear you're just doing that to get my goat. You know how much I don't like animals. They belong outdoors, not as pets."

She kissed Alaska's cute puppy face again. "Actually, Greg, it may be shocking to you, but I don't think about you much at all anymore."

He did look rather shocked at her bald statement, and then he sighed. "I didn't come here to fight, you know. I thought you might be feeling down and I wanted to come and make sure you were okay. I know how attached you get and how hard you fall. And even though you may not like me much anymore, I still care about you. I always have."

There was sincerity in his eyes, and that made her sigh. He was always very good at apologizing and she nodded and set the puppy down. "I appreciate you checking in, but I'm fine. I promise." The words almost sounded believable. Almost.

"I don't think you are," he said softly. "You're the most giving, loving person I've ever met, Becca, and if he gave you up, then he's an idiot."

For some reason, that made her lower lip tremble. "What does that make you, then?" she asked in a shaky voice.

"Oh, I didn't say I wasn't an idiot."

Becca chuckled, hugging her arms to her chest. Well, at least he wasn't denying that.

"I just . . . I hate that he hurt you." Greg reached out and put a hand on her shoulder, warm and friendly. "Whether you believe it or not, we've been friends for even longer than we were romantic, and I still want to be your friend. I miss you."

That touched her. He was right; they'd been friends since childhood, having both grown up in the small town. It was hard to hate Greg, especially when he was obviously trying his best to reach out to her. Suddenly having him as a friend again sounded really, really nice.

"And if I'm honest," Greg continued, "my hair has never looked worse and my stylist won't see me."

She laughed, and then suddenly she was laughing and crying both. He tugged her into a hug and she let him hold her, stroking her back. Of course, she compared that hug to the ones Hank gave her and found it lacking. Everything about Greg was lacking when compared to Hank, really. He wasn't as big and strong, didn't smell as nice, didn't hold her as firmly. She missed Hank. God, she missed him so, so much. Breaking up with Greg for the final time had been upsetting, but she'd been outraged and betrayed.

With the breakup with Hank? She just felt so hollow. Like she'd never be happy again. Funny how one person could bring so much light into her world so quickly . . .

And then just as quickly take it away again.

For a moment—for a crazy, brief moment—she wanted to call Hank and tell him that she'd changed her mind. That a hair salon wasn't worth her happiness and she'd go to Alaska with him. She'd give it a shot, living out in the rough, even though it wasn't the life she wanted. Suddenly, a life without Hank and Libby didn't seem like one she wanted, either.

But she'd confessed her love to him and had gotten nothing in return. He hadn't even called.

So she was just . . . sad. Clingy, like everyone always said.

Becca sighed.

A hand squeezed her ass and Greg buried his face against her hair. "I've missed you."

Becca froze. She jerked away and gave him a look of shock. "Did you come here to cop a feel? To scoop up the pieces and see if you could get laid? Seriously, Greg?" Why did she keep thinking a tiger would ever change its stripes?

"Sorry?" he said, posing it more as a question than a statement. He wasn't sorry, just saying whatever would defuse her anger.

She took another step back and saw a big body move away from her window, a brown Stetson perched on the man's head.

That was one of Hank's younger brothers. He'd been checking in on her—like they had for the last while, ever since she and Hank had been over—and he'd seen everything. He'd seen Greg grabbing her like a schoolboy.

It probably looked terrible.

She should have run after him and tried to explain herself . . . but why? Hank didn't love her. He hadn't even tried to keep her. She was surrounded by men who were just using her, it seemed. Becca laughed, the sound brittle and pained even to her own ears, and scooped her puppy up again, burying her face against her soft fur. At least this would keep Greg off her.

"I think someone saw us," Greg said, curious. "Pretty sure I just saw Hannah across the street. Should I go and try to explain? You know how she loves to gossip."

She shook her head. "Why bother? Let them think what they want." She didn't care anymore.

Hank stabbed his pitchfork into the square hay bale in front of him as if it had personally offended him. Sometimes it felt good to stab at things like that. After all, he couldn't shout at the world about how angry he was. He couldn't stomp around all day, because his daughter would get upset and the others would nag him. So he stabbed hay with pitchforks and tried not to think about Becca. Becca, who'd told him she loved him with shining eyes. Becca, who gutted him in the next moment by declaring she would never move to Alaska.

He stabbed at the hay again, spearing a clump and tossing it into the wheelbarrow. It had been over a week since he'd last seen her and it still felt as if someone had shotgunned him in the gut. Actually, that might have hurt less. The pain would have certainly been over a lot quicker. Dating Adria—ha, if he could even think of it as that—had never been this tough. He'd never been caught up in emotions. When he'd found out the truth about her and she'd admitted it, he'd just felt . . . stupid. Like he should have known better. But with Becca?

The pain kept going. On and on, like it was going to destroy him from the inside out.

She loved him.

She wouldn't live with him, though. Wouldn't leave to go to Alaska with him, because apparently cutting people's hair was more important than being with him. And wasn't that just the kicker? He wasn't as important as her business was. He wasn't as important as making money. Him and Libby both.

And he'd wanted her with him forever. He'd wanted to watch the gray hairs thread through her pretty hair. He'd wanted to fill her belly with the children she said she wanted. He wanted to turn into a wrinkled, horny old man right next to her and pinch her butt for the next seventy years and laugh about it. He wanted to have a life with her, damn it.

And she flat out refused.

"You think it's dead yet?" Jack drawled from behind him, voice flat.

Hank turned, the pitchfork in his hands. He glared at his brother. "What?"

"That hay you're stabbin'. You think it's dead yet?"

He just rolled his eyes at his sarcastic little brother. "I'm busy. What do you want?"

"Just wanted to tell you that I was in town."

Hank stiffened, waiting. Both Caleb and Jack had taken it upon themselves to spy on Becca while Hank moped at the ranch. They said it was their brotherly duty, and he hated that he was so eager for them to report back, but he was. He wanted to know what Becca looked like every day, if she looked sad, if her shop was busy, if she was taking care of the puppy . . . if she missed him. If she felt as destroyed as he did. So far, the reports had not been encouraging. Caleb had said that every time he saw her, she was always helping a client, her hands in someone's hair or slapping foil on their head—women and their beauty treatments, he'd never understand them. He'd also said she was super smiley and happy, and that made Hank want to stab even more hay. Couldn't she look the littlest bit sad that she'd stomped all over his damned heart? He was dying by inches and she was having the time of her life, it seemed.

Jack was silent, which irked Hank's already bad mood.

"Well?" he prompted when his brother kept watching him.

"You're not gonna like it."

His entire body tensed. Was she hurt? Sick? Did she need him? "Is she okay?"

"I looked in on that salon of hers and saw that blond guy was all over her, squeezing her ass and trying to cop a feel. You know, her ex? Didn't take him long to move in on her again."

Hank saw red. The entire barn was suddenly covered in a red haze. That creep was touching Becca? Trying to get into her pants? He knew Becca—she'd never indicated anything but anger and frustration at her ex. She'd told him plenty of times that the guy always came wheedling his way back, looking for another chance. "He was grabbing her? You're sure?" When Jack nodded, he clutched the pitchfork so hard that he could feel splinters digging into his calluses. "You think she's still up there at the salon?"

"I'm guessing so. Why?"

"Because I'm going to go murder him for touching her,"

Hank growled. He'd take the pitchfork with him, scare the daylights out of that little shit of a man—

Jack stepped in front of him—and nearly got a pitchfork tine in the belly. "Whoa there." He put his hands up. "How do you know she wants to be rescued?"

"Because she hates that guy. He embarrassed her in front of everyone. You think she wants anything to do with him?"

Jack carefully maneuvered around the pitchfork and put a hand on Hank's shoulder. "She's a grown woman. She can take care of herself. Besides, I'm pretty sure she told him off. I parked down the street and he left a few minutes after I did, all grumpy and shit."

That made Hank feel a little better, but only slightly. Every muscle in his body was tense with the need to protect Becca from someone trying to take advantage of her. It didn't matter that she didn't love him enough to move to Alaska with him. He cared about her. Hell, his whole body lit up just thinking about her. She was special and gentle, and she needed someone to champion her and protect her, and even if she didn't want Hank anymore, he'd still look out for her because he fucking loved her.

"You're growling."

"What?" he practically snarled at his brother.

"You're just growling at nothing." Jack frowned up at Hank. "You okay, man?"

"No, I'm not okay. Why would you ask something so stupid?"

"She's fine, okay?" Jack shook his head, a look of wonder on his face. "I don't get why you care. You said it's over, right? We're going back to Alaska, remember? Uncle Ennis is looking for new hands. One's coming next week for a dry run. The moment he's set up, we're back home in the wild. That's what we wanted, remember?"

Hank wasn't sure anymore. All he knew was that he wanted Becca, and some other jerk was trying to touch her and Hank wasn't there to save her. He flung down the pitchfork and stormed into the main house to check on his daughter. At least the sight of Libby would make him feel better.

Unfortunately, inside the house wasn't much better. Caleb sat in the kitchen with Libby, coloring with her. Uncle Ennis—who was supposed to be watching his daughter—was nowhere to be seen. "Where's Doc?"

"Someone had a horse emergency," Caleb said, shrugging. "He'll be back later."

"Look, Daddy." Libby held up her paper. "I drew a family!"

His jaw clenched when he saw the paper. It was him in a hat—if he squinted hard—but even with her childish scribbles of a drawing, he could see that there was a dark-haired woman at his side in a pink dress and a tiny girl next to them. "Good job."

"It's me and Miss Becca and you," she told him proudly, holding it out. "I want to put it on the wall with my other pictures at Miss Becca's job."

He could feel his nostrils flaring, his temper about to snap, and Libby wasn't at fault. "We'll do that later," he promised her, keeping his voice even, and took the picture and put it on the fridge, under a magnet. When he turned around, his daughter frowned at him.

"Miss Becca won't see it there."

"We'll show her later. Go play in the living room." Anything to distract her. For days, she'd been asking about "Miss Becca" and when they were going to go over and have pancakes. When they were going to have another Daddy-and-Becca sleepover. When they were going to watch a movie with her again. She asked about Becca constantly, and he didn't have the heart to tell her that Becca wasn't going to be in their life anymore. Hell, just thinking about it gutted him as it was.

How could one tiny woman change his life so damn much? Life was supposed to be simple. He knew what he wanted. He knew how to get there. Now he felt like he didn't know anything and it was making him crazy. He was starting to feel like a crazy man. Scratching at his beard, he watched his daughter hop out of her chair and bound into the living room.

"You okay?" Caleb asked. "You're not yourself. You almost snapped at her for drawing a picture."

He knew, and he was ashamed. Libby didn't deserve for him to lash out at her. He'd do his best to keep his frustration on lockdown, because she didn't need to know that he was dying inside. "I'm miserable, thanks for asking."

Caleb just grunted, ever quiet. "Not too late to change your mind, you know."

"About?" He practically snarled the word.

"Alaska."

Alaska. What would he do if he didn't go to Alaska?

Hank knew the first thing he'd do—he'd march right up to that salon, fling Becca over his shoulder, and take her upstairs to her pretty, girly bedroom. He'd toss her down on the bed, strip her clothing off in that way that made her eyes light up, and kiss every inch of her for hours and hours. Then he'd drag her into the nearest church—or the justice of the peace; he wasn't picky—and make her his. He'd stake his claim on her so no one else would ever think they'd have a shot. And he'd make a family with her.

But . . . that was the problem.

He already had a family—Libby. And he had to think about her. She hated school, and if he stayed in Painted Barrel, she'd have to go back. He loved his daughter. He'd do anything for her. If she hated school so much that she sobbed and bawled when he took her there, then she wouldn't go to school. It was as simple as that.

Libby was everything to him, and he had a responsibility to her.

It didn't matter what his heart wanted. He was a father, first and foremost.

CHAPTER TWENTY-TWO

"Am I a bother?"

"Not at all," Becca lied as Sage Cooper-Clements came in. The mayor had had her baby and then had promptly gotten pregnant again, a fact that everyone in town liked to tease her about and which made her blush constantly. Her belly was still in the early stages of showing, but her cheeks were rosy and rounded and she looked happy and healthy.

Becca was disgustingly envious of her.

The mayor held out a plate of cookies. "I wanted to bring these over for you. I heard you're having a heck of a month." Sage gave her a sympathetic look. "I know whenever I'm feeling awful, double chocolate chip always makes me feel better."

She couldn't help but smile at that. Sage felt like it was her duty to ensure that everyone in town was happy, so it was no surprise that the mayor had stopped by to discuss Becca's breakup. It was one of those things where it was just a matter of time. So Becca smiled—or tried to—and plucked one of the cookies off the plate. She could definitely use some chocolate therapy at the moment. "I appreciate it, Sage. How's the baby?"

"This one or the one at home?" She patted her belly. "Both are great. Jason's watching the little guy while I make my rounds here in town. Then I've got to head home and rescue him from poopy diapers." She grinned. "This is not entirely a cookie mission, though."

Becca paused mid-bite. "Oh?"

"Nope. So . . ." Sage twisted her hands. "One of our hands has been asking about you. He wanted to show up with some flowers and do the whole big, splashy ask-you-out thing, and I suggested that I test the waters out for him first." She grimaced. "Is this the worst timing ever or what?"

"One of your . . . hands?"

"Ranch hands, yeah. He says he met you before?" Her eyes were a tortured mixture of sympathy and curiosity.

Oh. The flirt. Becca vaguely remembered the wink, but she couldn't recall his face. "I think so." She shook her head. "That's really sweet of him, but tell him please no. I'm not ready to date anyone right now. I'm still . . . my heart's still occupied." Fresh tears started to come to the surface, so she shoved the cookie into her mouth and nearly choked on it.

"Of course." Sage reached out and rubbed her shoulder. "I thought as much, so I wanted to come and see how you were doing. I know it was hard when you broke up with Greg, so I can't imagine what you're going through right now." She hesitated. "I heard he came by, too, and . . ."

Becca shook her head. "No and no."

Sage exhaled with relief. "Oh good. It was going to be really awkward to tell you that you can do better than him if you'd have already taken him back."

Becca laughed, though there wasn't much that was funny right now. She swiped at her eyes. "No, this is ten times worse than the Wedding That Wasn't. My pride was destroyed with that one. With this, it's all heart." She squeezed a fist over her chest. She kept waiting for it to get better—for her to miss Hank and Libby just a little less with every passing day—but it wasn't. It still felt fresh, and awful.

Right now she'd give ten botched weddings for one right one with Hank.

"I just want you to know," Sage began gently, "that if you ever need a shoulder to cry on or just to talk—or vent—I'm just across the street in the municipal building. And I always have cookies."

She managed a smile. "Thank you, Sage. I really do appreciate it." It was frustrating that everyone in Painted Barrel was coming by for gossip, but it also made her feel oddly loved. Like she belonged. Like she was an important part of the community and she'd be missed if she left.

She had to stay. Had to.

But late at night, when she hugged Alaska to her chest, she started to wonder if she was making a mistake.

Sometimes, she didn't know. If she was positive she was doing the right thing, it'd feel right, wouldn't it? Nothing felt right anymore, though. Nothing at all.

Becca dreamed about Hank that night. Dreamed that he was at the airport, Libby in his arms, and he wanted to talk to her but she ignored him. He went to Alaska, but in her dream, his plane never made it there.

She woke up in a cold sweat, sobbing and miserable.

This wasn't working. She needed to talk to Hank. She loved him, and she thought he was growing to care for her, too. Maybe they could figure something out. Maybe he could visit her on holidays. Something. Anything. There had to be a way for them to meet in the middle, or she had to at least try.

If she didn't, she'd regret it forever.

So that morning, she took extra time with her appearance. She gave her hair a blowout, making sure it was full and as luxurious and shiny as she could make it. Her makeup looked fantastic, and she wore a sundress with tiny spaghetti straps and a suggestive back, even though the early morning was a little chilly. She wore strappy sandals that made her legs look longer, and she put Alaska on her leash and headed out to the Swinging C Ranch.

Or she started to. The moment she hit the edge of town, she turned around and went back to the bakery. She walked out five minutes later with an enormous box of doughnuts, her face burning. The woman behind the counter—Geraldine—had smirked when she'd put her order in, and soon she'd call Hannah and let her know that desperate Becca Loftis was bringing doughnuts back to the ranch in the mornings again. Well, it was too late to worry about that now. She didn't care about her reputation if this worked.

If it didn't, well, it'd just be another humiliating broken relationship failure tossed into her face, and she was getting awfully used to that.

She was nervous the entire drive out to the ranch, her hands sweating. When she got to the house, she knocked on the front door and there was no answer. Okay, she hadn't expected that. Of course, it was later than her usual early mornings, and the sun had been up for a few hours now. She headed down to Doc's office at the far end of the building, but when she saw a man waiting there with his bulldog, she quickly left again. Doc was obviously busy.

Frustrated, she headed back out to her car and noticed that Hank's truck was parked in its normal spot. He was there. Either he was out on the range or he was in the barn. She headed out to the barn, picking her way in her high-heeled sandals and regretting her shoe choice.

Becca clutched the doughnut box against her chest as she headed out to the barn with Alaska, feeling oddly vulnerable. What if she saw Hank and both of his brothers there? Would they laugh at her for being desperate enough to show up with baked goods? Would they chase her off and tell her she wasn't wanted? God, why had she shown up?

She knew why, though. She loved Hank and she missed him and Libby terribly. She wanted to see if this could be saved somehow, some way, because the thought of living without them in her life hurt too much to contemplate. She thought she'd just get over it, but that wasn't happening. Every day she missed them more. So she sucked in a deep breath and headed into the barn.

The smell of cattle, horses, and hay assaulted her, and she picked her way inside as carefully as she could. There were a few calves in a stall—bottle-fed babies, likely—and two of the horses were still in their stalls as well. One of the ranch dogs loitered, watching Alaska curiously with a slowly wagging tail, and at the far end of the barn, she could just make out a pair of big shoulders behind some equipment and a cowboy hat. She headed in that direction, trying to think of the words to say.

Hi, Hank, I just wanted to see if you were okay.

Hi, Hank, just checking in to see if Alaska was still on the menu or if you miss me.

Hi, Hank, contrary to what you might have heard, I'm not back with Greg. I promise whatever your brothers might have said isn't true.

But all of those sounded stupid and needy, and she kept spinning the words through her brain over and over again, looking for just the right opener as she walked toward him. All of it flew out of her head when she turned the corner and saw him standing in the middle of a stall with one of the cattle, his arm inside the thing up to the elbow. Oh dear.

"Uh, hi," Becca stammered. "Is this a bad time?"

Hank looked at her like she was crazy. "What are you doing here?"

"I should be asking that of you," she joked. "I guess you're lonely."

The look on his face grew even stranger. "I'm turning the calf. The hooves are stuck."

"Right. I know. I was just . . . making a bad joke." One that fell incredibly flat. She watched him as he continued to maneuver his arm inside the poor cow, the thing's head trapped in a grate specially prepared for such things. She knew this was normal. Her father and his cowboys had done such things dozens—hundreds—of times. It was just awful timing that she'd come by while he was arm-deep in cow uterus, because it was going to be difficult to have a serious, emotional conversation with a man during that. "I wanted to see how you were doing."

"Busy." His teeth were gritted, his face a mask of concentration.

"Of course." Becca waited, hoping for . . . something. *Tell me you love me, Hank. Tell me you miss me. Tell me you're not going to Alaska and we can give this another shot between us because I miss you like crazy.* She clutched the doughnuts and waited for him to talk.

He cursed under his breath, moving his arm ever so slightly, concentrating on the cow.

Right. The timing was terrible. She was stupid to show up here. He was busy. It wasn't like he didn't know where she was. She was in her stupid salon every day. He had her phone number if he wanted to talk. It was just . . . kind of obvious he didn't want to talk. That he was done with her.

She swallowed hard. "I'm just gonna go, I think."

Hank glanced over at her, sweating. "You okay?"

"Yeah. Great." She put a bright smile on her face. "Talk to you later."

And she hurried out before he could stop her. She passed the woodpile, hesitated, and then dumped the pink box of doughnuts there. The last thing she wanted to do was go inside and talk to Doc or the others about how she was recovering.

Because she wasn't recovering at all. In fact, she was just making a fool out of herself, chasing after a man that wasn't interested.

Damned cow seemed to take forever to give birth, but finally the calf was on the ground, breathing, the mother licking it clean, and Hank grabbed a towel, cleaned off his arm, and stormed out of the barn. While he'd been more or less trapped with his arm in the cow—and it truly was trapped, since her uterus had been contracting around his arm and the calf both, trying to expel them—he'd kept thinking about Becca. After well over a week of silence, she'd shown up, looking pretty, with doughnuts. Was that a peace offering? Had she changed her mind about wanting to go to Alaska with him? Did she miss him as much as he missed her? Because he fucking ached for her, constantly. The ache was something he kept hoping would go away, but it was ever-present, reminding him of what he'd lost. He hated that he was in the same category as that shithead Greg, who'd walked away from her when she was the perfect woman. Wasn't he doing the same thing? Making the same stupid mistake?

Alaska hadn't seemed half so important. Libby still was, of course, and he planned on making his daughter happy no matter what, but he could homeschool her here in Wyoming as easily as he could in Alaska . . . and Becca was here. Sweet Becca with her ready smile, generous heart, and soft body. Becca, who made him feel like everything was possible and he could conquer the world.

Caleb was staying, after all.

Maybe it was something Hank needed to look into, too.

He headed for the house. Caleb and Jack were out on horseback, checking on the fences of one of the more distant pastures. That meant he could talk to her alone. In quiet. Maybe they could figure out this thing between them and come to an agreement of some kind.

Maybe he could kiss the hell out of her until she was frantically reaching for his belt buckle, and then all his aches—both heart and body—would be soothed by her presence. But then he passed the box of doughnuts sitting on the woodpile. And frowned. She hadn't gone inside. He picked it up, noting that the contents were completely scattered, and headed into the house.

Uncle Ennis was by the coffeepot in the kitchen, pouring himself a cup. He turned to look at Hank, then frowned. "Did you get doughnuts this morning? Seems kinda late for that sort of thing."

"Where's Becca?"

"Was she here? I didn't see her." He smirked, raising his cup to his lips. "You two back together, then?"

"No." Hank tossed the doughnuts on the table, disappointed. She'd left without saying a word. She'd seen he was busy and still bailed out. That wasn't how a woman acted when she wanted to get back together, was it? Seemed like she was running from him, and that irked Hank.

His uncle sighed heavily. "Can I speak frankly?"

Hank's back automatically went up. "Can I stop you?"

"You're fucking shit up, boy."

He scowled. "That's your big statement? Just that I'm fucking stuff up? You do know it wasn't my decision to break up, right?"

"Yes, but you're letting her get away." Doc shook his head. "You can't let that happen. Let me tell you a story."

Hank bit back a groan. One of his uncle's long-winded

stories. Great. This was just what he needed—a fairy tale wrapped in a lecture. Like he didn't already know that things were a mess?

But his uncle didn't ask. He just launched into his tale, leaning against the counter. "Years ago, back when I was about your age, I fell in love with this pretty little thing that lived in town. She was a good friend, and we always saw each other at get-togethers and parties. I was a mite shy then, and I just admired her from afar, trying to decide when was the best time to get up my courage to confess how I felt. There was no rush, after all. We both lived here all our lives and she wasn't going anywhere. So I didn't tell anyone about my grand plan; I just thought about it real hard every time I saw her, and waited for the right moment. When it was all perfect, I'd confess my love and then she'd be mine. Except I never told her that I had feelings. I just treated her like a friend. And when there was a big barn raising for the Cavanaughs a few towns over, she went with another man. Fell head over heels in love with him and they were married within a month."

Hank continued to wipe at his hands with the towel, fighting back irritation. "Why are you telling me this?"

"Because that woman was your mother."

He looked up in shock, meeting his uncle's gaze.

Doc nodded. "Yep. Your father had no idea I was madly in love with the same woman, because I never said a thing. After that, it was too late, you know? She loved him, he loved her, and that was the end of it. I missed out on my chance . . . Where are you going?"

Hank had gotten to his feet as Doc spoke, and he paused. "Gonna tell Caleb and Jack that if they touch Becca I'll break their hands."

Doc snorted. "That wasn't what this story is about. Sit down." When Hank reluctantly sat once more, his uncle just gave him a thoughtful look. "I'm telling you this not because I think you should be suspicious of your brothers but because you're going to lose out on a good thing if you wait for the timing to be just right."

Hank clenched his jaw, frustrated. "It isn't about timing."

"It's always the timing, son." Doc shook his head. "Don't kid yourself. If you have feelings for her, then nothing else matters."

"I asked her to go to Alaska with me." He admitted the words slowly. "She wouldn't go."

"Why would she? There's nothing up there for her. She's not like your ma was. She's not into the fishing and hunting and living rough. You knew that, too, and you still asked her out."

"She asked *me* out—"

Doc threw his hands up. "But you said yes, right? My point is you knew who she was when you accepted. You were fine with her being a soft girly girl who likes hair and pretty clothes until it no longer suited your timing."

He hated to admit it, but his uncle was right. He'd known Becca was exactly the wrong kind of girl for him when he'd gone out with her . . . and he'd still done it. She was the kind of woman he said he'd always avoid, and yet he couldn't stop thinking about her.

Then again, Adria had been more his type, and look where it had gotten him. Meanwhile, Becca—who couldn't bait a hook or chop a lick of wood—loved and cared for his daughter. She loved Hank, too . . . or at least she had.

Even if he could change who Becca was, Hank wasn't so sure he would want to. He liked that Becca was soft and sweet. He liked that she loved to cook and curl up and watch movies. He loved that she was just a happy person, content to be exactly who she was.

They were at an impasse. He didn't want her to change . . . but she didn't fit into his life. "It's not just about me. It's about Libby—"

"Horseshit," his uncle said, disgusted. "You're hiding behind that as an excuse. Libby is four. She thinks Santa and the Easter Bunny are real. If you told her that school was amazing, she'd love it. But you and those brothers of yours have been telling her all along that school's crap and she doesn't need it, and of course she picked up on that. It's no wonder she hated it. Millions of kids go to school every year and they get by just fine. You think Libby's the one kid in the world that can't figure out how to play well with others?"

Hank stared at his uncle in surprise. The man was utterly vehement.

Doc raised a hand in the air. "I know. I'm cussin' up a storm. I just feel like you're making mistakes, Hank. And I care for you boys—all three of you—and I want to help. Your father's not around anymore, so it's my duty to look after all three of you, even though you're grown men."

"What do you suggest, then?" Hank asked. "She won't move with me."

Doc gestured at him. "What do you want out of life? Let's say you could have anything in the world. What would it be? What does your ideal situation look like? Is it a big house? Fancy cars? Seventeen children? What?"

Hank moved to the sink and washed his hands again as he thought. He'd washed them in the barn, but something about helping a cow give birth made him feel as if he had to clean them repeatedly, so he soaped up his arms to the elbow and thought. What did he want out of life? What was his perfect?

"I want Libby to be happy," he admitted after a long moment, rinsing off the soap. He shook off the water and turned to face his uncle. "She's my first priority."

Doc nodded. "And for you?"

The answer was surprisingly easy. He didn't want a big car or a big house, no. "I want a good woman at my side." He knew just the one, too. "I want a big family. I want to be able to provide for them and keep them safe. I want nights in front of the fire with my family at my side, and I want to take my kids fishing and raise them somewhere safe where they can run free and be happy. I want to grow old with my wife . . . with Becca."

"I'm not hearing Alaska in that fantasy of yours," his uncle pointed out. "So why are you so fixated on it?"

He had no answer. The truth was, he'd always pictured Alaska as his home, but he thought about having a wife and half a dozen kids in their log cabin and . . . it didn't work. The cabin was crowded with three men and a little girl. He couldn't imagine squeezing more people into it. Plus, what if someone got hurt? He thought of Libby and the time she'd cut her finger and Jack had had to bandage it up because Hank had been out in the field, checking traps. What if it was something worse than a cut finger and they were a full day's snowmobile ride to the most rudimentary of medical assistance?

What he claimed to want—Becca, Libby, more children, a quiet life—didn't necessarily have anything to do with Alaska. It was just him being stubborn. Alaska was easy to run back to because he knew what was required of him there. With Becca, he sometimes felt out of his depth. Like he wasn't going to live up to her expectations.

Doc just clapped him on the shoulder. "You think about it for a while, son. Maybe you stay here in Wyoming; maybe you don't. There's always a job for you at this ranch and a place to live. If that's not what you want, though, that's fine, too. But regret is a terrible bed partner, so make sure that you don't let a good thing slip past you."

CHAPTER TWENTY-THREE

Hank thought about his uncle's words all day. He cleaned the barn from top to bottom as he silently mulled his thoughts. What would his future look like if he stayed here? He tried to imagine it. There'd be cattle in his future instead of trapping, but he didn't mind ranching. It was hard work, but it let him be out in the sunshine and there was a satisfaction to tending a fat, full herd. Maybe he wouldn't keep living in the main house, though. Maybe he'd take one of the cowboy cabins and expand on it, make it a home.

Maybe he'd build Becca a new home right next to this one. Something with a big kitchen and a big wraparound sofa so they could cuddle up and watch movies together every night. He imagined a house with her in it, and it'd be full of scented candles and those silly throw pillows she was enamored with, but it'd also be full of her bright laughter and her joy. He pictured her holding Libby's hand, her other hand in his . . . and his chest squeezed so hard with longing it felt like a physical ache. Yeah, he wanted that.

He wanted to give her the children she wanted. He wanted to see her smile every morning and every night. He wanted to hold her close and love her with all his damned heart.

And she'd shown up that morning, all pretty, with a box of doughnuts, a shy smile of greeting on her face. He hadn't been able to figure out why she'd come by.

Had she . . . changed her mind about him, too? Did she miss him like he missed her? Because not having Becca at his side was like missing a limb . . . or having his heart ripped out of his chest. He wasn't surviving without it. He needed her.

The realization hit him like a load of bricks. He didn't need Alaska. He needed her.

Libby didn't need Alaska, either. If she didn't like school, they'd figure something out. But she needed Becca in her life, too. She needed two parents to love and look after her. With that thought swimming in his head, he dumped the rest of the fresh hay into the horse stalls and then headed inside.

"Libby?" he called out, and she came around the corner, riding on Jack's shoulders. Her giggles were wild, her face lit up with amusement. There was a half-eaten peanut butter and jam sandwich in her hand, and some of her curls were dragging through the sandwich. Her overalls were filthy, and she looked like a damned mess.

"We're just playing a bit of horsey," Jack told him, and did a mock gallop to make Libby laugh again.

Hank raised his arms. "Horsey time is over. You're a mess, Libs." She launched herself into his arms and he caught her, then settled her on his hip. "You and I need to talk."

"Okay, Daddy," she said brightly.

"What about?" Jack asked.

He frowned at Jack. His youngest brother had a good heart, but if anything, his stubbornness ran deeper than even Hank's. He wouldn't like to hear that Hank and Libby were going to stay in Painted Barrel, too. Best to hide that information from him until everything was settled. "Father-daughter stuff."

Jack put his hands up. "Sounds creepy. I'm out."

It wasn't creepy, damn it. But if that got Jack to leave, so much the better. Hank bit back a retort and took Libby upstairs to the bathroom, removing the squashed sandwich from her hand and washing her arms and face. "Daddy needs to tell you some important stuff, okay, Libs?"

She gave him a surprisingly serious look. "Are you okay, Daddy?"

"I will be," he promised her. "I've been . . . giving the future a lot of thought. And I was just thinking that maybe you and I will stay here for a while instead of going back to Alaska. What do you think?"

"Can I have a bubble bath?"

Clearly she wasn't understanding the gravity of the situation. He expected that, since she was four, but he needed to make her understand. "If we stay here, that means you have to go back to school."

Libby shrugged. "Okay."

That . . . was it? "I don't want you to feel anxious about it—"

"Can I have a bubble bath after school?"

". . . Sure?"

She beamed.

"You're not upset about school?"

Libby shrugged again and he decided not to press it. If she was happy, then going back to Alaska wasn't all that necessary, was it? He sighed deeply, a load of stress off his shoulders. Why was everything with Libby so simple and yet so complicated at the same time? "Let's get you in the tub, and Daddy's going to text Becca, okay?"

She wiggled with excitement. "Are we going to see Miss Becca?"

"That's my hope."

He peeled filthy clothing off his daughter and grimaced at the nest of dirty curls atop her head. He didn't want Becca to see what a mess his little girl was or make it seem like he was a wreck without Becca at his side . . . Then again, maybe that was the best idea. Nah. He ran the water for Libby and added soap, and while his daughter splashed and played in the tub, he sat on the toilet and texted Becca.

HANK: Bec cvcx aserer u therrte?

HANK: casn wwe talkk?

HANK: iu wanterdf to tsdlk tro youy

He cursed at his fat fingers. The phone keyboard was so small and his fingers so big that he was sending her nothing but streams of gibberish. Even so, he stared at his phone, waiting for her to respond.

Nothing.

All right, then, he was just going to show up and ask her to start over again. To give him another shot. Hank studied Libby's messy, sticky hair, and . . . an idea hit. He grabbed a towel. "Hurry up with the bath, Libby. You and I have somewhere to go."

"Where are we going?" She splashed, her voice rising in volume with excitement.

"Well, we're gonna go to a ring store, I think," he told her, because if he was getting back together with Becca—and he wasn't going to allow a "no" into his head—then he wanted to make sure the entire world knew she was his. That ring would stake his claim on her.

Provided she talked to him. She was probably mad about this morning. He'd gotten totally tongue-tied when she'd showed up, unsure what to say without spilling his guts at her. So he'd said not much at all, and it had somehow turned out worse than saying nothing.

What if she was mad at him now? What if that was why she wasn't responding to his texts? He studied Libby thoughtfully. "We might go by the store, too. How do you feel about pretending to put gum in your hair again?"

"No!"

"Just pretend—"

"No, Daddy!" She slapped her small fists against the water.

He raised his hands in the air. "It was just a suggestion." He could always just pull her hair into a messy knot and hint at it if nothing else. He'd never sabotage Libby's hair just to get into the door of Becca's salon, but he could pretend. "Come on, let's get dressed so we can go into town."

Two hours later, he had a ring box in his sweating hand and his daughter's tiny hand in his other one. Hank had tried to think of something clever to say, or a way to slide into the subject of marriage, but he was clueless. All he knew was that he was going to go through that door and talk to Becca, and if she wouldn't listen to him, he . . . well, he just wouldn't leave. She had to hear him out eventually, didn't she? After all, she'd come by that morning to talk and he'd been tongue-tied. Hopefully she'd still be in a talking mood this afternoon.

Libby skipped at his side, all excitement as they headed down the sidewalk toward the salon. He'd parked down the street so Becca wouldn't see just how nervous he was. He'd have a whole two hundred feet to pull himself together, after all. So he sucked in a deep breath, did his best not to squeeze the life out of his daughter's hand, and led her toward the salon. At the last moment, he shoved the ring box into his pocket, hiding it.

Becca was sweeping up underneath one of her chairs. She looked up as the bell clanged against the door, and her face went pale at the sight of him.

"Becca!" Libby squealed, rushing forward. She flung her arms out and raced toward the woman, and he wasn't surprised when Becca discarded her broom and hugged Libby, pulling her into her arms and showering her face with dozens of tiny kisses.

"Libby! I've missed you, baby girl! How are you?"

"Me and Daddy are here because—"

Hank cleared his throat, trying not to bark at his daughter before she spoiled the surprise. "Because we wanted to talk to you."

Becca's expression immediately grew wary. "Oh?"

He studied her. Couldn't help but notice that she'd changed clothing from earlier. She'd been wearing tall heels and a dress with entirely too much cleavage that had made him crazy to think about. He'd pictured her leaning over her male clients, shaving them with her big, bouncy breasts in their faces, and he'd nearly come unglued. It seemed like that dress had just been for his benefit, though, because she was wearing one of her favorite outfits—a tunic and striped leggings and a flat pair of sandals. Either she'd come that morning to flaunt herself in his face or there was hope for him yet. So he smiled, even though it didn't feel natural, and tried to flirt like Jack would. "Can I have a greeting like that?" he asked, indicating his daughter. He'd be all right if she peppered his face with a hundred kisses. He'd sit still for every one of them, too.

She flushed, looking nervous. With a quick kiss to Libby's forehead, she set the little girl down and took her hand. "I need to talk to your daddy, sweetheart. Why don't you look at the new coloring book I got for you? It's at your desk. Pick out a few pictures and we'll color one together in a bit, all right?"

Libby hugged Becca's legs and then skipped away to her little pink desk in the corner of the salon. He noticed Becca hadn't taken down any of Libby's art, either. It had been almost two weeks since their big fight, and that was . . . downright promising. If she'd thought they'd never see each other again, wouldn't she have taken that stuff down?

Or was he reading too much into this because he was desperate?

He licked his lips. "I . . . ah . . . think we need to talk. You came by earlier and I should have said something then. Shouldn't have let it go on for as long as it has." Because, hell, he'd missed her like nothing he'd ever experienced before. He'd thought he'd get over it, but every day it was just worse, and talking with Doc had made him realize that you didn't get over some people. Some people were permanent, in both good ways and bad. Hank wanted that permanent with Becca—that forever—so he had to get her to realize that she needed him as much as he needed her.

Becca grew even paler at his words.

Should he have said more? He wasn't sure how to lead into it. Hank took off his hat, nervous and utterly aware of the ring box in his jeans pocket. "Came here to settle it."

Becca burst into tears.

That . . . was not what he'd expected. It horrified him to see her sobbing, and Libby looked up from her desk like a deer in headlights, took one glance at Becca, and then started wailing, too.

"I . . . Becca . . . Libby . . ." He clenched the brim of his Stetson with frustration. "What did I say?"

Becca just waved a hand, sobbing, as she went to retrieve Libby. He watched, frozen, while she scooped up his crying daughter and tried to soothe her. "It's okay, Libby. It is. I promise." She pressed another kiss to the little girl's cheek even as she rocked her. "It's just hard for me to hear. I'm sorry."

Hard for her to hear? His belly suddenly felt like it was full of lead. Hard for her to hear because she'd already moved on? Was he making this awkward? Damn it, he didn't know what to say. "I . . . Becca, I'm sorry."

She shook her head, her hand going to the back of Libby's head as she stroked the little girl's soft curls. Her eyes closed and for a moment she looked utterly beautiful, just like a Madonna in a painting. "Like I said in the past, I just get attached easily. It's not you; it's me."

Now he was getting confused. "I like that about you."

"Yeah, well, it's hell when someone breaks up with you." She opened her eyes and a fat tear rolled down her cheek. "I'm sorry I came by earlier. I didn't get the hint. I get it now. I won't bother you anymore."

Wait.

She thought she was bothering him?

Did she . . . think he was here to break up with her? For good?

Ah hell, he was just messing all of this up. Hank rubbed his beard, frustrated. The sound of both of them crying was killing him, so he did the only thing he could think of to stop it. He was no good with words—that much was obvious. Better to just show her. Mutely, he pulled the ring box out of his pocket while she rocked his daughter in her arms, soothing her.

Then he dropped to one knee in front of Becca and held the ring box out.

She froze, her eyes going wide. After a long moment,

she sniffed, confusion on her face. "I think I missed something."

"I miss you," he said bluntly.

Her lips formed a circle of surprise.

She wasn't saying anything, though, so he continued. He had to get it all out before she changed her mind about him. Before she decided she was better off without him in her life. "I miss you so much that it makes my entire body ache," he continued. "I miss hearing your laughter. I miss your smile and I miss the smell of your hair and I miss the way you push your cold feet between my legs when we're sleeping together. I know I scared you off because I said I wanted to go back to Alaska, but I don't want to go there if you're not going to be with me. I want to be where you are, because that's the place that makes me happy."

Becca swiped at her eyes, gazing at him from over Libby's head. "But you said—"

"I know. I ran my mouth off without stopping to ask what you wanted. I know you have a business here and there's nothing for you up there but me. I was mad about it for a few days, I admit, but I also had to think about what I really wanted. I haven't missed Alaska all that much since I've been here. Sometimes I miss the weather or the quiet, but Wyoming's not so bad." He shook his head and then gazed up at her, devouring her face. "But I missed you every second of every day for the past two weeks. I couldn't sleep at night because you weren't with me. I heard that Greg guy came around and—"

"I'm not with him," she said quickly. "Never again."

"I know," Hank continued. "I heard he was sniffing around and I wanted to come by and kick his ass for thinking he had the right. And then I stopped being angry at him and started getting angry at myself. For letting you down. For thinking I could walk away and not be affected." He shook his head. "If you said no to me right now, I wouldn't blame you. I haven't been the best boyfriend, and I know I'm sometimes stubborn and hard to live with, and I can be frustrating and—"

"Yes," Becca said quickly.

His heart soared. "Yes?"

She bit her lip as their eyes met. "A few conditions first, though."

Everything inside him froze. This was when she dropped the hammer. This was when she'd make him grovel, make him beg to have her back and . . . hell, he'd do it. He'd do it because those tears shining in her eyes and the hesitation on her face were killing him. "Go on."

"Whether we stay here or we go, we discuss it together, okay?"

He relaxed. "I can do that."

"And two . . . I don't want a long engagement. I already did that once. This time I want to actually make my way to the altar and not just get dragged along—"

"Today?" he asked.

"What do you mean, today?"

"I'll marry you today, if you want. We can go right down to the courthouse and do this."

Becca looked astonished. "Today?"

"What's wrong with today?" He held the ring box out again, nudging it toward her. "Or tomorrow, I guess, if you want to wait."

She stared at him. Licked her lips. Hugged Libby closer. And then she hesitated once more. "I think I have one more condition."

"Oh?"

"I need to know if you love me," she blurted out. "Maybe that's just me being emotional and silly, but I don't know if I can do this if you don't love me like I love you."

Is that what she was worried about? Had he never said

the words? Hank reached out and took her free hand in his. She looked at him, all uncertainty, as he gently took his daughter from her arms. He set Libby down and she popped her thumb into her mouth, looking up at him. He took Becca's other hand in his, and then squeezed them both as he pulled her in close to him, dragging her forward until she was seated on his knee.

And then he wrapped his arms around her tightly, because he was never going to let her go. "I love you," he murmured. "I love you so much. Marry me?"

She smiled. "Okay."

CHAPTER TWENTY-FOUR

Two hours later, she had a ring on her finger and she was Mrs. Henry Watson.

It didn't feel real. Becca couldn't stop touching the ring on her finger as they helped Libby get ready for bed. They were at Becca's house, tucking Libby into her room after a long, long day. The little girl had been yawning for the last hour after they'd driven back from the courthouse a few towns over, and even a Happy Meal hadn't kept her awake. That meant that they'd get alone time together—which meant the wedding night.

Gosh, she was more than ready for a wedding night.

She twisted the oversize ring on her finger and gazed down at it again. Hank hadn't realized how small her fingers were, so the ring was far too big. She still wanted to wear it, though, so the backside of the ring was covered in a thick wad of wrapped tape to make the fit a little more snug. It was the perfect ring, Becca decided. It was a small cluster of diamonds in the shape of a flower, and it sparkled and danced every time she moved her hand. It wasn't enormously expensive, but she was glad about that. She didn't want Hank spending a fortune on a ring—she just wanted Hank.

He pressed a kiss to Libby's brow as he tucked her in. "Night, Libs." Hank looked up at Becca and gestured at his daughter.

She smiled and leaned in to give Libby a kiss. "Good night, princess."

"G'night, Mama." Libby had been calling her that since they'd left the courthouse, and it made Becca's eyes tear up every time. She really was a mama now. This was more than she could have dreamed.

Hank took her hand and they left the room together, tiptoeing back down to Becca's bedroom. She blushed with embarrassment at the mess—there were empty Kleenex boxes next to the bed from her crying binge, her trash can was overflowing, and there was an empty box of chocolates on the floor. She'd been a bit of an emotional eater in the last two weeks. "Sorry it's a mess—"

He sat down on the edge of the bed and pulled her against him, tucking her between his thighs. His arms went around her waist and he turned her around, easing the tunic over her head. "I don't mind the mess. You weren't expecting company. No, that's not right. Part of me hates the mess because I see what I did to you and it's awful. I wish I'd never made you cry." He touched her cheek. "And the small, selfish part of me likes it because it meant you were messed up as much as I was." He leaned in and pressed a kiss to the middle of her now-naked back. "I missed you something fierce."

"Me too," she breathed. "God, I missed you so much. That's why I came by."

"I was hoping. Distracted, too." He made a hand gesture, indicating how deep his arm had been in the cow, but that seemed like the wrong thing to do at the moment. Heck, even this he was messing up. He shook his head and kept talking. "I was just too tongue-tied to say anything. Didn't want to fuck it up more than I already had." He pressed another kiss to her back, sending shivers across her skin, and then undid the fastening on her bra. "Still can't believe you're mine forever."

"Forever."

He groaned, dragging the bra off her shoulders and letting it fall to the floor. "Never thought I'd have a wife. Never thought I'd get to touch someone as pretty as you, as perfect, as soft."

Just his words were turning her on, but his touch skimming over her skin? That just brought everything to another level. Becca moaned as he slid his hands into her panties and eased both them and the leggings down her thighs at the same time. She stepped out of them and kicked off her shoes, and then she was naked in front of him, her entire body quivering with excitement and need.

"I love you," she told him again, cupping his jaw and twining her fingers in his beard. It was still soft, and she arched a brow at him. "Did you oil this?"

"Was kinda hoping I'd get you back. I did a lot of thinking about all the makeup kissing we'd get to do." He gave her a sly look.

Becca giggled. She'd been thinking about it, too. They'd kissed briefly after the proposal, but Libby had been impatient and they'd only managed to sneak a few pecks. It was the same at the courthouse. He'd held her hand and they'd exchanged their vows, and he'd given her a quick, searing kiss. She was hungry for more now that they were alone and had all the time in the world. So she put a hand on his chest and leaned in, brushing her lips over his.

Hank's mouth met hers in a hard, delicious slant, and then he was devouring her with hungry, needy kisses, showing her just how much he'd missed her. She'd missed him, too, just as fiercely, and then she was kissing him back with all the pent-up frustration and need of the last few weeks. Her tongue met his and she twined her fingers in his hair, full of need and longing.

"Love you," he managed between kisses. "I'm gonna say it more often so you know it, but I love you, Becca. You're the most perfect woman ever."

His hand slid between her thighs and he cupped her sex, teasing the folds apart with light touches, stroking her until she was rocking her hips against his hand, her mouth frantic on his. She whimpered with every caress, until she was losing track of where she was. Her world had narrowed down to the hand driving her wild, the big body she pressed up against, and the mouth that possessed hers like he owned it. "My Becca," he told her over and over again. "All mine."

"Yours," she agreed, and when his hand left the warmth between her thighs, she whimpered, tearing at the buttons on his shirt. He needed to get naked, pronto. She had to touch his bare skin or she'd go mad. "Hank, I need you—"

He captured her mouth again, silencing her words, but even as he kissed her, he tore at his clothing, pulling first his shirt off and then ripping at his belt. She stepped backward as he cast off the last of his clothing, and then he was naked and glorious in front of her, the hard, thick length of his cock rising from his lap. He sat down on the edge of the bed again and pulled her forward, kissing her. "Straddle me," he told her in a low breath.

"Straddle . . . you?" She could feel herself blushing.

"I've got you," he reassured her, one big hand on the small of her back. "Want to look at you when I sink so deep inside you, Becca."

Oh, she wanted that, too. Feeling a little awkward, she nevertheless did as he asked, straddling him with her hips and creeping forward ever so slightly until his cock brushed against her spread folds. She felt exposed like this, vulnerable, and even more so when he reached between them and caressed her again.

"Love how wet you are, baby. You're coating my hand with your need."

She was; there was something about the way he touched her that just made her crazy with arousal, as if her body would never stop humming—and now they were going to have incredible sex for the rest of their lives. It seemed like a dream. He carefully lifted her up and then shifted his weight. She felt the press of his cock against the entrance to her core for a split second before he kissed her again, and then she eased her weight down, working him into her body.

And good lord, it was delicious. Whimpering, clinging to Hank, she forgot all about awkwardness as he locked an arm around her waist and began to slowly work his hips.

"Oh—wait," Becca gasped, remembering something important. "Hank, wait, you can't be inside me bare."

He thrust deep, her eyes nearly rolling back in her head with how good it felt. "You want me to get out now? When you feel so damned good?"

"Not . . . on . . . pill," she managed between thrusts. He really did feel amazing, and it was hard to concentrate. "I stopped taking it when we broke up."

"Good," he said, and buried his face against her neck as he pulled her closer. "Hope you want lots of babies, because I plan on taking my wife every night for the rest of our lives."

She moaned. "I want that. I want that so much."

He began to rock into her harder, and Becca used her own hips to work him deep. She lifted up and sank back down, trying to find a rhythm, but he was so distracting and delicious that she kept losing control. Eventually Hank gripped her waist and then rolled them over until she was under him on the bed, and then he began to take her with deep, hard strokes that made her feel as if he was claiming all of her. It didn't take long for her to come—the change in angles made that deep belly orgasm build almost instantly. She clung to him as the pleasure wracked her body, gasping out his name, and a few moments later, when he came, she held him as he shuddered over her.

Hank's big body collapsed on top of hers, and then Becca shivered at how good it felt to be pinned underneath him. Her husband had the most wonderfully huge body, and it felt so good over her. She was a little sad when he eased off her and then washed them both with a damp towel. Then he pulled her close against him and tucked her under his chin.

"Mrs. Watson," he murmured.

The name made her so damned happy.

He rubbed her naked back absently, his big hand curving up and down her side and then cupping her butt. "So when do you want to have the big church wedding?"

She looked up at him, surprised. "You want to do that?"

"If it's what you want. I'm fine with it. Figured you wanted the big white gown and lots of flowers and everyone staring as you make an honest man out of me."

Becca giggled at that, then shook her head. "I'm strangely in no rush." It felt good to just be his. She didn't have anything to prove to anyone. If they had a second wedding later on, that was fine. If not, well, that was fine, too. "We should probably talk about a few things first, though."

"Like when I get to meet your parents?"

"Ugh. I guess we do need to do that at some point." She made a face. "Maybe not yet, though." Her father would wonder about their relationship, and her mother, well, her mother would think the same thing her father did. "I meant more along the lines of where we're going to live. Do you want to move in with me or do you want me to move in with you?"

"Hmm." He traced little circles on her buttock with his

fingertips. "For both of us, it makes sense that we live near our jobs. But here, you have a room for Libby and we have privacy together. Doc won't care if I'm a little later than the others to show up for work every day. He'll just be happy I got my head out of my ass and married you."

Aw. Doc was such a good man. "Was he encouraging you to come talk to me, then?"

"I wouldn't say it was 'encouraging' as much as calling me a dumbass for letting you get away in the first place."

She was going to bake that man a million cookies as a thank-you. "I'm glad you came to your senses and didn't let me get away, too. So you really want to move in with me?"

"If it's all right with you."

"Hank, we're married," she said, chuckling. "Someone's going to have to move in with someone."

"The only thing I ask is maybe a few less doilies downstairs."

"I can do that." She tickled his side, loving the way his big body tensed against her. "What about . . . Alaska?"

"You want me to go walk her?" The puppy was asleep in Libby's bed with her, but she'd peed on the floor earlier after they'd left her inside for too long. It happened. Alaska was still a baby. She wasn't upset.

"No, I mean the state, Alaska. Your old home. The one you were going to go back to."

"Ah." He pressed another kiss to the top of her head. "It's not going anywhere. Caleb doesn't want to go back, either. Got his eye on some pretty girl in town. It'll just be Jack, and I don't know if he even wants to go or if he's just being stubborn." She felt him shrug. "Might be fun to go up there for a few weeks in the summer every now and then, but Libby needs a mama and I need my wife more than we need to go to Alaska."

She tucked her head against his chest, loving the sounds of those words. "I don't want you to feel trapped here—"

"The only time I felt trapped was at the thought that I might not get you back and I had my hand stuck inside a cow's uterus." He stroked her back thoughtfully, his fingers moving up and down over her skin in a way that was both comforting and arousing. They'd just had sex, but she'd be more than ready for another round if this kept up. "I suppose I should think about Libby and school a bit more. If she hates it there, I don't want to force her to go."

Becca picked her words carefully, not wanting to start a fight. "I understand. I don't want her to be miserable, either. Amy tells me that most kids cry the first day and then they get used to it, though. It's a big change for them. If it helps, I'd be happy to go for a few days and stay at her side so she knows there's nothing to fear."

He squeezed her tight. "You'd do that for me?"

"No, I'd do that for Libby." She looked up at him, beaming. "She's my daughter, too, now."

"Damn, I love you, woman," he growled. "Why is it you have the answer for everything?"

"Because the answer for everything is easy." As long as they loved each other, nothing else seemed to matter all that much.

EPILOGUE

Three Years Later

"Slow down," Becca called after Libby as her daughter raced ahead, the dog bounding at her side. The narrow trail wound through the trees, and in the distance, tall mountains loomed. Even though it was August, the weather was cool and the mountains in the distance had snowy caps. Everywhere around them there were green trees and rolling hills and the air felt clean and fresh. Becca took in a deep breath, smiling to herself. So this was Alaska.

"Listen to your mother," Hank called, heading down the path after Libby. He was laden with their gear, arms full of sleeping bags and clothing, a cooler, and fishing rods. He turned to give her an exasperated look. "She listens real well, doesn't she?"

"She's seven. I don't think her eardrums will fully develop until she's twenty-one or so," Becca teased.

"Da!" cried the little boy at Becca's side. "Da!"

"Someone's listening," she told Hank with amusement, and beamed down at her toddling son at her side. She was walking the slowest out of all of them, because Henry Junior was just now testing his little legs at the age of fourteen months, and it was darling to watch those chubby little legs move.

"You watch your mama," Hank told his son as he moved past with the bags. "I'll be back in a moment. Gotta make sure Libby remembers the way." He headed off after his daughter, disappearing into the trees after her.

"Da!" Henry said again, pointing after his father.

"That's right," Becca told him, proud. "That's your daddy." She wanted to reach over and smooth the cowlicks of dark hair crowning the baby's head, but it was more important to let him stretch his legs after so long in the car. All of them had felt the long car ride, but no one had wanted to leave the dog Alaska behind for weeks while they visited the cabin. Alaska was a long-legged, overeager goofball of a dog who tended to chew things she shouldn't and get into everything, but she was also fiercely devoted to Libby and it wouldn't be a bad idea to have another set of eyes on the rambunctious seven-year-old out in the woods. The older Libby got, the more trouble she got into, but it was just a phase, Becca hoped. She'd outgrow it at some point. And if not, well, they'd just have to learn to walk faster to keep up with her.

Henry lifted his arms, indicating that he wanted to be carried, and Becca scooped him up. "Oof, heavy little man," she murmured. "Come on, let's go catch up with Daddy."

She headed down the path that wound through the woods. The dirt road had ended about a quarter mile back, which meant that it was a long walk out to the cabin, but the path was clear, courtesy of Jack and his buddies. She knew the brothers still came up to the cabin regularly for fishing and hunting trips, or loaned it to friends in the area provided they'd handle the upkeep. She'd been surprised when all three brothers had elected to stay in Painted Barrel, but it was nice to have family around to call upon. Back home, Caleb and Jack were going to check in on the builders since Becca and Hank wouldn't be home for a while. The expansion on their house was coming along, and she was ready to have extra bathrooms and a bigger living room and kitchen. With three people in the house, it had been a cramped fit. With the new baby? Extra bathrooms and a bigger kitchen were a necessity. They'd looked at getting some land and Doc had offered for them to build on the Swinging C lands, but with Libby in school and Becca's business thriving, it just made more sense to stay in town for now.

Becca touched her slightly rounded stomach, where another baby was now growing. With frequent doctor visits between Henry Junior and now this baby, it was another reason to stay in town. She was only two months along and had yet to tell Hank. She'd tell him on this trip, and she hoped he was as excited as she was. Her dream of a huge family was becoming a reality, and she couldn't be more thrilled. She kissed Henry's head, thinking of pregnancy and childbirth and going through it all again. Pregnancy had been surprisingly easy. She'd gotten pregnant after about a year of marriage, and Hank had been so excited that her normally taciturn husband had told everyone in town. The pregnancy itself had been a breeze. She hadn't been sick, hadn't felt bloated or had weird cravings—she'd just plumped up like a Christmas turkey. And, really, that was all right, too. Most of the weight had come off with breastfeeding, and what hadn't, Hank loved to squeeze. He said he loved her big butt and thick thighs, and she hoped he was ready for them to become even thicker. Just thinking about the baby filled her with anticipation.

"Da!" Henry said, pointing ahead.

"I see him," she murmured, watching Hank's hat bob through the trees.

She headed down the path, and Libby came racing back

toward her, Alaska dancing at her heels. "Mama, the stream is so close! I forgot how close it was! Can I go fishing?"

"Wait for your father," she advised her, heading toward the cabin. "He needs to put our things down and then I'm sure he'd love to go fishing with you."

"I'll go find the skinning cabin, then—"

"No," Becca said, using her firmest mom voice. "Stay where your father or I can see you. Stick to the trail. Remember your uncle Jack said he saw a bear out here a few months ago."

"Okay," Libby said, and then skipped back down the trail again, Alaska eagerly bounding behind.

She just shook her head at the girl. Libby was all skinny legs and blond curls now, and her love of pink and princessy things had turned right back around to fishing and horses and tomboy things. Hank was delighted, and Becca missed being able to give Libby "princess" hair, but that was all right. Her daughter was happy and she had her hands full with Henry most of the time anyhow. Libby's grades in school were excellent, though, and she loved reading. Just last night at the hotel, Libby had insisted on reading a Marguerite Henry book to the baby for his bedtime story. He was far too young to appreciate the stories about ponies, but he'd sucked his thumb and listened to his sister as she turned pages, and Becca's heart had felt so, so full.

Was it possible to be this happy? And tired? She chuckled to herself. Because she was both.

Her family was growing, and Hank was still working at the Swinging C, which meant he put in long days. Her own business was as steady as could be, as Painted Barrel had grown over the last year or two and more people seemed to drift through town for haircuts thanks to good word of mouth. She'd hired one of the local girls who'd just gotten out of beauty school, and while Henry was little, she was working half days and on the weekends. She used a few local babysitters, and Hannah at the hotel was always thrilled to watch Henry, but sometimes she was just tired from constantly being on the go.

That was why this family vacation was so worth it. They'd spend a few weeks in Alaska at the cabin, roughing it and connecting with nature, and then school would start for Libby. Once school started, there was cheerleading, soccer, PTA meetings, and an endless stream of "mom" duties in addition to her regular schedule, but she wouldn't change a bit of it.

She loved being a busy mom and having a busy schedule.

Hank appeared as she meandered down the path, his brows furrowed as he approached. "Is he getting too heavy for you, baby?" He'd gotten rid of the bags he'd been laden down with and came to her side to take Henry from her.

"Nope, I'm fine," she told him. "Just enjoying the scenery." She'd been a mite distracted. Pregnancy brain, she told herself. "Libby at the cabin?"

"Yep. I told her once we were settled in we could start fishing, so she's busy unpacking absolutely everything." He gave her a crooked grin that melted her heart. "Sorry in advance for the mess."

"Oh boy." Becca chuckled. Sometimes the "help" from her daughter was less helpful than it was just straight-up messy. "I guess we'd better walk faster to see what we can salvage."

They got to the cabin a few moments later, and Becca loved the picturesque sight of it. It was nestled into the trees, the roof thatched with moss, the walls log and mud. It was cozy and adorable. Once she got inside, though, she just started laughing.

It was one room.

With a dirt floor.

"This?" she told her husband, sputtering through her laughter. "This is what you wanted to move our entire family into? It's one room!"

Hank looked sheepish. "It's cozy in winter."

"I'll bet." She looked at the bed against the wall and shook her head. Libby had already dumped all their carefully packed clothing out on it and had scattered their things. Somewhere outside, Alaska was barking. "Can you watch the baby for a few? I'll straighten up in here."

"You got it." He leaned down and gave her a kiss. "Love you, Becca."

She smiled. He told her that at least three or four times a day, and it was better every time she heard it. "Love you, too."

She fell asleep in the bed.

At least, she was pretty sure she did. All Becca knew was that one minute she was folding laundry, and then it seemed like a really good idea to lie down and just close her eyes.

"Becca? Baby?" Hank's soft chuckle woke her up. He sat down on the edge of the bed as she rubbed her eyes. "Long day?"

"Mm, sorry. Just tired. Have I been asleep long?" She sat up, fighting back a yawn.

"About an hour. You okay? You never nap unless . . ." He gave her a suspicious look and then reached over and squeezed her breast. "Aha."

She batted his hand away. "Don't 'aha' at me. I was going to tell you."

A big grin creased his face. "You were, huh?" He dragged her into his lap and gave her an enormous kiss. "How far along?"

"About two months," she told him, unable to stop smiling. "Are we happy?"

"We are." He kissed her again. "I'll make sure you get plenty of naps on this trip, then. And maybe some alone time together."

She snorted. "Alone time? You do realize we have a seven-year-old and a one-year-old?" She stiffened, alert. "Where are they, by the way?"

"Just outside. I told Libby to keep an eye on Henry while I retrieved you. The sun's going down and Libby wants to roast marshmallows. You know she'll be on her best behavior for that."

"Marshmallows? Before dinner?" Becca protested. Actually, to her pregnant belly, marshmallows sounded pretty amazing. "Did you put bug spray on them?"

"Not yet."

"Hank!" She climbed off his lap. Or tried to. He pulled her right back down again, ignoring her irked expression. "Let me up, Henry Watson, or our children are going to be eaten alive by bugs."

"I will. I just wanted to kiss you one more time first." He cupped the back of her head and gave her the softest, sweetest kiss. "I love you, Rebecca Loftis Watson. You make me the happiest man alive."

And she decided that she could stay for maybe just one more kiss.

Her life was busy and chaotic . . . and wonderful, and she wouldn't have it any other way.

Turn the page for a sneak peek at
Jessica Clare's delightful
holiday romance

HER CHRISTMAS COWBOY

Coming October 2020 from Jove!

Caleb Watson had skills. Or so he told himself. He could rope a runaway heifer from horseback. He could keep even the most ornery herd of cattle together. He could ease a breech calf out of its mother without blinking an eye. He could saddle a horse faster than anyone he knew.

And those were just his ranching skills. Back when he lived in Alaska, he could track anything, fix a snowmobile out in the field, survive on his own for weeks. Heck, he could even build a log cabin and have it fully functional within a short time frame.

He was strong. Capable. Self-sufficient.

He stared at the front doors to the elementary school and wished he would stop sweating.

Because Caleb had to acknowledge that when it came to skills in the field or in ranching, he could handle himself with the best.

But when it came to talking to people . . . ?

He was the worst.

The absolute worst.

His younger brother, Jack, was smooth. He could talk the pants off anyone and always managed to get his way with a smile and a wink. His older brother, Hank, wasn't much of a talker, but he was still better than Caleb.

It wasn't just that Caleb clammed up around people. His mind went blank and nothing would come forward. It was like the moment he was required to give a response, he forgot what words were.

Most of the time he didn't care. He was a cowboy; the cattle didn't mind if he was silent. His brothers didn't mind if he wasn't chatty.

But around women, it was a problem.

Caleb had never had a girlfriend, which was fine when you were a kid, or when you lived in the remote wilds of interior Alaska and might not see a single woman for months on end. Here in the town of Painted Barrel, Wyoming, though, he felt his lack of social skills acutely.

Very, very acutely.

Because Caleb was in love.

Just thinking about love made him reach into his pocket and pull out his bandanna to mop the sweat on his brow. Love was difficult even in the best of times, but when you had trouble speaking to women, it was pure torture. Every time he got up the nerve to talk to a woman, it ended badly.

There was that time he had a crush on a cute bar waitress back in Alaska whom he'd blushed and stammered over until she thought he was mentally unsound.

There was a girl who had worked at her uncle's game-processing shop one summer. He'd gone there often all summer just to try to speak to her. He'd paid other hunters through the nose for their kills so he'd have some excuse to go into the shop. When he did finally get up the nerve to talk to the object of his affections, she thought he was creepy because he was "killing so many animals" and she wanted nothing to do with him. There were a few other passing women he'd managed to somehow insult without meaning to.

And now there was Miss Amy Mckinney, one of two elementary school teachers in Painted Barrel.

The moment he'd looked at her, he'd been in love. Amy had a gorgeous face and a smoking-hot body, but what he liked most about her was that she was kind. Or she seemed to be. He hadn't quite got the nerve up to talk to her himself. He'd been around when she was talking to other people, though.

He might have showed up at several PTA volunteer meetings just to hear her talk. Not that he had kids. He didn't usually volunteer, either. But he showed up anyhow, because he'd get to watch her from afar, see her smile at others as she talked easily, and wish he wasn't such a damned idiot the moment he talked to a pretty woman.

Today, though, he had a reason to talk to her. His brother Hank was out in one of the distant pastures, and Caleb had been cleaning out the barn when Hank had texted and said his horse was limping and he was going to walk it in, but that meant he'd be a few hours, and Hank's daughter, Libby, needed to be picked up from school.

Caleb had immediately volunteered to go pick her up. It was the perfect opportunity. Miss Mckinney was Libby's teacher, so he'd stroll into class, tip his hat at her, announce he was there to pick up Libby, and strike up a conversation.

His mind went blank. A conversation about . . . what? What did one talk about with a schoolteacher? The weather? Everyone was going to talk about the weather with her. He needed to say something different. Maybe something about school? But he didn't have children that went to the school . . . Maybe Christmas?

Surely he'd think of something. He wiped his brow, sucked in a deep breath, and then got out of the truck.

* * *

Most of the parents at Painted Barrel Elementary knew the drill for picking up their children. Amy took the ones that rode the bus out to the bus driver's line in front of the principal's office. She quickly counted heads and then went back to her classroom, where the other children waited with their backpacks for their parents to pick them up. Picking up their children in the classroom instead of outside was better all around, Amy figured, since it was cold and snowy in Wyoming in December, and little hands needed gloves and those were the first thing that her students tended to lose.

Plus, it gave Amy a good chance to talk to the parents, to pass along notes about behavior, and to make sure everything was going well. With a small class of twelve students, she could do such a thing. It was one of the main reasons she'd moved out to Painted Barrel and accepted the teaching job that had the lowest salary instead of taking a far more lucrative one in a big city. She really wanted to connect with her students. She really wanted the opportunity to influence her kids and watch them grow. She wanted to be a teacher that they remembered.

Plus, she was starting over—her life, her career, everything. What was better than starting over in all ways? She'd lived in bigger cities all her life. Now Amy just wanted to blend into a tight-knit community and be part of things. Maybe being part of a community would help choke down that black hole of loneliness inside her that had just gotten bigger and bigger since her divorce.

Maybe.

This wasn't the time to think about her divorce from Blake, though. Right now she had to focus on her kids. So as the first parents showed up, she went into teacher mode, chirping about how wonderfully this or that kid did in class today, helping put on little jackets, and finding mittens.

More parents showed up, and then her classroom was an absolute cluster of people bundling small children in warm outdoor gear, and so she got her clipboard and checked off names and parents while one of the PTA moms chattered in her ear about the upcoming school Christmas Carnival. It was another one of the ways Amy was probably a bit too anal-retentive about her kids, but she was able to get away with it because it was a smaller class. She carefully kept track of who picked up who every day and made notes in a logbook in her desk. Safety was important.

As parents left with their children and the room started to clear out, she tried to focus on the woman talking non-stop in her ear. She kept an eye on the children left in the classroom as Linda talked about Santa's Workshop and the plans to give each child a small present from the teachers.

"Don't you think that's a good idea?" Linda asked as Amy gazed at the empty rows of desks in her classroom.

"Great," Amy enthused, noting that she was down to two students. One was Billy Archer, whose mom worked a bit later on Wednesdays. The other was Libby Watson, though, which was unexpected since her enormous bear of a father was usually there right on time. Libby was calmly coloring at her desk, unconcerned.

"So you'll be Mrs. Claus?" Linda asked as Amy headed toward the school hallway. "We really need a volunteer and I think you'd be great."

"I can do that. Would you excuse me for a second? I just want to make sure I didn't miss someone." Tucking her clipboard under her arm, Amy headed out into the hall and looked around. Occasionally a parent would get distracted by their phone and wander into the wrong classroom, so it was worth checking. She peered down the hall and didn't see anyone, then turned around—

—and nearly ran into a large, bearded man with a cowboy hat in his hands.

Amy bit back a yelp of surprise, hating that she jumped. Her hand went to her chest, where her heart was hammering. "Oh, freaking heck, you startled me."

The man clutching his hat flushed a deep red. "Sorry," he mumbled.

She bit her lip, because she'd almost cussed a blue streak—and right in the middle of an elementary school filled with students and parents. Trying to compose herself, she smoothed a hand down her skirt. "Can I help you find a classroom?"

The man opened his mouth. "Libby," he managed to croak out after a moment.

She waited. When he didn't say anything else, she tried to fill in the blanks. "Are you saying you're here to pick up Libby? Mr. Watson didn't leave me a message."

"He's . . . lame."

Amy blinked. "What?"

The man cleared his throat and looked distinctly uncomfortable. "Horse. Lame."

"Oh." She studied him. "And you are . . . ?"

"Brother. Caleb." He stuck out his hand, then blurted out, "Weather's Christmas ain't it."

She took his hand gingerly and tried not to notice that it was sweaty. He was nervous, poor man. It was obvious from his actions and the way he stumbled over his words, then closed his eyes after he spoke, as if he were regretting every syllable that came out of his mouth. Her heart squeezed with sympathy.

"Well, Mr. Caleb, I appreciate you coming by, but I can't release the students to anyone—even family—without one of the parents' permission. If you'll come inside and wait, I'll call Mr. Watson or his wife and make sure it's all right before I send Libby out with you." She gestured at the door, indicating he should go inside her classroom. This was usually a test on its own. If it was a creep of any kind—not that she'd met any in their tiny town—calling the parents would normally make someone run. But this man simply ducked his head in a nod and followed her in, which meant he was likely legit.

She was still calling the parents anyhow.

As he walked inside, Libby jumped up from her seat. "Uncle Caleb," she called, beaming at him. "I drew you a horse! Come see!"

The man's face creased into a broad smile at the sight of the little girl. He glanced at Amy.

"Please, have a seat. This won't take long."

She watched as the big cowboy pulled out a child-sized red chair and perched on it, his long legs folded up against his thick, puffy cold-weather vest. Uncle Caleb—which meant he was Hank's brother. She could see it. Hank was a massive, massive man with a grim face and a thick black beard. He was utterly terrifying looking at first, but the way he doted on his petite wife and his equally tiny daughter meant he was harmless. Caleb was obviously cut from the same cloth—he was as tall as his brother, if not as broad. His face wasn't as hard, but maybe it was because he had dark, dark eyes framed by thick lashes that made him look soulful. He had the beard and the build that his brother did, though.

Handsome, too, not that she was supposed to be looking. Handsome and shy, she decided, when he glanced up at her and immediately turned bright red again. She'd seen him around town and had probably met him before, but had never realized he was Libby's uncle. She was bad with faces, which was why she had the clipboard. Both he and Libby looked entirely at ease together, so Amy pulled out her phone and texted Becca Watson—Mr. Watson's recently married bride and Libby's stepmother.

AMY: Hi Becca, this is Amy. A man named Caleb is here to pick Libby up and says Hank has a lame horse? Does this sound legit to you?

Linda cleared her throat, sidling in next to Amy. "Did you hear what I said?"

"Oh. I'm sorry." Amy looked over at her, forcing an apologetic smile to her face. "I didn't catch it."

"I asked if you had a boyfriend. We need a Santa Claus to go with our Mrs. Claus." Linda's expression was avid.

Amy tried not to flinch. Being that it was a small town, relationship stuff came up a lot. "No. I'm sorry, I'm divorced."

Her phone pinged and Amy quickly glanced down at the text.

BECCA: Caleb is totally fine. Do you need a description? Big bearded guy, stumbles over his words. Looks like a shy Hank. Or I can come get her. Let me know.

She smiled down at her phone and glanced up at Caleb and Libby. The man was watching her with those dark eyes, his expression unreadable. For some reason, it made her feel a little flustered and shy herself. "You're good to go, Mr. Watson. Thank you for waiting."

He nodded in a jerky way. "Libby's mine . . . ah, my pleasure." He coughed and then slowly closed his eyes again.

She bit the inside of her cheek not to laugh. "Stumbles over his words" was right.

Amy started to text Becca back when Linda nudged her, continuing to talk about the Christmas Carnival. "Do you know of anyone that can do it? Curtis is running the popcorn machine and Jimmy said he'd be in charge of the midway. Terry dressed up last year, but his wife is insisting that we find someone else. She thinks he's flirting with the elves." Linda tittered at her joke, missing Amy's horrified expression.

The last thing she wanted was to cause problems in someone's marriage. She knew how that felt. "Maybe I shouldn't be Mrs. Claus, then—"

"Me."

Both of the women looked up at the same time.

The cowboy stood up next to Libby's desk, his face flushed. His hat was practically crushed in his big hand as he spoke. "I'll do Mrs. Claus."

"You mean you'll be *Mister* Claus," Libby called out, giggling.

He looked for a moment as if he wanted the floor to swallow him up, but managed to nod. His gaze remained locked on Amy, as if trying to silently communicate something to her.

What it was, she didn't know. But she put on her best teacher smile. "Sounds like you and I are going to make quite the pair."

Ready to find
your next great read?

Let us help.

Visit prh.com/nextread

Penguin
Random
House